WOLF INSTINCT

PAIGE TYLER

sourcebooks
casablanca

Published by Sourcebooks Casablanca, an imprint of Sourcebooks
P.O. Box 4410, Naperville, Illinois 60567-4410
(630) 961-3900
sourcebooks.com

Printed and bound in the United States of America.
OPM 10 9 8 7 6 5 4 3 2 1

With special thanks to my extremely patient and understanding husband. Without your help and support, I couldn't have pursued my dream job of becoming a writer. You're my writing partner, my sounding board, my idea man, my critique partner, and the absolute best research assistant a girl could ask for.

Love you!

Prologue

"WE HAVE TO KEEP MOVING, OR THEY'RE GOING TO CUT OFF our escape route!"

Even though the city around them was coming apart at the seams from the explosions and automatic weapons fire, somehow Corporal Zane Kendrick still heard Lance Corporal Oliver Shipley's warning. But while he'd heard it, there was nothing he could do. He was too busy watching one of his best friends in the world dying in his arms.

Lance Corporal Harry Redfield was already unconscious, which was almost certainly a saving grace. The horrific shrapnel wounds covering the front of his body—courtesy of a 107mm rocket warhead—would have had him screaming in agonizing pain. Even in the middle of the war zone Sangin had become, those cries would have only brought more Taliban fighters down on them. And as Oliver had implied, that would mean the end of them all.

They'd considered carrying Harry, but as British special forces soldiers, they'd seen enough men die on the battlefield to know he wasn't going to make it. Calling in a medevac wasn't an option, either. With wounds this bad, it wouldn't have mattered anyway.

Hoping there was a God up in Heaven to hear him, Zane prayed Harry would die quickly, without ever regaining consciousness and seeing how badly he was torn apart. It was a horrible thing to wish, but in this situation, it was the best they could hope for.

"Dammit, Zane!" Lance Corporal Billy Gordon snapped. "I know you don't want to hear this, but we're going to have to leave Harry behind, or we'll be as dead as he is."

Zane knew Billy was right, but he couldn't leave Harry to die here in this dirty alley alone. Zane's fiancée, Sienna, would have said it was because he cared as much about his men as he did his family. She said that was part of what made him a good leader…and a good man. Zane wasn't so sure about that. Sienna might have been a little biased when it came to her future husband. He loved her like crazy, but to say she only saw the best in him was an understatement.

This had started out as a simple rescue mission but had quickly gone bad. Earlier in the day, a group of British paratroopers from the third battalion had been ambushed by a large force of Taliban fighters while clearing a compound full of weapons and improvised explosive devices. There had been multiple injuries, and the paratroopers had been forced to retreat. It wasn't until later they'd realized one of their corporals was missing. Zane and the three other members of their Special Air Service patrol had volunteered to go back for him.

Fortunately, they'd found the injured soldier fairly quickly, even though he'd been hiding. Then that rocket had streaked in out of nowhere and Harry had gotten hit.

"He's dead, Zane." Oliver put a hand on his shoulder. "We need to go."

Zane gazed down at Harry in the darkness, tears burning his eyes. He and Harry had gone through basic recruit and common military training together, then met up again in SAS assessment. They'd gone through the rigorous special ops training and ended up in D Squadron together. They'd been on every training exercise and deployment together for the past six years. Now, Harry was dead. Just like that.

He wished they could bring Harry with them, but he knew they couldn't. It would take a weapon out of one of their hands and increase the likelihood that none of them would make it home. But there was no way in hell he'd leave Harry lying in the street, not with the way the Taliban treated captured enemy soldiers—dead or alive. So he and his friends hid Harry's body under some metal sheeting in the alley. Hopefully, that would be enough to keep him safe until they could come back in the daylight and recover the body.

"We all need to remember this location," Zane said. "That way, someone will be able to come back and take Harry home to his family."

Oliver and Billy solemnly nodded. There was a lot of dangerous ground for them to cover between here and base camp. The chance of all of them making it back wasn't good.

It tore him up to even think about, and his thoughts immediately turned to Sienna. They were supposed to get married when he got back from this deployment. He'd gone out of his way to reassure her he wasn't in a lot of danger over here—not because he wanted to lie to her, but simply because she wasn't the kind of woman who could deal with the reality of what he did for a living.

If he didn't make it back, he didn't want to imagine what it would do to her.

"Let's go," he said, pushing thoughts of Sienna aside and hefting his L119A1 carbine, ignoring Harry's blood covering the front of his uniform. "Watch yourselves. This city is full of people looking to kill a coalition soldier, and we're the only ones here to shoot."

Zane led them west, toward the river, sticking to the shadows to avoid the groups of armed men roaming the streets. Oliver kept the District Centre apprised of their location as they moved, whispering into his radio to keep from giving their location away.

While Zane tried to stay focused on the present and the need to get the rest of his team back home safely, he couldn't stop thinking about how crushed Harry's parents were going to be when they found out he was dead. Zane had spent a lot of time with them over the years, and he would rather be the one to tell him, but that wasn't the way it worked. Some officer in the regiment who'd probably never met Harry would be the one to do the notification. Zane couldn't imagine how horrible it would be to learn your son was dead from a total stranger.

He and his team were still two kilometers from base camp when they ran into a group of armed men on a narrow street. The first round caught Zane in the left hip, spinning him halfway around. He grunted as pain gripped him, but he ignored it, putting everything he had into getting his weapon up and aimed at the men. Then he pulled the trigger, carefully putting down one target after another. Billy and Oliver did the same, even as Oliver shouted into the radio that they needed backup.

Zane felt two additional spikes of pain as more bullets slammed into him, but he couldn't for the life of him say where he'd been hit. It scared him that they didn't hurt like they should. He dropped his spent magazine and loaded a new one, squeezing the trigger again and again. A few minutes later, the last man fell, and the echo of gunshots slowly faded.

Knowing they needed to get the hell out of there before more bad guys showed up, Zane turned to tell Billy and Oliver as much. At least he tried to. Unfortunately, his whole left side refused to cooperate. He glanced down to see that he'd been hit once in the thigh and once in the stomach, right below his tactical vest. He knew the one in his stomach was bad, but since it didn't hurt that much, he wouldn't worry overmuch about it. It wasn't as if things could get worse.

But when he finally managed to turn around, he realized things could, indeed, get worse. Billy and Oliver were on the ground, and they weren't moving.

Shit.

What energy he had left drained away. He took a few careful steps, then dropped to his knees between his friends. Behind him, he heard the light thud of feet running across broken ground. It looked like Taliban reinforcements were on the way.

Zane rolled Billy over on his back but knew before seeing his lifeless eyes that it was too late. A round had caught Billy in the neck. He'd probably bled out before even hitting the ground. Another piece of Zane's soul tore away as he thought about Billy's pretty girlfriend and the baby they had on the way. She'd wanted Billy to get out of the regiment and get a job at her dad's clothing store. But Billy had insisted retail wasn't for people like him and had reenlisted for another tour.

Zane should have talked him out of it. Billy's unborn child would still have a father if he had.

He forced himself to stop thinking and turned to Oliver, dreading what he'd see. Relief flooded though Zane when his friend groaned. Then he saw the shattered ballistic plates of Oliver's tactical vest and the blood pouring everywhere. The first shot had broken the protective ceramic plate. The second had punched through his chest. It was amazing he was still alive.

"Stay with me, Ollie," Zane whispered, sliding his arms under his friend's shoulder and pulling him up. It struck him then that he was desperately holding on to the last friend he had. The last member of a team he'd been sweating and bleeding with for years. "I'm getting you home. I promise."

Somehow, Zane got both of them to their feet. Draping one of Oliver's arms over his shoulder, he gripped the back of his friend's belt. Oliver tried to help, shuffling like some kind of zombie as they headed toward base camp. They still had a long way to go.

"Help is coming," Oliver gasped. "I got through to District Centre before it happened. They're sending help."

Zane nodded, hoping his friend was right. Because there were a lot of Taliban fighters between here and base camp. Those fighters would do everything they could to slow any vehicles moving this way.

Within minutes, Zane was breathing so hard from exertion he missed the insurgents creeping up behind them…until the shooting started. He spun, emptying his carbine in the general direction of the group of people trying to kill them. He had no idea if he hit anyone, but it made them duck. He would have had to let go of Ollie to reload the assault weapon, and he sure as hell wasn't doing that. Dropping the carbine, he pulled the Sig Sauer from a holster on his right thigh.

He popped one round at the group of men starting to reassemble behind them, then took off running toward base camp, though with his injuries and Oliver's dead weight, it was more of a shamble. But they moved. That was all that mattered.

Time became little more than a messy blur of stumbling, gasping for breath, and pain—interspersed with the occasional shots coming at them from the shadows. Zane fired back when he could, taking out a few of the bad guys, but mostly he tried to keep moving. He was carrying limited ammo for his 9 mm. When he ran out, he and Oliver were dead. The goal now wasn't to wipe out the bad guys. It was to hold them off until help arrived.

A few minutes later, Oliver faltered. His friend was fading fast.

"Go," Oliver rasped. "I'm slowing you down."

"Shut up!" Zane snapped. "I'm not leaving you!"

Zane's first magazine ran out when three men jumped out of a side street. He got the one holding the grenade launcher right before the slide locked back. The other two men ran away, probably not realizing they could have dropped Zane and Oliver without too much effort now that they were defenseless. Reloading the Sig with one hand was complicated. The regiment made them train for stuff like that, for situations like this. Still, practice was one thing. Reality was totally different.

He had fifteen rounds left. That's all that stood between him and Oliver and certain death.

Zane was so focused on moving forward he barely saw the Taliban fighters slipping out of the darkness. The ground all around them flared with the sparks of ricocheting bullets, and Zane spun Oliver to the side, heading toward one of the buildings lining the street and trying to shield his friend with his body as much as possible.

It didn't work.

Zane heard the whoosh of the rocket-propelled grenade coming their way a fraction of a second before it impacted the wall of the nearby building and exploded. They both went down, but Oliver took the brunt of the blast wave—and the frag.

Zane hit the ground so hard he thought it would kill him, but he wasn't that lucky. He didn't even pass out. He bounced and slid a few feet, then lay there, numb. Frag from the RPG had gotten him, too, and blood was leaking out of him at an alarming rate. The fact that he didn't feel anything even closely resembling pain still worried him, but he couldn't focus on that. Oliver needed him.

He crawled on his hands and knees to his friend's side, stopping every so often to shoot at the insurgents coming at them.

Oliver was a mess, and Zane was sure he was dead. But when he rolled Oliver over, he was still breathing.

"Don't let them take me alive," his friend whispered, gray eyes locking desperately on his. "I'm not scared to die, but I don't want to go out that way."

Tears filled Zane's eyes. He knew what Oliver was asking. The Taliban would have no problem torturing his friend, even if it was only for a few minutes before he died. But Zane wasn't sure this was something he could do. He was supposed to save his friends...not kill them.

But as one bullet after another hit the ground near them, Zane realized he didn't have to worry about it anymore. Oliver closed his eyes and let out one last, shuddering breath.

Something inside Zane died then, the final piece of his soul withering away. Harry, Billy, and Oliver—men who'd depended on him to bring them home—were all gone.

How the hell does a person go on after this? Why would they bother?

Zane lifted his Sig out of pure instinct, squeezing the trigger and killing the four men charging him. He wasn't sure why he did it. There had to be others roaming around. But shooting people who were trying to kill him was what he'd been trained to do, so he'd keep doing it until he couldn't do it anymore.

But when the part of his mind that had been counting rounds reached fourteen, he stopped. Once he fired the last round, he'd be defenseless, almost certainly captured and tortured by Taliban fighters who would make him pay for every insurgent who'd died tonight. He hated the idea of putting Sienna and his family through the horror of knowing he'd spent his last few hours being tortured.

But before he could fully consider placing the barrel of his 9 mm under his chin, he knew he couldn't do it. His whole team had gone down swinging. There was no way he could do any less.

He straightened his arm and aimed at the nearest of the men coming at him. There were at least a dozen more behind that guy. Zane would get the first one. Whatever happened after that would happen.

Zane had started to squeeze the trigger when he heard the thrum of big diesel engines followed by the chest-rattling throb of multiple heavy machine guns tearing up the world around him. The rescue party had finally arrived. But as the crowd of Taliban fighters continued to charge at him without slowing, he knew it was too late. The best he could hope for now was to die fighting.

"I'm sorry, Sienna," he whispered, then aimed at the men again and pulled the trigger.

Zane sat bolt upright, gasping for breath, his muscles twitching like there was a living thing inside him trying to escape. For a few moments, all he could smell was the acrid scent of smokeless gunpowder mixed with the nearly overwhelming stench of sweat and blood. His heart hammered in his chest as he realized he was lying in bed in the two-story cottage in Hempstead he and Sienna shared.

It was the same nightmare every time, reliving the night his friends had died. It always ended right before the rescue party arrived, so he never got to the moment when he realized he was going to live.

Zane breathed deeply, letting the scents and sounds of Afghanistan and the battle slowly fade away. His throat was raw from growling, and he had the coppery taste of blood in his mouth from where he'd bit himself with his fangs.

He knew he was dealing with PTSD from everything that had happened to him in Sangin. He couldn't make sense of the fangs or the growls, though. Sometimes, he thought he was going insane.

He glanced at Sienna's side of the bed to find it empty. That wasn't surprising. She tended to leave the room when he had a nightmare. A quick glance at the clock told him it was barely past two in the morning, and he considered lying back down, desperate for more sleep. But it'd be a waste of time. There was no chance he'd be able to get any shut-eye tonight. He'd rather check on Sienna anyway.

He didn't bother with shoes or even a shirt, slipping into the hallway in the shorts he usually slept in. Well, the shorts he slept in now. He and Sienna used to sleep naked all the time; that had changed since he'd gotten back. A lot of things had.

Zane glanced down the hall toward the bathroom, wondering if Sienna was in there, but a soft noise from downstairs convinced him she wasn't. He listened for a moment, expecting to hear the murmur of the telly. Instead, he picked up on the subtle tread of bare feet on wood in the kitchen downstairs. He headed for the steps, not bothering to wonder how he knew something like that. His weird hearing was merely another thing he had no explanation for.

The lights in the living room were off as he moved down the stairs, but the soft glow coming from the kitchen was more than enough to light up the entire first floor of the house.

He slowly padded the rest of the way down, hearing Sienna moving about in the kitchen, likely making cocoa. The thought of his fiancée dressed in her long, blue bathrobe and fuzzy, pink slippers, standing in front of the stove, stirring a pot of chocolate, brought a smile to his face. Things hadn't gone the way they'd planned upon his return from Afghanistan. Instead of squeezing their wedding into a few short weeks of leave time, Zane had spent endless days in the hospital recovering from wounds that should have killed him. When they didn't, he'd been promptly and efficiently separated from military service. The official cause was "combat-related disabilities." The real reason was because the doctors thought he was a fucking nutjob.

He and Sienna had postponed the wedding while he dealt with his *issues*. Considering the number of *issues* he had, he wasn't sure when things were going to get back on track, but Sienna seemed willing to stick with him through them. He had no idea why. It certainly wasn't anything he deserved. He'd be the first to admit he was a bloody mess.

He was still smiling as he reached the bottom of the steps. But when he caught sight of the two suitcases by the door, his heart started to thud hard in his chest. Then he saw the engagement ring on the coffee table.

Zane was still processing the scene when Sienna walked in from the kitchen. Instead of her bathrobe, she was dressed in a skirt and blouse, a pair of low heels dangling in one hand, her red hair up in a bun. She saw him standing in the shadows of the stairs and froze in her tracks.

"You're awake," she said.

"You're leaving," he pointed out.

The realization of that was like a wound spreading

across his soul. He wished he could say he was surprised, but he wasn't. A part of him had known.

"I'm sorry," she whispered, looking like she genuinely meant it. "I wish I was strong enough to be here for you, but I'm not."

Sienna walked over to her suitcases, then turned to look at him. "You push everyone away. Your family. Your friends. Me. You won't let anyone help you."

He supposed that was true, so he didn't try to deny it. He gestured at her suitcases. She'd done a good job of packing quietly. He hadn't heard a thing. "So you were going to leave in the middle of the night without saying anything?"

At least she had the decency to look chagrined. "I was going to leave you a note."

He didn't respond. Because really, what was there to say?

Sienna gazed at him, her gray eyes sad. "You're different than the man I used to know. The one I fell in love with. The one I wanted to marry." The softly spoken words felt a lot like the bullet wounds he'd received in Afghanistan—painful but muted. "I don't know what happened to you over there because you won't tell me. You won't tell anyone. But you've changed into something I can't recognize. It's like you're some kind of…"

Her voice trailed off as though she couldn't quite put a name to what it was he'd become.

Zane considered the reflection he'd caught in the mirror after he'd woken up from one of his nightmares and gone into the bathroom. He'd seen what he was now. Sienna had obviously seen it as well.

"I think the word you're looking for is *monster*," he said quietly.

Sienna stared at him, emotions roiling in her eyes. But she didn't disagree.

Sighing, she slipped on her shoes, then opened the door and picked up her suitcases. She hesitated for a moment, as if she wanted to say something more. But there weren't words for a situation like this. She must have known that, because she turned and walked out without saying anything, closing the door behind her.

Zane heard her footsteps tapping away across the sidewalk and parking lot. A few moments later, a car started, then drove away. Damn, he really hated how good his hearing was now.

Walking over to the coffee table, he picked up Sienna's engagement ring and stared at it. He remembered picking it out with her before the deployment. She'd been absolutely gaga over the thing. He wanted to be angry with her for walking out, but he couldn't find it in himself to blame her. She was right. He'd pulled so far away from everyone that sometimes it seemed like he wasn't even living in the real world. It was like he was floating around the edges of it, waiting for something to come along and convince him there was a reason to keep going.

He'd thought that something would be Sienna, but apparently he was wrong about that.

Zane rolled the ring back and forth in his hands for a while, then flipped it across the room and into the fireplace, where it was lost in the ashes of the smoldering fire.

Like everything else in his life.

Chapter 1

"THIS ISN'T MUSIC," ZANE SAID TO FELLOW WEREWOLVES and SWAT teammates Rachel Bennett and Diego Martinez, practically shouting to be heard over the throbbing beat coming out of the club they were heading toward. The sign above the entrance read *Attitude* in big, bold, splashy letters. "I'm not sure what the hell it is, but it's definitely not music."

Rachel laughed. Tall and athletic with long, blond hair she always wore up in a ponytail, she was the newest member of the Pack. "My grandma used to say, 'When the music starts to get too loud, you know you're getting old.'"

Rachel seemed to have a lot of sayings from her grandma, but that merely went along with her relaxed, southern twang. Zane frowned at her over his shoulder as they passed the long line of people waiting to get into the club and walked straight to the door. The crowd complained loudly—some of them more vocal than others—wanting to know what was so special about him and his friends. Zane ignored them.

"I didn't say it was too loud," he pointed out to his pack mates. "It's that bloody backbeat the LA clubs add to every song they play. It makes my teeth ache."

Diego laughed as he and Rachel moved ahead of

Zane. Originally from southern California, his dark-haired pack mate had a unique way of appearing intense and laid-back at the same time. "Do you think the reason he can't stand the music is because he can't dance?"

"You might be onto something there," Rachel said, slowly rolling her hips to the sound coming out of the big doors as she walked. "He's just mad because he doesn't have any rhythm and the rest of the Pack does."

Zane snorted. He was used to his pack mates on the Dallas SWAT team ragging him because he couldn't dance. He'd never fancied dancing anyway, so it wasn't like he cared, but his pack seemed to think it was an insult to all werewolf kind. Like being able to gyrate your body around a crowded dance floor in time to a crappy song was some kind of valuable skill. He much preferred focusing on abilities that had some purpose in his life—like being able to run down a speeding car full of bad guys. Or having complete control over his fangs and claws. Fortunately, those were things he excelled in.

"Do you think there's anything we can do to help him?" Diego asked thoughtfully, acting like this was a serious problem that needed to be fixed.

Rachel shook her head in fake despair as she glanced over her shoulder at him. "Unfortunately, no. I think we're going to have to accept that there's no chance for a recovery. Zane will never be able to dance."

"Very funny," he grumbled as he and his friends approached the two bouncers standing guard at the door.

The guys were big and no doubt imposing to a normal human. Zane and his friends weren't normal or human.

One of the men moved to block their path, but a low growl from Zane made him rethink that decision. The bouncer glanced at Rachel and Diego, then at Zane again before stepping aside. The people at the front of the line protested, saying they'd been in line for an hour, but Zane ignored them, too. The suspect they were after had gone in the club. Zane and his pack mates didn't have time to wait in line.

Once inside, Rachel and Diego went their own way. They were pretending to be a newlywed couple in LA for their honeymoon, while Zane was undercover as a lone British tourist. This was the third club they'd been to in as many nights. Their target's routine was becoming seriously repetitive.

Zane wandered deeper into the club, nearly gagging from the myriad scents assaulting his nose. There must be five hundred people in there, drinking, dancing, and sweating out dozens of different illicit drugs. Even if he weren't a werewolf with a nose good enough to pick up the scent of a rabbit from a thousand feet away, he would have been overwhelmed.

He tried to block out as many of the scents as he could, pushing them to the background one by one. He momentarily picked up on one that was decidedly pleasant, and any other time, he would have liked to follow it. But meeting the woman giving off those pheromones wasn't in the cards tonight. He reluctantly pushed her scent out of his head and kept walking. He picked up another one as he went that was somewhat familiar, but there were too many competing smells to nail it down clearly, so he dismissed it as well.

"Our guy and his crew are standing at the far end of the bar," Diego's voice came over the earpiece Zane wore.

"Copy that," Zane said.

Turning, he headed that way, skirting the dance floor. Several women eyed him with looks that could only be called *hungry* as they gyrated to the music. One of them, a tall, slender brunette in a tight dress that didn't leave much to the imagination, grabbed his left bicep through his leather jacket with both hands, giving it a squeeze and trying to drag him onto the dance floor. Searing pain shot through his arm, almost bringing him to his knees, and it took every ounce of control to keep his fangs and claws from coming out. So much for always being in control. He wasn't as successful at hiding the growl that escaped. The woman couldn't possibly have heard the sound over the noise, but the look on his face was enough to scare her off. Releasing his arm, she quickly retreated and went back to dancing with her friends.

Zane stopped in his tracks, waiting for the throbbing pain in his arm to recede. Taking a deep breath, he wiped away the sweat beading on his forehead with the back of his hand. It was difficult to believe that after two months it could still hurt so damn much.

"What's Stefan doing?" Zane asked into the mic clipped on the inside of his shirt when the pain finally became a dull ache.

"Same thing he's done every night since we started following him," Rachel answered. "Staring at people like a frigging pervert. He makes my skin crawl."

When Zane finally got to the far side of the club, he found Stefan Curtis leaning back against the bar, regarding the crowd of people on the dance floor with an appraising eye. Four big guys stood guard, two on either side of him. They looked vigilant, even though the vibe they put off was enough to keep everybody far away from their boss.

Based on the way many of the women eyed Stefan, they obviously considered him attractive. With his perfect blond hair, classic features, and tailored suit, he could have easily been a model for *GQ* or *Gentleman's Journal* magazine. But at the same time, Zane could understand why Rachel's skin crawled when she was around the guy. It was difficult to put into words, but there was something unsettling about the way Stefan looked at people. Like he was mentally dissecting them to see what made them tick. It made Zane's fangs ache to come out, as if his inner wolf instinctively recognized a threat when it sensed one.

That wasn't surprising, considering Stefan's uncle was Randy Curtis, the former chief of police of the Dallas PD and current member of the FBI's top ten list of fugitives. It was tough to get your name on there, but trying to murder an entire SWAT team, as well as their friends and family, was a good way to do it.

Six months ago, no one in the Pack even knew what a "hunter" was. But in September, they'd learned that groups of men roamed around the country, killing any werewolf they stumbled across. Within weeks, werewolves had shown up in Dallas looking for protection. No one thought the hunters would be bold enough to try anything in a city guarded by a pack as big as the Dallas SWAT team. Seventeen alphas strong at the time, equipped with weapons and tactics only SWAT cops possessed should have been more than enough.

But in November, the hunters had attacked them, almost killing several members of the Pack, including

Zane. He was still missing a major chunk of tricep muscle from his left arm and likely always would, regardless of all the experimental drugs the Pack's doctor had tried. But as bold as that assault had been, it paled in comparison to the blatant attack on the SWAT compound in December. It had been a miracle any of them had survived it.

Knowing there were people who wanted to kill werewolves simply because of what they were was bad enough, but it had been even more crushing to learn their own police chief had been in league with the hunters the whole time. Zane and his pack mates had no clue what his connection to the hunters was or why he wanted the Pack dead, but they'd tracked him to LA three weeks ago and had been searching for him ever since.

They'd learned a lot about Randy Curtis in that time, though nothing to suggest his current location or his connection to the hunters. But they had discovered why he'd run off to LA. Turns out this was home for him and the entire Curtis family. Zane came from a large one himself, but the Curtis family tree put his to shame. There were dozens of brothers, sisters, cousins, nieces, nephews, and various in-laws who called this city home. And all of them worked for the same international conglomerate based in LA—Black Swan Enterprises. Eric Becker—the Pack's resident hacker—had spent hours digging through the company's computers and still had no idea how far their financial reach might be. But it was obvious that whoever ran Black Swan Enterprises was filthy rich and powerful as hell.

Zane wondered why Randy Curtis had become a cop in Dallas instead of working for Black Swan like the rest of his family. If Curtis had come back here asking his relatives to hide him from the authorities, they'd done a bloody good job of it. In fact, Zane had begun to think this whole trip to LA was a waste of time when they'd stumbled across Curtis's nephew, Stefan.

While Stefan had gone to the same Ivy League college as the rest of the Curtis clan, he didn't have a position on the Black Swan board. And while he had money, fancy cars, and high-priced security, he didn't work for the company. As far as Zane could tell, the man wasn't connected to Black Swan Enterprises at all.

Stefan also had a police record with multiple charges of assault, battery, attempted rape, larceny, and burglary. He'd never made it into a court of law because he had the best attorneys money could buy, but it was obvious he was the black sheep of the family. Like his uncle.

Who better than a black sheep to hide another black sheep?

Zane and his teammates had assumed Stefan would lead them to Curtis at some point, but he and his crew spent every evening out crawling around the city's underbelly from nightclubs and backroom gambling dives to drug dens and strip joints. The funny thing was, Stefan didn't partake of the entertainment in any of those places. Instead, he stared at people—and skeeved Rachel out, of course. If Stefan wasn't here to hook up, why bother? And why did he always travel with security?

"We might have something," Diego murmured in his earpiece, distracting Zane from his musings.

That's when he realized Stefan had moved away from the bar and was now talking to two young women. They seemed a little nervous, but Stefan must have turned on the charm—or maybe gave them a compliment—because after a moment, they both smiled at him. Identical twins, they were tall, slim, and attractive, with big, expressive, blue eyes and long, straight, platinum hair. The girls looked like they couldn't be more than eighteen. It made him wonder how the hell they'd gotten past the bouncers.

Over the radio in his earpiece, Zane heard Rachel curse as Stefan leaned in close to one of the girls and whispered something in her ear.

Zane moved closer, so he could step in if Stefan tried something. That's when he caught the same familiar scent he'd picked up before and immediately realized it was coming from the twin girls. He stared at them for a few minutes, testing the air, unsure what he was picking up on. Then it hit him as he remembered where he'd smelled that unique scent before. Selena Rosa, his best friend's mate, put off the same scent during the first few days of her change, when she'd still been more human than werewolf. Bloody hell, those two girls were brand-new werewolves, probably only days into their change.

Stefan caught a nearby waitress's eye and lifted his hand. The waitress immediately walked past Zane and over to the trio, a tray with two mixed drinks in her hand.

Zane's inner werewolf growled as a pungent odor wafted from the glasses to sting his nose. Shit. This was a damn setup, and it was getting worse by the second.

"Something's going down," Zane said into his mic as Stefan handed a glass to each girl. "He's drugging them—*and* those girls are brand new werewolves."

"I knew that chucklefuck was up to no good," Rachel muttered.

"Think he's grabbing the girls for Curtis?" Diego asked. "Payback against werewolves or something?"

"There's no way Stefan could know they're were-wolves," Zane said. "I doubt they even know themselves yet. If he's getting them for Curtis, it's because they're attractive women."

The thought made Zane want to retch and he was heading for the table before he could take another breath. He couldn't let Stefan slip those girls roofies—even if it meant blowing his cover.

Unfortunately, his planned rescue went to crap when the twin girls downed the drinks like they were lemon-ade. Biting back a snarl, he had no choice but to stop where he was and go with plan B—stand back and save the girls at the first opportunity that presented itself.

The twins started showing effects of the drug within minutes, which only made Zane more convinced they were brand-new werewolves. Drugs and alcohol didn't affect werewolves. He watched their eyes getting glassy as they laughed at something Stefan said. Zane over-heard him mention taking them to another party across town, one that'd have a lot of famous Hollywood movie stars and producers.

The twins exchanged looks, as if unsure whether to accept the invitation. But then one whispered in the other's ear, and after a moment, they both nodded at Stefan. Instead of whisking them out of there, Stefan told them he needed to make a quick stop on the way and that his "personal security" would take them to the party.

The girls giggled and nodded, apparently thinking Stefan must be someone famous if he had bodyguards.

Stefan headed for the exit with one of his crew, leaving the other three guys there.

"Rachel and Diego, you stay with Stefan," Zane said into his mic. "I'll stick with the girls."

"All three of those guys are big and packing heat," Diego pointed out. "I'll stay here with you."

Zane ground his jaw. Before he'd gotten shot in the arm in that drive-by, Diego never would have suggested he needed backup. What Diego was subtly trying to say was that he didn't think Zane could handle those three muscle heads on his own.

He resisted the urge to tell his pack mate to mind his own fucking business. They didn't have time to argue. Besides, he knew Diego was only trying to have his back.

"Stefan is the whole damn reason we're here," Zane said. "He said he had to make a quick stop. Maybe he's going to see Curtis. If there's even a chance of that, we can't let him out of our sight for a minute. You two go. I'm good here."

There was a moment of silence over the radio, but then Diego grunted. "We're on it. Be careful. And call us when you get the chance."

Out of the corner of his eye, Zane saw his pack mates head for the exit, shadowing Stefan and his bodyguard. Zane breathed a sigh of relief. While everything he'd said about Rachel and Diego keeping an eye on Stefan was true, there was another reason he wanted them to stay together. He hated to even let his mind go there, but he wasn't sure they could trust Rachel.

She'd shown up in Dallas right before the hunters attacked the SWAT compound. She'd immediately fit right in, but that night, she hadn't taken a shot at one of the hunters when she'd had the chance, and the man had gotten away. Instead of telling SWAT commander Gage Dixon—their pack alpha—Zane figured he'd talk to her about it, then he, Rachel, and Diego had come out here and he hadn't found a chance.

Zane knew he needed to find the time soon, because the more he was around Rachel, the more concerned he became. He'd caught her glancing over her shoulder more times than he could count, her heart thumping out of control like she thought someone was about to jump her. Other times, she'd stare off into space like her head was a million miles away. Zane didn't know what trauma she'd gone through when she'd become a werewolf, but his gut told him she was dealing with some serious post-traumatic stress. He had enough experience with PTSD to know it when he saw it.

He turned his attention back to the two girls. The drug must have fully kicked in because they both looked really out of it.

Even as he focused all of his attention on them, a part of his head casually noted the same pleasant scent he'd picked up when he'd first come into the club. Only it was closer this time. It completely overshadowed the scent of the new werewolves, and Zane couldn't remember ever smelling anything so delicious. It was almost enough to make him drool. He probably would have, too, if he didn't have a job to do.

Over by the bar, the twin werewolves swayed a little on their feet. The same waitress who'd given them the drinks immediately rushed over, saying something about helping them to the restroom. The girls nodded, sudden panic in their eyes as they realized something was off.

The shorter and stockier of Stefan's three bodyguards disappeared into the crowd, no doubt heading for their car, while the other two casually followed the waitress, maintaining their distance as the woman led the girls to the back of the club.

Zane had hoped to help the girls without completely blowing his cover, but he stopped giving a crap about that the moment the waitress led them away like sacrificial offerings. His fangs extended a little as he strode after them. He was going to save those werewolves, to hell with how much of a mess he made.

As he expected, the waitress led the twins past the restroom, steering them down a dark hallway, toward the back door. There was a metal click and a gust of fresh air—well, as fresh as it could be in a city like LA—as the woman opened it and urged the girls outside. The three men followed, closing it behind them.

Zane hit the door at a full run, slamming it open with his right hand and bursting into the alley. He immediately turned right, his nose telling him that was the way they'd gone.

The waitress was nowhere in sight now, but there was a big, black sedan parked fifteen feet away that the three men were stuffing the two girls into. The girls were little more than limp zombies now, neither putting up a fight of any kind.

Growling, Zane raced down the alley. When he reached the car, he grabbed the first jackass by the back of the neck, digging the claws of his right hand into the thick muscles there and yanking the man off his feet, then slinging him toward the building behind them. The thud when the guy slammed into the brick was incredibly satisfying, and Zane had a crazy urge to grab the guy and do it all over again.

Bloody hell. He was losing control of his inner werewolf. He hadn't done that since he'd first turned into one. But the aggression, not to mention the growling, fangs, and claws, were seriously out of character for him.

Zane was so distracted he didn't realize the other two wankers had pulled their guns and were pointing them at his chest. He wasn't worried about getting shot. Nothing less than a bullet through the heart or one in the head would put a werewolf down. But still, getting shot wouldn't feel good. Not only that, but the men would quickly figure out Zane wasn't exactly human.

Not something he wanted their boss to know about, especially if Stefan was the one helping Curtis.

But as Zane took a step forward to close the gap between him and the two men with guns, he realized he didn't have a choice. He could almost certainly take out one of them before the guy pulled the trigger, but he'd never deal with both in time. Not with his bum arm.

He prepared himself for the unpleasant sensation of a large copper-jacketed slug tearing through his body when a beautiful blond appeared from behind the car, quickly moving up behind the men like a bloody ninja. She wrapped an arm around one man's neck, flipping him over her hip and slamming him onto the pavement *hard*.

That was when Zane figured out she was the woman putting off that pleasant scent he'd picked up inside the club. Except now that he was close to her, he decided it was a lot more than pleasant. In fact, it was a yummy combination of cinnamon, chocolate, and roses.

Zane wanted to take a minute to figure out how she

could smell like all of those things at once—and what she was doing out here in the alley—but the last asshole standing made up his mind about who to shoot first. Turning his weapon on Zane, he started to squeeze the trigger.

Bloody hell.

Perhaps he should stop drooling over the blond and do something before the guy shot him.

———

FBI Agent Alyssa Carson pegged the tall, good-looking, muscular guy with the dark, piercing eyes as a cop the moment she saw him. There was something about the way he carried himself. He had an aura of authority that screamed *law enforcement*. Then, when she saw him move across the dance floor, all animalistic grace and power, she started thinking maybe he was CIA or some other three-letter agency. Because he slipped through the crowd like a trained killer. Either way, she was stumped as to why someone like him would take a sudden interest in two random girls heading for trouble.

Alyssa doubted the man could be there for the same reason she was. To the best of her knowledge, Christine Howard, her friend in the LA FBI field office, was the only other law enforcement official in the state who knew about the case Alyssa was investigating. In fact, it had been Christine who'd called and told her about the three young women who'd gone missing two weeks ago.

Los Angeles was a city with a population of almost four million people. They disappeared at a terrifying rate there—so many that, after a while, it seemed like nothing more than a blur of pictures appearing and disappearing on a host of websites and the occasional billboard. But when the body of one of those missing women had been found in a landfill with a bizarre cause of death, Christine had called Alyssa. Because, unlike most people in the bureau, Christine knew Alyssa specialized in the strange and bizarre.

In fact, Alyssa was at the club tonight thanks to a rumor Christine had heard. It wasn't much to go off of, mostly whispers suggesting the missing women might have been there around the time they disappeared. But it was all Alyssa had to go on, so she'd trusted her instincts.

When she'd seen the player in the expensive suit charming the two girls, she knew those instincts had been right. The way the man eyed them was creepy to say the least. Alyssa had no doubt the guy was planning to grab the girls. Considering he had four big Neanderthals with him, Mr. Creepy had all the help he needed to make it happen.

The guy she thought might be a cop seemed to figure that out, too. He didn't seem too happy about it.

Is Tall, Dark, and Gorgeous also looking for the missing girls?

It seemed unlikely, but then again, those two young women at the club tonight definitely matched the profile—attractive and a little naive. No doubt, they were runaways from Small Town, USA, who'd come to LA to become famous.

Alyssa parked herself in a dark corner, so she could keep an eye on the situation and try to figure out exactly what was going on. She frowned as Mr. Creepy gestured a waitress over, one who already had a tray of drinks ready and waiting. That wasn't suspicious at all, was it?

Within a few minutes, the twin girls were going

glassy eyed, and it was obvious they'd been drugged. Damn, sometimes Alyssa hated that her instincts were so good. On the other hand, this was the break she'd been looking for. If these guys were the ones who'd grabbed the other women, maybe Alyssa could follow them and put an end to this before any more bodies found their way into the landfill with all the blood drained.

When Mr. Creepy left with one of his Neanderthals, Alyssa saw Tall, Dark, and Gorgeous look back and forth between the two girls and the rich guy, a torn expression on his face. Like he was trying to make a decision. Then his lips moved, like he was talking to himself. A moment later, she saw a man and woman on the far side of the club follow Mr. Creepy out the door. The pair moved with the same dangerous grace as Tall, Dark, and Gorgeous as they slipped through the crowd.

That's when it hit her—Tall, Dark, and Gorgeous wasn't there for the girls. He and his friends had been following Mr. Creepy. Not shocking, she supposed. If Mr. Creepy was making people disappear, he was probably doing other illegal crap as well.

But if Tall, Dark, and Gorgeous was there for Mr. Creepy, why hadn't he gone with the rest of his team? Why was he ghosting down the back hallway, one-hundred-percent focused on the girls and the waitress herding them out of the building? Especially since it seemed like he didn't have any other backup.

She didn't have any backup, either. But who was keeping score?

Alyssa had to practically run to keep up as she heard the back door open and close. Tall, Dark, and Gorgeous might be big, but he was damn fast. A part of her realized her original plan to let the men grab the girls, then follow them was shot now. Tall, Dark, and Gorgeous was going to put himself right in the middle of everything and wreck any chance of tracking those Neanderthals anywhere.

But it wasn't like she could stand by and let him do it on his own. The thought of him going up against those three men made her stomach twist up in a knot. Which was a little strange considering he was in the middle of mucking up her case.

Alyssa felt a tingle race up her spine as she quietly slipped out the back door. She had enough experience with weird to know when she saw it, and something weird was definitely about to go down.

She was already moving through the shadows when she saw Tall, Dark, and Gorgeous sling one of the Neanderthals through the air. The crunch as the man hit the brick wall was nearly deafening in the silence behind the club. Tall, Dark, and Gorgeous was big, no doubt about it, but so was the Neanderthal. No one should be able to toss someone around like that, no matter how strong they might be. And normal people didn't growl, even in the middle of a fight.

Why did everything she got involved in have to turn out to be bizarre?

She put that thought from her mind when the guns came out. That's when she realized Tall, Dark, and Gorgeous wasn't carrying a weapon. Instead, he strode toward the other two Neanderthals like he planned to tear them apart with his bare hands.

Alyssa rolled her eyes. Another guy with more testosterone than brains.

She slipped from the shadows and around the back of the sedan, noticing that the twins were completely out of it now and slumped in the backseat in a boneless heap. That made things easier. At least they wouldn't give away the element of surprise as she grabbed one of the men and flipped him over her hip. The moment he was on the ground, she pulled out the Sig Sauer holstered behind her back and thumped him in the temple with the butt of the weapon. Not hard enough to crack bone, but more than hard enough to put him out.

She spun around, bringing her gun up, knowing the other Neanderthal was probably already pulling the trigger on the big guy she felt a stupid need to protect.

Everything happened so fast. Which was crazy, since she'd been through enough training and real-life situations like this. But one second, the remaining Neanderthal had his weapon pointed straight at the big guy and the next, Tall, Dark, and Gorgeous...moved.

There was another growl, a flash of reflected light off some seriously intense eyes, then Tall, Dark, and Gorgeous knocked the man's gun hand aside. After that, there were about a half dozen quick strikes she recognized as some kind of martial arts style. Part of her noted Tall, Dark, and Gorgeous barely moved his left arm, instead, doing all the damage with his right. It didn't seem to matter as bones crunched and the gun went flying into the darkness.

Maybe he wasn't a cop.

More like a soldier.

Or a trained killer.

Tall, Dark, and Gorgeous bounced the guy's head off the side of the car door, then picked him up and tossed him into the same wall his buddy had crash tested. Yup. Brick was still tougher than human. Alyssa winced.

Tall, Dark, and Gorgeous spun around to look at her, his body taking on an aggressive stance. Alyssa instinctively brought her weapon up, only to have him grab it out of her hands before she even saw him move.

She rolled backward on the pavement, going for the backup piece holstered at her right ankle, dragging it out and jacking the slide back in one smooth motion. She brought it up straight and level, green night-sight dots aligning in the center of the man's chest.

"I'd prefer if you didn't shoot me," he said in a deep voice.

Alyssa wasn't sure what was more distracting, the way the words rumbled out of that muscular chest or the sinful British accent that made her think of some kind of decadent chocolate commercial.

"It would probably hurt," he added.

She hesitated, making sure that none of the three Neanderthals were a threat before putting the weapon's safety on and slipping it back in her ankle holster. She knew it was insane to approach a guy who clearly had danger written all over him without her weapon drawn, but her instincts were saying this was the way to go. Bottom line, she trusted her instincts more than her training.

"The thought of shooting you hadn't entered my mind until you jerked my gun out of my hand," she said. "Then I didn't have a choice."

"Sorry about that." He held out his right hand, her Sig sitting casually in the middle of it. "I kind of did it without thinking. Bad habit of mine."

Alyssa stepped closer, understanding a little something about acting without thinking. That was when
she realized just how attractive he really was. Like
Hollywood-movie-star attractive. And holy crap, he was
even taller and more muscular than she'd thought. He
wore his leather jacket unzipped, allowing her to make
out some of his broad shoulders and all those pecs.
Damn, they seemed to go on for days.

Maybe she should pat him down for weapons, start-
ing with that chest. Purely for safety's sake, of course.
Okay…no…bad idea. She didn't even know his name.
Groping him would be rude.

So instead, she carefully reached out and took her
gun from his hand, checking the magazine before putting it away. She hadn't seen him messing with it, but
then again, she'd seen how fast he could move. She
backed away from him, not bothering to comment on
the fact that he'd taken her weapon away from her. She
didn't like thinking about how easily he'd been able to
do it. Then again, she hadn't shot him, so as far as she
was concerned, they were even.

Alyssa checked on the three unconscious men, kicking their weapons away and making sure they weren't
going to be waking up anytime soon. Once that was done,
she walked over to the sedan and the two drugged girls
lying in the backseat to find Tall, Dark, and Gorgeous
already checking the twins' heartbeats and respiration.
The calm, confident way he moved suggested he'd done
this more than a few times before.

"They're both doing okay right now, but they could
still have a bad reaction to the drugs," he said, his concern obvious. "We need to get them to a hospital."

Alyssa knew that was true, but unfortunately, it wasn't that simple. Because of the direction her investigations sometimes took, they were conducted under the radar. Christine was the only other person in the LA field office who knew she was there and what she was looking into. If word got back that she was running an op like this without alerting the local special agent in charge, things could get complicated.

"We'll get them to the hospital." She pulled her phone out and sent a text to Christine before slipping an arm under the first girl and gently tugging her out. Christine would be up worrying about her, so she'd see the text without a doubt. "But we can't call an ambulance."

"Why's that? You're a cop, right?" he asked, as if he already knew the answer.

She turned to look at him, trying to make sure she didn't dump the unconscious girl on the hard ground at the same time. She was about to ignore his question or, even better, redirect him by asking if he was a cop, but when she opened her mouth to go that route, her damn instincts took over and she found herself saying the exact thing she shouldn't.

"I'm a fed, not a cop," she said, handing the first girl off to him. While Alyssa had struggled a little with her, Tall, Dark, and Gorgeous scooped her up in one arm like she weighed nothing more than a bag of groceries. The girl's eyes fluttered open and she gazed up at the big man holding her. She smiled, then passed out again. "But we still can't call an ambulance. I have someone I know who can take them to the ER."

"Why?" he asked, his voice more curious than suspicious.

"It's…complicated," Alyssa finally said, ducking into the sedan for the second girl.

She expected him to press for an explanation, but when she had the second girl out, she found him gazing down at her with a slightly amused expression.

"I'm okay with complicated," he said softly.

The way his British accent sounded out the phrase had her wishing he would say it again, possibly while leaning over and breathing softly along the bare skin of her neck. Or tracing patterns on her skin with those long fingers of his. Oh yeah, that would do it.

"I'll get my SUV and meet you at the head of the alley," he said, setting the girl down beside the sedan. "We can put them in the backseat."

"I don't think so," Alyssa said, handing him the second girl before he could say anything. "We'll put the girls in the backseat of my car, and you can follow me to the drop-off point if you want."

"What's wrong with my SUV?"

She didn't answer right away, taking a few moments to pull the tracking device out of her coat pocket, then move to the front of the car. Flipping the tiny on/off switch with her thumb, she leaned down to attach it to the underside of a radiator mounting bracket. The heavy-duty magnet made sure it stayed put. She stood up to find him regarding her with an arched brow.

"It's complicated, right?" he asked, mouth quirking.

It was all Alyssa could do to keep an answering smile off her own face. That was all she needed, for things to be more complicated. So she nodded and headed for the alley exit.

"By the way, you never answered my question," he said. "About why we can't take my vehicle."

She turned back to look at him. "I'm not putting those two unconscious girls alone in a vehicle with you. You could be a psychopath for all I know."

He snorted. "I can't be a psychopath. I'm British."

She was about to ask exactly what the hell that was supposed to mean when he continued.

"By the way, I'm Zane Kendrick." He smiled, perfect, white teeth flashing in the darkness. "And before you ask, yes, I'm a cop."

Alyssa ignored the interest her mind was taking in that amazing smile of his, because hello…*complications*! Instead, she nodded and kept heading toward her car.

"Alyssa Carson," she said casually over her shoulder. "FBI. But you already knew that part, right?"

She expected him to say something snarky in that delicious British accent of his. Instead, all she got was what sounded like a growl, and yeah, that was pretty okay, too.

Chapter 2

"I'm guessing Christine is FBI, too?" Zane asked as he perused the menu at the quaint, old-fashioned diner where they stopped for dinner an hour later. "As well as being one hell of a good friend?"

"What makes you think she's a fed?"

Alyssa made a show of scanning the menu, even though she already knew what she was going to order. She'd known the moment Zane had suggested going to a diner to grab a bite to eat. What could she say? French fries were her jam.

Of course, she was also keeping her eyes fixed on the menu so she wouldn't be caught staring at the man across the booth from her. Now that she had him under some better lighting, it was obvious he was seriously droolworthy. Then there was that accent. She felt an incredible urge to strip naked, lie back on the table, and let him talk her to orgasm. She was sure she'd read something in *Cosmo* about that being possible.

The hunky cop with the British accent glanced over the top of his menu at her, making her peek up to see a knowing expression on his face. Yeah, he knew the effect he had on her.

"You sent Christine a text in the middle of the night asking her to meet you in a dark parking lot behind an old warehouse. When she shows up, she calmly helps us transfer two unconscious girls to her car after you tell her they've been drugged and need to be taken to a hospital ASAP. Then she leaves without asking a single question," he pointed out. "A person that unshakable is either law enforcement or a criminal. Since you're a fed, I'm assuming it's not the latter. That makes her FBI. And one hell of a friend for not asking for details."

Alyssa set her down menu, giving up on the whole ruse of looking like she'd been reading it. Besides, who was she trying to impress? "I'm guessing you must be a detective. Since you're so clever and all."

"I'm not a detective. I'm SWAT. The clever part is due purely to my British DNA." He smirked, making her want to do seriously naughty things to his lips. Or have him do seriously naughty things to her with those lips. She wasn't sure which. "What, you never heard of Sherlock Holmes? Being clever is in my blood."

She shook her head, trying to shake loose her attraction to his witty charm. Damn, this man was dangerous. "I could care less how clever you think you are. I'm just trying to figure out what an LA SWAT cop was doing in a nightclub following a group of men who spend their nights kidnapping girls for fun."

"Who said I'm an LA SWAT cop?"

"You're not?"

"No," he said. "I'm from Dallas."

Okay, that made even less sense. She opened her mouth to ask Zane what the hell he was talking about, but the waitress chose that inopportune moment to show up to take their order. Actually, there were two waitresses. Apparently, they really wanted to get the order right. Or more likely, both women had a thing for British accents. She supposed she couldn't blame them.

As Alyssa ordered a Diet Coke and a plate of seasoned fries, she was shocked Amy, the redheaded waitress with the notepad, could take her eyes off Zane long
enough to write it down. Zane ordered steak and eggs,
pancakes, bacon, sausage, toast, and a plate of fries,
because those sounded "bloody good."

"I love a man who likes to eat," the older of the two
women said with a smile. African American with curly
hair piled atop her head and a warm smile, her name tag
read *Edna*. She asked Zane to repeat his order, to make
sure they'd gotten it right. Alyssa didn't necessarily
mind. Even words as simple as *eggs and bacon* sounded
sexy when he said them.

Then he made the evening complete by asking if they
had Earl Grey tea. Because...British!

"Normally I'd ask about the insane amount of food
you ordered, but I'm more interested in why a Dallas
SWAT cop is in LA saving damsels in distress," Alyssa
said after the waitresses left.

Zane flashed her a grin. "Maybe I'm on vacation
and saw something that looked a little suspicious, so I
decided to help."

The look he gave her was so angelic that for a
moment she found herself wanting to believe him. Then
she remembered the way he'd growled and thrown those
Neanderthals around in the alley behind the club and
reminded herself, while Zane might be attractive, he
certainly wasn't an angel. He might not even be human.

"By the way, I probably should have mentioned I saw
the man and woman with you," she said. "The ones you
were talking to over that expensive-looking commo rig
under your shirt. Are they Dallas SWAT, too?"

The smile never left his face, but those chocolate-brown eyes sharpened, becoming appraising. "Is it normal to run FBI operations without backup? What about hiding everything that happened from your fellow agents? Is that standard, too?"

She returned the smile that wasn't really a smile. "Is this how we're going to do this? I ask a question. You ask a question. I ask another one. But neither one of us answers. If so, I'm not sure why we're here, other than to get something to eat."

He lifted a brow. "Anything wrong with a man and woman having dinner with each other?"

"Oh, you mean like a date?" Alyssa laughed. "Well, crap. If I'd known this was a date, I would have worn something nicer. Maybe even done my hair."

Zane chuckled, his eyes taking in the long, blond hair she had pulled back in a ponytail and the dark-blue blouse she wore. Her hairstyle was all about practicality because she never knew when she was going to have to chase after a bad guy—or smash one in the side of the head with the butt of her weapon. Her blouse was standard work issue. It wasn't like she'd brought fancy clothes with her. In fact, she never packed anything dressy when she was working cases…which was pretty much all the time. Hoping to blend into the club, she'd left the top two buttons undone to flash a little skin and show off the white gold necklace she had on. That bit of skin suddenly seemed to attract Zane's attention and his gaze became almost predatory.

"You look good just the way you are," he said softly.

The compliment made her heart suddenly start beating faster. *WTF?* If she had any sense in her noodle, she'd be out of the booth and running for the door. But she stayed right where she was.

She didn't say anything in response. Seriously, what was she going to say after a line like that? Thankfully, Amy and Edna showed up with the food then, giving them a reason not to talk for a while. The aroma of bacon and sausage wafted over from his side of the table to tease her even as the fries commanded her attention. Alyssa dumped half a bottle of ketchup on a separate plate, then added a good puddle of mayo on top of that. She dipped a few fries in the mixture and bit into them. Mmm, they were delicious. A little crispy on the outside, tender on the inside and perfectly seasoned.

Alyssa watched out of the corner of her eye as Zane dug into his steak and eggs. He didn't bother with salt or pepper, or even steak sauce. He simply started eating. She expected him to pause and say something, but after a few minutes of silence, she decided coming to this diner had been a mistake. She had no doubt he and those two SWAT cops with him knew something about Mr. Creepy. It was equally obvious he wasn't telling her jack. And as much as she liked the fries, she could get them anywhere, including back at her hotel.

Which was where she should have been right then, instead of wasting time at the diner. She could use the sleep. She'd been running on fumes the entire time she'd been in LA. She shoved another handful of fries in her mouth—holy crap, they were good—then started to slide out of the booth. She'd pay at the counter, then get the hell out of there.

"My teammates and I are out here trying to track down the man who attempted to kill us," Zane said casually, pushing his empty plate aside and sliding the pancakes in front of him.

Wait, where had the steak and eggs gone?

Alyssa slid back into the booth. Yeah, the question he'd answered was one she'd asked ten minutes ago, but it was progress.

"This guy who tried to kill the three of you," she said. "Does he hate cops or you three in particular? I haven't met the other two yet, but I can definitely see a person coming to dislike you enough to try killing you."

Zane snorted but didn't look up from his stack of pancakes. He carefully layered the crisp bacon in between the fluffy pancakes, then slathered on gooey butter before dumping nearly an entire bottle of maple syrup over the top of the pile. He cut off a wedge from the stack that was way too big for a lion to eat and shoved it in his mouth. The sounds of happiness he made as he chewed were patently unfair. The man even made gluttony sound sexy.

Alyssa was beginning to think she'd have to wait another ten minutes to get more information out of him when he looked at her with those mesmerizing, dark eyes.

"The man we're after didn't just aim for the three of us. He led a group of men who were attempting to kill my entire SWAT team."

Something clicked in her head then. Dallas SWAT team…terrorist attack…corrupt city official. Alyssa didn't watch much in the way of news since her work was in the category most people would describe as *all-consuming*, but she vaguely remembered seeing something about a group of psychos trying to murder cops at a wedding.

"That was you, huh?" She gave him an apologetic look. "Since I'm a fed, you'd think I'd have figured it out the moment you mentioned you're Dallas SWAT, but I'm a little disconnected from the real world these days. Sorry."

He took another bite of the high-sugar-diet killer in front of him. "You have nothing to be sorry about. You don't stay glued to the TV and social media. In the world we live in, that's probably a good thing."

Alyssa ate some more fries. Because they were there, and everyone knew it was bad luck to leave uneaten fries on your plate. "The man was a high-level city official or a cop, right?"

Zane nodded. "Randy Curtis, chief of police."

Her eyes went wide. "Your own chief tried to kill you? Why?"

His mouth edged up. "It's…complicated."

She wanted to get pissed at his nonanswer, but she'd started that particular defensive strategy, so she supposed she couldn't complain if he used it on her.

"Every law enforcement organization in the country is looking for Curtis," she said. "What makes you think he's in LA?"

Zane regarded her thoughtfully for a moment, then turned his attention to his fries. Alyssa watched in amusement while he made french fry sandwiches with the toast, then slathered them with mayo. How could he eat this much and stay so fit?

"A teammate of mine who's good with hacking tracked a text message on Curtis's phone to LA," he said.

"So, you came out to LA to find him yourselves," she surmised. "I'm just guessing here, but I'm assuming you didn't share this little tidbit of information with anyone else, right?"

He shrugged. "When your boss tries to execute your entire team, it's a little difficult trusting outsiders."

Alyssa could understand things becoming personal. It was a weakness of hers, too. "You obviously must have gotten some more leads since arriving in LA, since the three of you were scoping out that club."

He gave her another long look, his eyes boring into hers as if evaluating how much he should tell her. "It turns out Curtis has family here, with lots of money, power, and connections."

It didn't take long for Alyssa to figure out where this was heading. "You think he came out here looking for help from one of his rich relatives. The creepy guy in the expensive suit?"

Zane nodded. "Stefan Curtis, his nephew. He's the black sheep of the Curtis family—as in the Black Swan Enterprises Curtis family."

Alyssa didn't bother to hide her surprise. She wasn't even from LA and still knew the name. Black Swan Enterprises was some kind of worldwide conglomerate, existing for no other reason than to make a buttload of money. She had no idea they were even based out of LA, or that a single family ran the group.

"Stefan has lots of money, but no obvious position within the Black Swan organization," Zane continued. "More interesting than that though is his criminal record. He even has his very own goon squad."

She nodded. "If someone in the Curtis family is capable of helping someone hide from the po-po, it'd be him. But where does the kidnapping angle come in?"

Zane pushed his empty plate aside and gestured toward Alyssa's, arching a brow. She nudged her plate closer to him.

"That's the part I'm hoping you can help with." He picked up a handful of fries from her plate, careful not to cross-contaminate. And who said chivalry was dead? "We've been following Stefan, hoping he'd lead us to his uncle, but he doesn't do much beside hang out in clubs, gambling joints, and strip clubs, staring at attractive women and looking like a bloody pervert."

Stefan's behavior tonight, along with the criminal background Zane mentioned, painted this particular pervert as a good suspect in the recent disappearances she was investigating. And maybe the other ones Christine had been tracking as well. Alyssa had no idea how the body in the landfill drained of blood or the Curtis family–slash–Black Swan Enterprises angle played into this yet.

"This is the part where you share what you know," Zane pointed out. "Since I'm being so friendly and all."

Alyssa considered pulling the *it's complicated* card but decided against it. The Dallas cop had done his part. She had a name to work with now. She knew how to play nice when she had to—even if she couldn't tell him everything.

"Three attractive young women disappeared about a month ago." She pulled out her phone and flipped through the photos she had of the girls. "Lindsay Carr, Stacie Bryant, and Georgie Sparks. Over the past few years, other people have gone missing in this part of LA, all fitting the same profile. All attractive and young. All the kind of people who can disappear without anyone noticing."

Zane grimaced at that. She knew the feeling. It sucked they still lived in a world where some people were invisible and didn't seem to matter. She considered telling him about the blood-drained body in the landfill but checked herself. That piece of info was too valuable to let go of right now.

"Something tells me the twins at the club tonight fit your profile, too. Girls that wouldn't be missed."

"That's my thought," she said. "Christine will look into it once she gets them IDed."

"What brought you to the club tonight?" he asked.

She shrugged and sipped her Diet Coke. "A rumor. Some street kids suggested the three girls might have been in there the night they disappeared."

"Not much to go on."

"I've made do with less."

Zane gestured at the remaining few fries on her plate. She nodded, watching as he devoured them.

"You ever notice how food from someone else's plate always seems to taste better than the stuff on yours?" he asked.

"Really? Huh." She considered that. "Maybe next time, you'll let me try something from your plate, so I can see what I think."

That charming smile curved his sensual mouth again, his expression suggesting he was still hungry even after everything he'd already eaten. She wasn't sure if it was food he was hungry for, though.

"Is that your way of saying you'd like there to be a next time?" he asked.

She hadn't been thinking anything like that. *Are you sure?* a little voice scoffed. Regardless, she didn't bother to respond to the subtle nudge.

"So, is the LA field office so overloaded with

missing persons cases they've started sending agents out completely on their own?" He picked up his tea, gazing at her over the rim of the cup. "Or is there something I'm missing?"

Alyssa hesitated. How could she explain she had nothing to do with the LA field office and that all the agents in her division worked alone until they had something concrete enough to justify calling in for backup? That's how things worked when there were only eight agents covering these kinds of cases for the entire United States.

But Zane was regarding her expectantly, so it wasn't like she could completely ignore the question. Especially since she blew off his barely disguised dinner invite.

"Just a matter of too much work and not enough people to do it," she said.

Zane regarded her thoughtfully, his right hand coming up to rub the slight scruff covering his jawline as his gaze drifted from her eyes, down her neck, then centered on her chest for a while. Okay, he was seriously gawking at her boobs. She'd expected him to look at some point, because, hello...men and boobs! But she had to admit, she hadn't thought he'd choose this moment to do it.

"What were you planning to do with those men who were kidnapping those girls?" he asked, lifting his gaze to hers again.

"I was planning to follow them, hoping they'd lead me back to the other three missing girls," she said, knowing even as she said the words that her answer wouldn't be well received.

His eyes narrowed. "You were going to let them kidnap the girls?"

She didn't need to hear him say the words out loud to make her feel like crap. She already had that covered. "It's not a scheme I'm proud of, but I need to do something to find those three missing girls—maybe even find out something about the other people who've disappeared. I was going to stay right on their tail."

"And if you'd lost them in this charming LA traffic?" he asked in a flat tone. "Then you'd have five missing girls, not three."

"Like I said, it wasn't my preferred plan. Trust me, I know what it's like to get grabbed by a bunch of low-lifes." She also knew what it was like to be afraid for her life, terrified those lowlifes were going to kill her. She shook off the memory. "But those girls have been missing since December. I had to do something or accept that the next time I saw them would be in a morgue in a condition no one should have to deal with."

Alyssa silently cursed herself for letting him get to her. Since when did she lose her cool so easily? And when the hell did she start allowing personal history to slip into a conversation she was having with a man she'd met a few hours ago? Especially a man she had no reason to trust.

She was still trying to breathe through the anger bubbling up inside her when Zane leaned forward and rested his right hand on top of her left. His was much bigger than hers. Warm and strong, too. Alyssa almost shook off the contact, but then his gaze caught hers and she stopped herself. Those eyes of his made it damn near impossible to think.

"I'm sorry I second-guessed you," he said. "I've had people do that a few times and never thought much of it. You were in an impossible situation. If you stopped those guys and had them arrested, Stefan would have hired some fancy lawyers to get them out within a few hours. They'd never tell you anything about those other girls, and worse, Stefan would know the FBI was looking at him. It was a no-win. You had to act on your feet and make the call. You did what you had to do. I get it."

Alyssa had no idea why she cared what a SWAT cop from Dallas thought, but for whatever reason, she did. "Thanks."

Amy chose that moment to stop by the table with the checks. Zane pulled his hand away from hers, giving Alyssa a chance to get her bearings back. By the time she did, she realized he'd grabbed her bill and was slipping a couple twenties into the cheap plastic folder to cover everything.

"You don't need to do that," she said, reaching across the table.

Zane put a single finger on it and slowly moved it farther away from her. Wow, that single-finger thing was sexy. In a tempting I-could-be-running-this-same-finger-all-over-your-body kind of way.

"Don't worry about it," he said. "You can cover it next time."

She lifted a brow. "What makes you think there'll be a next time? I understand what you're trying to do here, I really do. But this is an FBI case. You and your two friends from Dallas don't have any jurisdiction out here."

Alyssa expected something witty and charming out of Zane. Instead, he stood up, reminding her just how tall he was. "It's obvious there's some kind of overlap between the missing girls and our missing police chief. It's also obvious we can help each other, regardless of our lack of jurisdiction. But if that's not something you're interested in, fine. You do your thing. We'll do ours."

"You know that if I see you again in an official capacity, I'm not going to be able to ignore the whole jurisdiction thing. I can't."

She felt crappy for going down that road. But the truth was, Alyssa had no idea if she could trust Zane. Even if she could, there was no way she could let him get involved in this case. Not when her instincts were screaming this thing was going to get freaky. He was a cop from Texas. He wasn't ready to deal with her world. Unless he was freaky himself. In which case, she definitely didn't want him involved.

Zane's mouth quirked. "What makes you think you'll ever see me again if I don't want you to?"

She opened her mouth to answer, but he was already pushing open the glass door of the diner with its tinkling bell and stepping out, leaving Alyssa with the craziest sensation that he was right about her never seeing him again if he didn't want her to. For some crazy reason, that left her feeling disappointed.

Alyssa didn't know she was up and moving until the two waitresses behind the cash register caught her eye, making her slow.

"Damn, girl," Edna said. "Don't walk after that man. Run!"

Alyssa tried to stop herself, knowing it was a stupid idea, but her feet refused to listen. Before she knew it, she was running across the diner parking lot. Then she did stupid one better and jumped in front of his SUV to force him to stop.

"I'm staying at the Westin near the airport, off West Century Boulevard. Room 381," she said, breathing harder than the limited exertion dictated as Zane opened his window. "You should stop by in the morning, so we can figure out how we can make this work."

He was silent for a moment, then smiled. And just like that, her breathing suddenly seemed easier. "See you in the morning, then. If you want, you can pay for breakfast."

Alyssa nodded and watched him drive away, wondering why she was disappointed she hadn't gotten a first-date kiss. Then she caught a movement out of the corner of her eye and turned back to find the two waitresses, the short-order cook, and half a dozen customers standing there with big smiles on their faces and their thumbs up in the air.

Yeah, she should have gotten that kiss.

Alyssa was so tired by the time she got back to her room she almost skipped the mandatory check-in with her boss. But she did the right thing and yanked out her phone to send him a text, asking if he wanted to Skype. If she didn't, he'd be calling her nonstop for the rest of the night, interrupting what little sleep she hoped to get.

Pulling out her agency-issued laptop from the bag she kept it in, she clicked on the Skype icon and waited for her boss to connect. Her computer buzzed less than a minute later. She opened the call to see her oh-so-chipper boss staring back at her. Damn, it was like four o'clock in the morning in DC. She could see kitchen cabinets behind him, so she knew he was still at home, but sheesh, did the man ever sleep?

Obviously, he did. Just not when his agents were about to go into unknown situations completely on their own. Which was frequently.

Alyssa pretended not to notice the sigh of relief he let out when he saw her in one piece. Within the agency, Special Agent in Charge Nathan McKay had the reputation of being a tough man to work for, even bordering on scary. When it came to the standards he set for his team and the effort he expected from each of them, it was probably a well-earned reputation. But when it came to caring about his agents and doing anything and everything necessary to protect them, there was no one she'd rather work for. He was one of the senior federal agents in charge of the joint FBI-CIA task force she worked on known as the Special Threat Assessment Team—aka STAT—and he'd hand selected every member of the team. He'd gone to the mat for each of them on more than one occasion. He treated them as more than just people who worked for him. He treated them like family.

"Everything go okay tonight?" he asked, moving his head a little to the side like he could somehow get a better view through the laptop camera that way. "Did you find anything worthwhile?"

"Yeah. I think I might have gotten lucky."

Alyssa had to hold in the laugh threatening to slip out. Talk about a Freudian slip.

Nathan stood at his kitchen counter, looking at her expectantly from behind his wire-rimmed glasses. "And?"

Crap, she'd been so busy thinking about Zane and that kiss she didn't get she'd zoned out for a second. But hell, she'd chased him down like some woman in a romantic comedy. The least he could have done was lean forward with an offer. It's not like she would have actually accepted.

"Alyssa?" Nathan prompted. "Everything okay?"

"Sorry." She gave him a small smile. "I was just trying to get my thoughts in order. Anywho, tonight was…different. I was at the club and saw this extremely rich, extremely creepy guy blatantly setting up two girls for an abduction. He had four Neanderthals with him, and it was obvious they'd done this before. Everything was matching the profile for the other abductions, so when Mr. Creepy split with one of his Neanderthals, I was all set to follow the other three out the back with the girls when things got interesting."

Nathan picked up his coffee mug and took a sip. "Define interesting."

"It turns out I wasn't the only one watching Mr. Creepy. There were three SWAT cops there, and while two of them stuck with Mr. Creepy, the other one took it upon himself to rescue the girls."

"By himself?"

Alyssa shrugged. "I ended up helping, but I'm not sure if it was necessary. This guy was impressive. And maybe a little different. He put two of the Neanderthals down without breaking a sweat."

Nathan's blue eyes narrowed. "You think he's special?"

She considered that, hesitant to say it out loud. But she finally nodded. "I think so. He's a big man, but still, no human could be that strong. He growled, too. And I'm pretty sure I saw a flash of yellow coming from his eyes at one point."

Alyssa considered mentioning he ate food like it was

going out of style but decided against it. That admission would invariably lead to questions about her having dinner with him, and she didn't want to get into that with her boss.

"Any idea exactly what we're dealing with?"

"None," she admitted. "But for what it's worth, we talked, and while he's definitely dangerous, he doesn't strike me as a threat. In fact, I think he can help with this case. There's definitely something strange going on here with these disappearances."

Nathan regarded her for a few moments. "I trust your instincts, Alyssa, but I think you need to start from the top, maybe without skimping on the details this time."

She sighed, then did as he asked, trying to make logical sense out of everything that had happened that night…minus most of the diner stuff. She couldn't say why she didn't want to tell her boss about that part, other than the fact that breaking bread with a possible supernatural creature wasn't normal protocol. In some ways, it felt like she was lying to her dad, but her instincts told her to stick a sock in it, so she did.

Nathan frowned throughout a good portion of the conversation, but he did that most of the time anyway. He interrupted frequently with pointed questions, and more than once, he gave her a look suggesting he knew she was keeping stuff from him. But in the end, he promised he'd do complete background checks on Zane, Stefan, ex-police chief Randy Curtis, and Black Swan Enterprises. Though he said he'd have to tread carefully around Black Swan.

"They're a big organization with a lot of lawyers and IT security types on the payroll," her boss said. "We have to do this the right way or risk tipping them off we're looking at them."

Alyssa knew Nathan was right about that. A company like Black Swan was savvy enough to pay attention to every little ripple in the web that concerned them. But still, she chafed at the idea of going slowly on something like this.

"I understand. Do what you can. And while you're busy digging, see what you can find out about the Dallas SWAT team, too," she suggested. "Something tells me you're going to find a whole bunch of weird around anything they're involved in."

Nathan nodded and added a few more lines of scribble to the notes he'd been taking. When he was done, he looked up with a worried expression on his face. "You going to be okay handling this one on your own for a while longer, or should I get some backup out there?"

Alyssa smiled. "Do you really have anyone free to send?"

Another frown. "Not really. But I'll pull someone off another case if I have to."

She'd known that was what Nathan was going to say before the words were even out of his mouth. There were never enough people to do the job. Hence, the unwritten rule of *you're on your own until you confirmed there was a reason to send in other members of the team.*

"Don't worry," she said. "I got this."

Nathan hung up a few minutes later, leaving Alyssa sitting on her bed, tired, thinking about tomorrow's meeting with Zane, and wondering if she really did have this.

Chapter 3

ZANE STOOD OUTSIDE ROOM 381 IN THE WESTIN WITH HIS eyes closed, no doubt in his mind he had the right room. The scent slipping from beneath the door in front of him was obviously Alyssa's. There was no other woman in the world with pheromones that amazing. He let the incredible flowery, chocolatey, cinnamony aroma wash over him. He refused to consider why she smelled so damn nice when other women simply smelled...normal. But it would be a lie to say the thought of Alyssa being *The One* for him hadn't intruded on his thoughts as he lay in bed at the motel last night. An appealing, impossible-to-ignore scent had been how all the other guys in the Pack had described the smell emanating from their soul mates.

But Alyssa wasn't his soul mate. Zane was certain of that. For one thing, he had no damn time to be thinking about anything other than finding Curtis and putting an end to the bloody hunters trying to kill everyone he cared about. For another, it was a safe assumption a person had to have a soul to have a soul mate. His had been burned out long ago.

Even so, he had to admit the fight in the alley behind the club last night had been sort of fun. Yeah, he'd tussled with some guys back in Dallas when he'd helped his pack mate Jayden Brooks save the woman he loved, but that had been two idiot gangbangers who barely knew what they were doing. Those men behind the club had been trained killers. Cutting loose against them had felt good, even if he still couldn't do much with his left arm. He'd tried to get a backhand swing with that arm at one point, and the pain had been so severe his vision had gone a little dark for a few seconds. But he'd fought through it and had taken down three armed men before they could fire a shot.

Well, he'd taken down two. Alyssa had handled the other one.

Zane snorted. He probably looked ridiculous standing there in the hallway with a big grin on his face, but watching Alyssa put that wanker on his ass had been kind of hot. That little verbal fencing he'd gotten into with her after the fight, when neither of them had wanted to give up anything to the other, had been a turn-on, too. He hadn't realized it before, but clearly, he had a thing for strong, feisty women. Even if she represented nothing more than a way to keep an eye on those twin werewolves and find Curtis faster, he could still appreciate the attraction.

That was the line he kept telling himself whenever he started wondering why he'd agreed to have that late-night snack with her at the diner and why he hadn't been able to keep his damn mouth shut after getting there. He'd ended up telling her a lot more about his SWAT team and the search for Curtis than he'd planned. But sitting across from her and breathing in her scent, all the filters that usually limited what he said to anyone outside the Pack stopped functioning.

At least he was smart enough to recognize how dangerous that made her. He hoped.

Zane was balancing the tray of cups on the box of donuts he was holding so he could knock on her door when his mobile phone buzzed. He thought about ignoring it in favor of seeing Alyssa, but he knew that would be stupid. There weren't many people who had his number, and the ones who did were all important.

His mobile vibrated again as he moved down the hall and pulled it out. When he saw Becker's name on the screen, he thumbed the green button eagerly. He'd called the team's resident hacker after getting back to the hotel last night and asked him to do a little digging on Alyssa. He'd hoped the other alpha werewolf would have gotten back to him before this, but in the end, he was glad Becker was calling before Zane met with her this morning.

"What do you have?" he asked as he slipped into an alcove near the vending machines. "And what took so damn long?"

There was a growl from the other end of the line. "Bite me, you grouchy Brit. Maybe you haven't noticed but doing background checks for you isn't my day job. I was out until four this morning on a domestic violence hostage situation, then had to stop by the compound to help out a small beta pack who showed up in town. So excuse the fuck out of me if I didn't get your crap to you as fast as you wanted."

Zane pulled back and stared at his mobile. If he didn't know Becker's voice so well, he'd think he was talking to someone else. Becker was one of the easiest-going members of the Pack. He rarely lost his cool or snapped at anyone. Even less so now that he'd met his soul mate, Jayna. Zane couldn't remember the last time he'd heard his friend growl at someone, much less a fellow pack member.

"You okay?" Zane asked after the silence had stretched out for several long seconds. "Did something happen?"

More silence, then a sigh. "Those betas I mentioned used to have an alpha until a group of hunters cornered them in a warehouse outside Wichita, killing the guy right in front of them."

Zane closed his eyes and cursed silently. To the best of their knowledge, hunters had been tracking down and killing random werewolves for decades, maybe even generations, but it had become so prevalent in the past year that werewolves had showed up in Dallas hoping they'd be safe there. Word had somehow gotten around that the Dallas SWAT pack was strong enough to keep the hunters at bay. For the most part, that was true. There had been the two attacks in Dallas, but those had resulted in heavy losses for the hunters. There'd been nothing since.

Unfortunately, the hunters had found a way around the issue by hanging out around the northern part of Texas and ambushing werewolves heading to Dallas.

"Are the betas okay?" Zane asked.

Beta werewolves were smaller than alphas and not quite as strong. To make up for that, they formed much tighter bonds with their pack mates, so much so that sometimes it seemed like betas could read one another's minds. They never strayed too far from the group, either. Their bond with their alphas was equally strong.

"Not really," Becker said. "The girls had the alpha's blood all over their clothes, and the boy with them is barely keeping it together. Jayna tried to comfort them for hours, hoping they'd calm down, but it didn't help. I don't think any of them are ever going to be all right."

"Damn."

Zane leaned his head back against the wall. He knew Becker hadn't told him any of that to make him feel like shit, but that was the end result regardless. The whole reason Zane, Rachel, and Diego were in LA was to find Curtis and figure out who'd hired the hunters to come after them. What they were going to do after that was a little vague, but one way or the other, Zane was damn sure going to find a way to stop the assholes.

But they'd been out here for weeks and hadn't learned anything that got them closer to stopping the hunters. While they had been wasting time, innocent werewolves had been dying.

"What do you have on Alyssa?" he finally asked. "Anything interesting?"

"Yeah, I dug up some stuff on her. Not sure if it's anything you want to hear, though."

Zane tensed. Becker knew he was attracted to Alyssa because he'd all but come out and admitted it to him last night. If his pack mate was hesitant to get into the information he had on her, it couldn't be good.

"Did she lie about being in the FBI?" he asked warily.

"No, she's definitely in the bureau," Becker said. "I was able to confirm that through her Quantico training records, W-2s and other tax records, pictures from various crime scenes, and about a half dozen other documents and databases that'd be damn near impossible to fake. But she doesn't work at the LA field office. That's the problem. As far as I can tell, Alyssa Carson isn't assigned to any FBI field office anywhere in the United States."

"What do you mean?" Zane frowned. "She has to be assigned somewhere. Where does she work cases out of? Who's her boss?"

"That's the part I haven't figured out yet," Becker admitted. "Up until about a year and a half ago, Alyssa Carson's life was an open book. She got a bachelor's in criminology in 2009, a master's in criminal psychology in 2010, graduated Quantico in 2013, and got assigned to the Sacramento field office that same year. She got some serious commendations over a four-year period and looked to be on a fast track for advancement within the bureau."

When Becker slowed to take a breath, Zane almost growled in frustration. "And then?"

"And then she left the Sacramento field office and simply fell off the official FBI radar," Becker said. "She's definitely still working for them. Like I said, I confirmed that. But there's no record of where she's currently assigned or who she works for. I can't find anything related to cases she's worked on or trials she's testified at during that time. Hell, I couldn't even find anything to indicate she's gotten an award or commendation in all that time. Which doesn't fit the pattern for her."

"So she's completely fallen off the grid?"

"Not really. I found her name on an apartment lease in DC, but I'm thinking it's some kind of fake address because the rent and all the utilities are paid automatically. Plus, I could only find her on one or two DC traffic cams, which means she probably hasn't been there more than a few times since leaving Sacramento."

Zane's gut clenched, though he couldn't say why. All

he could say for sure was that something felt seriously off. "Where has she been?"

"She's been traveling almost nonstop all over the world for the past year or so," Becker said. "I have airline and rental car records putting her in about forty different cities around the globe in that time. It appears she travels alone, and the longest she's ever spent in any one place is about three weeks."

"What was she doing in all those places?" Zane asked, trying to understand where all of this was leading. "Were they related to missing persons cases? That's what she's doing here in LA."

"I don't think that's it," Becker said slowly, like there was something he wasn't sure if he wanted to say out loud. "Especially since the FBI doesn't have jurisdiction in the overseas locations she's visited."

"What is it then?" Zane demanded, fighting to keep another growl from slipping out.

"I don't want to make too much out of it because it could all be a big coincidence," Becker started, still choosing his words carefully. "But more than a few of those places on her travel itinerary just so happen to be places where hunters tracked down and killed werewolves."

Zane knew Becker was still talking because he could hear his pack mate's voice buzzing in his ear, but he stopped listening as the implications of what his friend had said filtered in. A fed showing up at the murder scene of one werewolf could be coincidence, but an agent traveling all over the country to multiple scenes went way beyond coincidence. Throw in the fact that Alyssa had started running around the globe at the same time the hunters' activity had started to increase, and it all became impossible to ignore.

Was Alyssa a hunter? Or a fed working with the hunters?

The thought made him feel physically ill, and he was glad he was leaning against the wall. Otherwise, he might have fallen down.

"Do you think it's possible she's—" Becker began, but Zane cut him off.

"No! She was in those places because she was investigating the murders. She isn't a hunter, I'm sure of it."

No way she could be a hunter. The woman he knew did not murder werewolves for a living. He'd never believe that.

"Okay." Becker sighed. "Look, maybe we're reading way too much into this. From what I can gather, most of the places Alyssa went involved unsolved deaths or disappearances that have no obvious connections to the hunters or werewolves. The circumstances around most of those deaths were a little bizarre to say the least. Gage thinks it's possible the feds have put together a team to look into unusual cases. If so, it's possible the U.S. government knows about our existence."

Bloody hell.

Did Alyssa know he was a werewolf? Had the whole fight in the alley behind the club been a setup to lure him into the open and get him to reveal his true nature? Had there been cameras back there in the darkness? Worse, what if she was in that club for those werewolves? Had Alyssa been playing him the entire time they'd been at the diner?

There was only one way to find out for sure.

"Becker, I'll talk to you later," he said. "Make sure you get Rachel and Diego up to speed on all of this. I'm not even going to try and explain it."

Zane didn't wait for a reply. Hanging up, he headed toward Alyssa's room.

———※———

Zane was ready to rip into Alyssa the moment she opened the door, but the sight of her standing there in a pair of shorts and a well-worn T-shirt, her long, blond hair tousled and down around her shoulders, completely took his breath away. The shorts showed off plenty of leg and the T-shirt was thin enough to suggest she wasn't wearing a bra. Bloody hell, she looked amazing.

"What are you doing here so early?" she snapped as he walked in. "I have a gun and I will shoot you. You know that, right?"

Zane opened his mouth to tell her eight o'clock wasn't early, but then her sweet scent distracted the hell out of him, leaving him momentarily speechless. He held up the tray of cups and the box from the bakery.

"I brought donuts," he pointed out, not sure where the righteous anger he'd felt had disappeared to. "You can't shoot a man who brings you donuts."

She eyed the box in his hand. "I thought I was supposed to buy breakfast."

"Donuts aren't breakfast. They're the things you eat on special occasions. Like your birthday or Christmas. Except you get to experience it every morning."

She considered that answer for a few seconds, apparently trying to work through the logic. Finally, she gave up and shook her head.

He turned one side of the tray in her direction. "Coffee with cream and two sugars."

Alyssa looked a little surprised but nodded, taking the cup from the tray and padding barefoot over to the tiny table in the equally tiny kitchenette in the corner. She took a seat and motioned him toward the other one. The act of sitting made her shorts ride up a bit, exposing even more of those extremely nice thighs. He had a sudden image of those well-toned legs wrapped around him and immediately went hard in his jeans.

He quickly sat down across from her before she saw the bulge in his groin, placing the box of donuts on the table between them. He sipped his tea and glanced around the room. It was a lot nicer than the place he and his teammates were in. There was a small travel bag by the bathroom and another suitcase, not much bigger than the first, set up on one of those hotel luggage racks against the wall by the TV, clothes neatly folded inside it. From the way her scent pervaded every corner of the room, overwhelming all others, it was obvious Alyssa had been there for at least a week, maybe ten days. Yet she hadn't unpacked. Maybe she wanted to be able to bounce on a moment's notice.

He surveyed the rest of the room, his gaze settling on the bed. The sheets and blankets were still lying where she'd shoved them down when she'd gotten up to answer the door. The scent wafting off those sheets was so feminine and mesmerizing he wanted to walk over, shove his face right into the middle of them, and breathe deeply. He could only imagine how she'd look at him if he did something like that.

Then again, maybe she wouldn't be surprised at

all. Maybe she'd immediately recognize his werewolf behavior for exactly what it was—because she already knew what he was.

On the other side of the table, Alyssa had opened the box of donuts and was regarding them with amusement. While the confections smelled delectable, it couldn't compare with her intoxicating scent. "I hope you don't think I'm eating half of these, because that much sugar in the morning would have me bouncing off the walls."

Zane snorted as she reached in and grabbed one of the glazed chocolate cake donuts. He went for a cream-filled number, but instead of taking a bite, he set it down on a napkin in front of him. Alyssa must have seen something on his face because she put her donut down, too, her eyes narrowing.

"What?" she asked.

"You're not assigned to the LA field office."

He wasn't as good as some of his other pack mates at knowing when someone was lying, but Zane could pick up on it occasionally. When someone lied, their pulse and breathing rate sped up a little and the scent they gave off changed a bit.

Alyssa regarded him thoughtfully for a moment, then picked up her chocolate donut. "Never said I was."

She took a bite, and Zane was distracted for a second by the way her lips moved as she chewed. He stopped focusing on how sexy she made something as simple as eating a donut and concentrated on whether she was lying or not. He didn't pick up anything to make him think she was. Then again, it wasn't like she'd given him a real answer. For what it was worth, her breathing and pulse were normal. Her scent was the same, too. Not that he could trust it. She'd probably smell like heaven in a skimpy pair of shorts even if she told him she was a pygmy lemur from Madagascar.

"So where are you based out of?" he asked. "Because you sure seem to move around a lot."

Alyssa took another bite of donut, chewing slowly, then sipped her coffee. "I see you've been checking up on me. Should I be thrilled you've taken such a personal interest in my busy work schedule or pissed that you obviously don't trust me?"

"Is there a reason I shouldn't trust you?"

"Is there a reason so many of the bad guys you and your SWAT teammates go up against end up becoming some coyote's chew toy?" she shot back.

He was glad Alyssa didn't have a werewolf's enhanced hearing because his heart immediately began pounding harder as the implications of her question hit him.

"What's that supposed to mean?" he asked, making his voice sound casual even though he was close to hyperventilating at the realization that the federal government had been snooping into his and his pack mates' lives. Yeah, he'd been snooping into Alyssa's, but that was different.

"Oh, nothing," she said, sitting there opposite him looking like butter wouldn't melt in her mouth. "I know coyotes are smart animals, but the ones in Texas are clearly bold as well. How many times have those critters shown up at the scene after a SWAT-involved shooting and nibbled on the bodies? Three or four at least that I saw." She sipped her coffee again. "Funny how I didn't see any other reports about coyotes doing that to dead bodies at other crime scenes. Just the ones involving your team. If it didn't sound ridiculous, someone might think those coyotes follow you guys around."

Zane ground his jaw, forcing himself to keep it together as Alyssa looked him right in the eye and pretty much called BS on the biggest lie in Dallas—that wild coyotes were to blame for the mauled and mangled bodies that were the natural outcome of a pack of werewolves going up against a group of armed bad guys. No one in the police department had ever questioned the theory that coyotes had clawed and chewed on the bodies—not even the medical examiner—as absolutely implausible as the idea of coyotes going after dead bodies might be. But Alyssa and her FBI friends seemed to see the lie for what it was—a complete and utter fabrication.

How much did Alyssa really know? If the hints she was dropping were any indication, somehow, she was aware that Zane and his pack mates had torn those men apart. But did she know Zane and his teammates were werewolves?

For half a second, he considered telling her the truth—or at least confirming what she already seemed to know. He had no idea why he'd even contemplate doing something like that, especially when he realized the risk it would pose to his pack mates. Alyssa was more than a little dangerous if she could make him think about doing something like that. Cursing his own foolishness, he shoved the idea back into the darkest corner of his mind and told it to stay there.

What should he tell her then? Well, as he'd learned in the SAS, when you find yourself in an ambush, the best course of action is to figure out where the gunfire is coming from and go there.

"Speaking of dead bodies, I couldn't help but notice that all those places you've been to over the past year seemed to have a lot of them," he said. "Funny that no arrests were ever made. If it didn't sound ridiculous, someone might think your whole purpose for going there was to make things disappear. No muss, no fuss. Just another example of Big Brother in action."

When her heart rate spiked, he knew he'd struck a nerve.

"So we're doing this again?" she said. "I ask a question. You ask a question. I ask another one, but neither one of us answers?"

Zane shrugged. He didn't know why he felt so shitty about playing that game with her, but he did. "It's obvious we both have things we can't talk about. So, yeah. It seems that's how this is going to go."

As an uncomfortable silence filled the room, Zane finally gave in and bit into his cream-filled donut. It didn't have enough cream for his liking. On top of that, his bloody tea was cold.

Suddenly, he was overwhelmed with two competing desires. One told him to get up and leave. The other wanted him to get up, pull Alyssa into his arms, and kiss her until she told him every secret she possessed. Or passed out from lack of oxygen. Bloody hell, maybe he'd just kiss her until her clothes fell off. How long could that take?

Zane finished that donut and reached into the box for another—cinnamon cake this time. As he chewed, he decided kissing her would be a very bad idea. He couldn't walk away from Alyssa, because he needed her help to figure out what the hell Stefan was involved in and so his team could find Stefan's uncle, but he wasn't stupid enough to try and kiss her. She'd probably kick him in the balls.

He wasn't thinking straight, that was the problem. He knew why, too. At least, he thought he did. There was the terrifying possibility Alyssa was that one-in-a-billion soul mate he was supposed to spend the rest of his life with and being near her was making him stupid. Or there was a chance he was having an adverse reaction to the latest batch of drugs the Pack's doctor had sent him to help regrow the muscle in his injured arm. Saunders had been shipping him a different cocktail of experimental drugs every few days the whole time Zane had been in LA. None of them seemed to work and almost always came with unpleasant side effects. Maybe the latest combination was making him insane.

As unsettling as that thought was, Zane decided he still preferred that explanation to the first possibility.

"So, what happened with Stefan?" Alyssa suddenly asked. "Last night after your teammates followed him, I mean."

Zane recognized an olive branch when he saw it. Alyssa was trying to move the conversation to safer ground. It wasn't much, but it was a start.

"Unfortunately, he went straight from the club to his fancy home in the Hollywood Hills, where he remained the rest of the night." Zane helped himself to another donut. The cake kind with pink icing and sprinkles. "He wasn't too happy when those muscle heads called and told him they lost the girls."

Alyssa looked up from her donut in surprise. "How do you know that? Do you have his phone bugged?"

Zane shrugged. "The FBI isn't the only one with high-tech toys."

She made a face. "What did they tell him?"

"Oddly enough, they talked mostly in code, like they were worried someone was listening in. They told him there was 'trouble with the product' and that they ran into some 'unknown players.' Stefan immediately shut the conversation down and said the subject would be discussed during the next scheduled meeting."

She did a double take. "That's kind of weird. I assumed Stefan would be the type to get pissed and throw things when stuff didn't go his way."

"Oh, he was mad," Zane said. "After he hung up, he cursed for a good five minutes. Then he threw things."

She lifted a brow, her coffee cup halfway to her mouth. "You have his house bugged, too?"

"You know what they say—in for a penny, in for a pound." He smiled. "A cliché I'm allowed to use, by the by, since I'm British."

Alyssa snorted but didn't point out all the laws he and his pack mates were breaking with their illegal wiretaps and listening devices. If it wasn't for the fact that none of her cases seemed to ever reach a courtroom, Zane would have been worried their actions would torpedo any case the feds put together against Stefan. That raised the question as to what the FBI planned to do with the guy, assuming Alyssa ever found those missing girls. Considering all those dead bodies she seemed to leave in her wake, maybe Stefan would simply end up in an unmarked grave somewhere.

Then again, maybe Alyssa was lying about being in LA to find those missing girls. Maybe she was really here to confirm Zane and his pack mates were werewolves—maybe those twins, too. Then all five of them would end up in an unmarked grave somewhere.

Wasn't that a cheery thought?

He was still imagining the trouble Alyssa would have stuffing him, Rachel, and Diego in the boot of her rental car to dispose of the bodies when she spoke.

"Those two girls Christine took to the hospital are okay. But for some reason, they want to talk to you. In fact, Christine said they were insistent about it, threatening to take off if I didn't bring you to see them."

The girls must have figured out he was a werewolf, he mused as Alyssa pulled the box of donuts closer. Or maybe the one who'd woken up for a few seconds had smelled something familiar and wanted to talk about it.

"Are they still in the hospital?" he asked.

Alyssa scanned the selection. She glanced at his sprinkled-covered one enviously, then settled for the plain glazed. He didn't get that. What good was a donut if it didn't have cream, frosting, and/or sprinkles? Maybe plain glazed was the diet version or something.

Donuts and *diet*. Fairly close together in the dictionary. Miles apart in reality.

"Yeah. They slept straight through the night, not coming to until early this morning. Christine is in the process of moving them to a hotel as we speak, but from the text she sent to me a little while before you showed up, those girls freaked out when they realized they'd been drugged and nearly kidnapped."

"I take it Christine was able to keep it all quiet without anyone reporting it to the police?"

If some random cop decided to pay Stefan a visit,

asking why his security team tried to kidnap two girls, that could tip him off he was being watched.

"No police report," Alyssa confirmed. "The girls were scared and more than a little pissed that Stefan played them with some stupid line about being a Hollywood producer, but more than anything, it seems they want to put this incident behind them. Other than talking to you, of course. Not sure what that's about."

He smiled. "Probably the accent. It does it for everyone. So what'd you get from the tracking device you put on their car?"

Surprise flashed in her eyes. What, did she think he'd forgotten?

"Truthfully, I haven't had a chance to check yet," she said. "Let's take a look,"

Setting her donut down on a napkin, she got up and walked across the room to grab her laptop from the desk where it had been charging. Coming back over to stand beside his chair, she set the computer on the table, then opened the lid and booted it up. There was a map of the city on the screen with a little, blinking, green light sitting off of South Broadway, halfway in between New Downtown and Little Tokyo.

"What am I looking at?" he asked.

He wasn't familiar enough with the city to know where exactly the car was. All he could say for sure was that the car wasn't parked in the middle of LAX or the Pacific Ocean.

She used her long, nimble fingers to enlarge that part of the map on the screen. "The car is in a parking garage near the middle of town, where it's been sitting since about three o'clock this morning."

Zane leaned closer to her, trying hard to ignore the mouthwatering scent she put off. He wondered if he could get away with licking her neck. He could say he was trying to clean a bit of glaze from the donut off...

She'd probably shoot him. She *had* been quick to remind him that she had a gun and knew how to use it.

"You think they abandoned the car there?" he asked, deciding to keep his tongue in his mouth where it belonged. Getting shot hurt at the best of times. If Alyssa shot him, it would hurt even more.

She nodded as if she'd been thinking the same thing. "Likely."

He sighed. "There's only one way to know for sure. We could go check on it after we see the girls, if that's okay with you? Maybe we'll get lucky."

"*We?*" She regarded him thoughtfully. "You honestly think it's a good idea for us to work together?"

"Why not?" he asked, even though he already knew the answer. "That was why you asked me to come over here this morning."

"*Why not?*" Alyssa snorted. "I think Dr. Phil would say it's because we have trust issues. Maybe it would be better if I check out the car on my own and call you when I learn something."

The thought of Alyssa going anywhere near Stefan and his crew without backup made his inner wolf howl. He knew she could handle herself—all those awards and commendations Becker had told him about, not to mention the way he'd seen her move last night, proved that—but the idea of her being in danger made his chest tighten up so much it was hard to even breathe.

Zane refused to examine why she made him feel that

way and focused on dealing with the present situation, pushing everything else to the background.

"I guess we're just going to have to work through those issues, because whether you like it or not, we're joined together at the hip for the time being," he said. "At least until we both find what we're looking for."

Alyssa considered that, then finally nodded. "Okay, we can work together. But there's one condition."

He let out a snort. "Only one?"

"Yes. And it's important. I'll work with you, watch your back, and trust you to watch mine. But I need your word that you'll be honest with me. If you lie to me, it's over."

"What would I lie about?"

"I don't know." She shrugged. "Like you said, we both have things we can't talk about. I can live with that. But I'm trusting you to tell me if there's something I need to know to do my job. Anything that has to do with getting those missing people back safely. Anything that involves my safety. Anything you know I wouldn't be able to overlook. As a federal agent and as a human being."

Zane knew he was going to lie before he even opened his mouth. He felt badly about it, but it wasn't like he could tell her that he was a werewolf. She was a fed, which meant she was the last person in the world he could trust with information like that. Even if she already knew what he was, he couldn't admit to it. Despite the possibility of her being terrified when she learned he was a monster, like his former fiancée had been, he still had an almost overwhelming urge to tell her everything. But this wasn't only about him. This was about his pack, too. And he'd do anything to protect them. Even lie.

"I'm not keeping anything from you, and I won't," he said.

Alyssa regarded him thoughtfully for a few uncomfortable seconds, like she was going to call him out, but then she nodded. "Okay. Let me check with Christine and see if she's still at the hospital or has already moved the twins to the hotel, then we can get out of here."

Chapter 4

"WHAT DO WE KNOW ABOUT THE GIRLS SO FAR?" ZANE asked as he and Alyssa walked along the hallway on the second floor of the Fairfield Inn and Suites.

Alyssa shrugged. Before they'd left her hotel, she'd changed out of her T-shirt and shorts into jeans, a simple top, and a jacket. Even though she'd covered up all that perfect skin, she looked just as delectable.

"Not a whole hell of a lot," she answered. "They've told Christine that their names are Zoe and Chloe—they wouldn't give up their surnames—that they're eighteen years old, and that they're from Utah. Other than that, they're not very forthcoming with information. And they didn't have ID on them, either. They're extremely eager to talk to you, though." She gave him a sidelong glance. "You must have made one hell of an impression in those three or four seconds that one girl was conscious."

Zane chuckled. "Don't take it too hard. I have the same effect with puppies and kittens, too."

Alyssa laughed, and he got goose bumps from the sound. Crap, he was such a wanker.

Zane could pick up the extremely slight werewolf scent before they even reached the door. Christine opened it as soon as Alyssa knocked. Not quite as tall as Alyssa, she had straight, dark hair and a no-nonsense way about her.

The twins were sitting on one of the two queen beds, eyeing him and Alyssa curiously as they stepped inside.

"Since we didn't have the time for formal introductions last night, I guess I should do it now," Alyssa said. "Christine Howard, Zane Kendrick…and vice versa."

"Nice to meet you," Zane said, shaking the woman's outstretched hand. "Thanks for all the help last night. I know it was late when we called."

She laughed. "Hell yes, it was late, but for Aly and her adventures, I don't mind losing a little sleep. I was happy to hang out with Zoe and Chloe. Come on. I'll introduce you."

The twins stood, both of them regarding him intently with their big, blue eyes as he shook their hands. While they might have been eager to meet him, Zoe and Chloe also seemed to be a little nervous. Up close, they looked even more fragile and…lost…than they had in the club last night. How the hell had they gotten into that place? That probably wasn't the question to lead with today, of course, but he planned to get to it at some point.

After the introductions were out of the way, the twins moved over to sit on the couch, while he and Alyssa leaned back against the counter of the small kitchenette and Christine took the chair by the desk.

Zane waited for the girls to say something, but they only continued to gaze at him before exchanging looks with each other. One of the twins—Chloe, he thought— tilted her face up a little like she was testing the air with her nose, then looked at her sister again.

"So, Christine said you wanted to talk to me?" he finally said, figuring if he didn't break the ice, they never would. "I was hoping you could tell us your full names and where you're from in Utah so we can help you get back home to your family."

"We can't go home," Zoe said firmly. Even though they were twins, Zane considered her the older of the two girls. Maybe because she tended to place herself in front of her sister, like she was the protector. "We don't have anyone to go home to."

He frowned. "What do you mean?"

"Our parents were killed a week ago this past Friday," Zoe said softly, her eyes haunted. "We don't have any other family to go back to in Provo. Mom and Dad were all we had."

Zane cursed silently. When he'd seen the twins in the club last night, he'd thought they were two local girls out for a night on the town hoping to slip into a Hollywood party so they could meet someone famous. Then, over dinner with Alyssa, he'd agreed with her that maybe they were runaways. He definitely hadn't seen this coming.

Alyssa and Christine looked just as surprised as he did.

"What happened to your parents?" he asked gently.

Zoe reached up to wipe a tear off her cheek. "Chloe and I went to the movies that night, and when we came home, there were four men in hockey masks waiting for us in the living room. Mom and Dad were already…gone." She took her sister's hand, holding on to it tightly as tears filled Chloe's eyes. "We tried to run, but the men grabbed us and shoved rags over our faces. We woke up in the back of an SUV. It was still dark, so I figured we couldn't have gone that far. The four men weren't around, so Chloe and I managed to get each other untied, then ran. We didn't realize we were all the way in Santa Fe, New Mexico, until the next day."

While their story was heartbreaking to hear, even

harder than hearing the words was seeing Chloe's expression while her sister spoke. It was like the poor girl was reliving the experience all over again.

"If you were in Santa Fe, how did you end up in LA?" Alyssa asked. "Why didn't you go to the cops there?"

Zoe glanced at her sister as if silently communicating with her. A moment later, she turned her attention back to him and Alyssa. "When we got out of there, we just ran and couldn't stop. We had to keep going."

Zane had no doubt seeing their parents' bodies, getting kidnapped, then being forced to run for their lives was the thing that had turned them into werewolves. He could see the trauma in their eyes. And considering how slender and lithe they were, he also had no doubt they were beta werewolves.

"Isn't there anyone back home for us to call?" Christine asked, her distress clear. "Cousins, uncles, aunts, close friends...somebody?"

The girls shook their heads in perfect synchronized rhythm. It was a little disconcerting how connected they were. Betas were really close anyway. He couldn't imagine what they'd be like after they'd fully turned, then found an alpha.

That thought bounced around in his head for all of two seconds before coming to a dead stop. Bloody hell, what if the two girls were here looking for their alpha?

"Is there a particular reason the two of you headed to LA?" he asked, interrupting whatever Christine had been about to say. "Do you know someone out here?"

The girls looked at each other again, then back at him.

"Could we talk with you alone?" Zoe asked.

That seemed to catch Alyssa and Christine by

surprise, but Zane had seen it coming. "Yeah, sure." He glanced at the two FBI agents. "Could you ladies give us a minute?"

It was their turn to exchange looks. Alyssa nodded and pushed away from the counter beside him. "We'll go grab some drinks and snacks from the vending machine for the girls." She glanced at the twins. "Any preference on candy bars?"

"Peanut M&M's," they said in unison.

"There's something different about you," Chloe said the moment the door closed behind Alyssa and Christine. "What are you?"

Zane moved over and sat down on the chair where Christine had been sitting, keenly aware of the twins' gazes on him and trying to use the time to organize his thoughts. Unfortunately, he was drawing a blank. He really wasn't good at stuff like this.

He took a deep breath and let it out slowly, meeting their eyes. "What I'm going to tell you is going to sound crazy, but please don't freak out, okay?"

Both girls stared at him, patiently waiting for him to continue.

"I'm a werewolf," he said, trying to make that sound...not insane. "And whether you realize it or not, so are you. You've just started going through the change, so you're probably not experiencing any of the more obvious things that come with it. But it's happening nonetheless."

Zane braced himself for the fireworks he was sure were coming. He expected them to tell him was crazy and that there were no such things as werewolves, but instead, the two girls looked at him, then at each other,

and then back at him. Bloody hell, he wished they'd stop
doing that. It was weirding him out.

"That explains why we feel safer when we're with
you," Chloe said thoughtfully. "But I don't think you're
the person we came out here to find."

"Or are you?" Zoe asked.

Now, it was his turn to sit there and stare. "I don't understand anything you just said. So, let's start over, okay?"

They nodded, still in perfect rhythm. He told himself
to ignore it.

"First, why aren't you freaking out about learning
you're werewolves?"

"We realized that something was happening to us
before we even got to LA," Zoe said. "The scratches,
cuts, and bruises we got when we escaped healed up in
a few hours. Then a couple days ago, we both started
being able to smell things we shouldn't be able to smell.
And last night, we realized we could see in the dark. We
didn't know what it was, but if you say we're turning
into werewolves, we'll believe anything right now."

Well, that was way too easy. Then again, it was
probably because they hadn't experienced the fangs and
claws yet.

"Your change is just starting," he told them. "It will
get more…real."

Zoe tucked her hair behind her ear. "Like what?"

He held up his hand and slowly let his claws extend.
Their eyes went a little wide at that, but they didn't freak
out. Apparently, they were okay with that. He decided
not to press his luck with the fangs. Nail extensions were
one thing—a mouth full of fangs might be a bit much
right now.

He let his claws retract. "What did you mean when you asked if I was the person you'd come out here to find?"

Chloe was the one who answered. "Within hours of escaping, we both felt something telling us we had to find someone. We don't know who it is, but that instinct has been pulling us to LA for the past week. When I woke up and saw you last night, I thought you might be that person." She gave him a sheepish look. "Don't take this the wrong way, but you're not quite…right. There's someone else out there, and I get the feeling they're looking for us, too."

Zane was about to point out how crazy that sounded, then realized he'd just told them they were both turning into werewolves. At this point, crazy was relative. Unfortunately, he didn't have any idea how betas found their alphas. Or vice versa. It didn't work that way for alphas. Gage had asked him to join the Pack and he had.

"I think," he said slowly, still working it all out in his head, "that maybe you two are looking for your alpha."

"What's that?" Zoe asked even as Chloe's eyes sharpened with interest.

"Alphas are a kind of werewolf." He knew he was going to muck it up if he tried to get too deep into the details, so he'd keep it simple. "They tend to be bigger and stronger, like me, and usually have a protective instinct. There are other werewolves called betas that are smaller and gentler, which usually form tight packs with an alpha. You're beta werewolves."

Chloe nodded. "That makes sense. And the pull we've been feeling is our alpha trying to find us while we've been trying to find him."

It wasn't a question, but he answered anyway. "Yes.

Though, in the interest of full disclosure, I should tell you that your alpha might not be a him. It might be a her."

Zoe eagerly scooted forward on the couch. "Can you help us find him or her?"

As much as Zane didn't want to take on the burden when he was already dealing with enough stuff on his plate, he couldn't turn his back on them.

"Yeah, I'll help you." He sighed. "In fact, I'm out here in LA with two other alphas from my pack, so maybe one of them is yours. If not, we'll come up with some way to find him. Or her."

Zane prayed it would be as simple as either Diego or Rachel being their alpha. Because it wasn't like he could look for whoever it was in the phone book under "werewolf, alpha."

"Wait a minute," Zoe said, her eyes narrowing suspiciously. "I thought you said alphas form packs with betas. Why are you in a pack with other alphas?"

How the hell did he answer that when he still wasn't quite sure how he and sixteen other alphas could live in harmony? Finally, he shrugged and replied with something close to the truth: "It just kind of happened."

Luckily, Alyssa and Christine came in with a handful of sodas and candy, saving him from any more questions for the time being.

"So, did you guys clear everything up?" Alyssa asked, handing him a candy bar while Christine gave the twins several bags of peanut M&M's and two bottles of soda.

Zane nodded. "I think so. But it means Zoe and Chloe need to stay in town for a while." He looked at Christine. "Do you think it will be a problem if they hold on to the room until then?"

Christine threw a curious look at Alyssa but nodded. "No, that's fine."

Zane glanced at the twins to see them already munching on their candy. They looked more relaxed now that they'd talked to him. He only hoped he could find their alpha.

~~~

Alyssa was stunned at how quietly Zane moved. For a guy his size, he slipped through the lowest level of the parking garage like a ghost. Maybe she should have agreed to let him come down here on his own. He was seriously good at this stealthy stuff.

He stopped and held up his hand, motioning for her to do the same, his head held high as he listened to the sound of a vehicle moving somewhere else in the garage. All Alyssa could make out was the squawk of car tires taking tight turns on smooth concrete. She had no clue if the vehicle was five levels above them or about to run them down any second. He must have decided everything was okay because he motioned for her to continue following him, heading down the incline toward the lowest level of the garage.

"You sure the vehicle we're looking for is down here?" he asked.

"The truth is, I'm just guessing," she admitted. "The program on my laptop only shows the location in 2-D. The sedan I put the tracker on could be on any level in here. I had no idea this place had five levels underground, but since we haven't seen it yet, it makes sense they parked down on the lowest level. Especially if they were planning to dump it."

That answer seemed to suit Zane, and he continued on ahead of her, his head swiveling side to side as they passed behind the few cars parked down there. It wasn't surprising this level of the garage wasn't filled to capacity. Even in a city as crowded as LA, with its lack of available parking, this section was too creepy for anyone to want to come down there.

As they walked, Zane would lift his head every once in a while, and he'd do this weird thing where he closed his eyes and sniffed. Like he was testing the air with his nose. Okay, that was damn odd.

After reading the information Nathan had found on the Dallas SWAT team, Alyssa had been convinced Zane—and probably the rest of his team—were special. She had no idea what they were, but after seeing copies of the autopsy photos of some of the criminals they'd dealt with, she got the feeling they were something that could be scary as hell if you got on their bad side.

One of the reasons Zane and his team were so good at taking down bad guys might be because they seemed indestructible. While there was nothing in any of the official incident reports the team wrote, Alyssa could read between the lines. It was almost a certainty that Zane and his teammates had been shot in the line of duty—multiple times in some cases. Yet only one of them had ever been taken to a hospital. Even after getting shot with a high-powered rifle round through the chest, the guy had literally run out of there less than a day after surgery and right back into the action, going up against a psychotic killer.

The funny thing was, even though she was sure Zane wasn't entirely human, she didn't feel concerned for her safety when she was with him. It was probably crazy, but as they'd talked over donuts earlier this morning alone in her room, she hadn't been worried for a second. Not even when things had gotten a little tense as they'd asked questions they both refused to answer.

The FBI agent in her wondered if Zane was using a spell to lure her in and make her feel safe when she shouldn't. She'd certainly seen enough over the past year to suggest something like that was possible. She'd dealt with things recently that could trick otherwise careful people into walking right into a trap.

But as Zane moved ahead of her in the dimly lit garage, she decided it wasn't some kind of supernatural spell that made her so comfortable with him. It was her instincts telling her she was safe with him. And Alyssa never doubted her instincts. They'd saved her butt more times than she could count.

Then again, as handsome as Zane was, it was also possible she was simply overlooking the danger because she was too busy gazing at him. It might be shallow of her, but in her defense, she hadn't slept with a guy in over a year and a half, and the last time she had, it hadn't been all that.

If they hadn't been in stealth mode, she probably would have laughed out loud. Deciding to trust a possible monster because she was horny was ridiculous. Then something twisted inside her and she mentally backtracked. He wasn't a monster. She wasn't sure what he was, but he wasn't a monster.

If nothing else, the way he'd handled that situation with Zoe and Chloe earlier made her sure of that. Those girls had been through the most horrible situation Alyssa could imagine anyone having to deal with, and Zane had been the one they'd turned to for help. Truthfully, she didn't blame them. It was obvious he was the kind of man who cared about people and would do anything to help them.

Alyssa only wished she knew what they'd talked about while she and Christine had been getting sodas and snacks. Even though she'd done a bit of casual prodding during the drive over to the garage, Zane wouldn't say. He'd kept the conversation focused entirely on what those two girls needed now, which mostly included Christine taking the twins' statements, so she could start getting everything cleared up with the police back in Utah.

"There it is," Zane said softly, jerking her out of her confusing thoughts. "Against the far wall."

This level of the parking garage dead-ended in a concrete wall, and the sedan was parked alongside a row of vehicles just like it, right down to make, model, and year. As she and Zane hurried across the garage, she was tempted to ask how he knew this was the car the girls had been in, but she decided against it. She was worried he might say something she couldn't ignore—like admitting he could smell which vehicle was the right one. That was something she didn't want confirmation on right now.

When they got to the sedan in question, Alyssa crouched down beside it and slipped her hand under the radiator, confirming it was the one with the tracking device. She straightened up to find that Zane had opened the passenger door and was searching the glove box. He rustled around for a few seconds before coming up with the vehicle's registration. He handed it to her without a word, then moved over to the next vehicle in the line. While he dug around in there, she took out the small flashlight she always carried with her and searched the first vehicle. It was super fancy, with all-leather interior and heavily tinted windows all around. It even had one of those privacy partitions, so the driver couldn't peek into the backseat.

"Well, if the line of identical sedans weren't a dead giveaway, this is," Zane said, coming back over to hand her another piece of paper. "The cars are registered to a company called Curtis Unified Parking Services. The address for the company is the same as the garage. They didn't dump the car here. They parked it here."

She frowned. "Stefan owns a parking garage? The guy comes from a family with more money than God, and he spends his free time running a parking garage? Kidnapping women isn't enough to keep him occupied?"

Zane shrugged. He looked as stumped as she was. "And before you ask, I didn't know about this place. We knew he was loosely connected to several legitimate businesses in the city, but not this one. Someone's done a good job of hiding it."

That someone would be either the Curtis family or Black Swan Enterprises.

"That's got to mean something," Alyssa said. "I'm not sure what, though."

"Me, either," Zane murmured. "But I'm curious about why they own so many vehicles. I'm pretty sure a company that manages a parking garage doesn't need a fleet of luxury sedans."

She leaned into the car to put the registration back in the glove box. "Do you think Stefan is kidnapping even more people than we thought?"

"I hope not. But my gut tells me he's using these cars for

something shady. We need to get out of here and do some digging. See what we can find out about Curtis Unified Parking Services. I'd be interested to know if there's a link between this place and Black Swan Enterprises."

Alyssa had a hard time believing a link like that would exist. Not when Stefan was using these same vehicles to kidnap people. The chances of something like that coming back on the powerful company was a risk no sane person would tolerate. All it would take was one of those vehicles getting in a traffic accident while carrying kidnap victims, or even pulled over for speeding. Why risk it? Regardless, it was still a place to start looking.

While she attached tracking devices to the other sedans, Zane slipped away to see if there was a direct access to the Curtis Unified offices somewhere nearby. No way in hell a man like Stefan would walk an inclined parking ramp to the next level to get the elevator. She didn't see a door anywhere, though.

Would Stefan have brought those girls here last night? If so, had he brought other people here, too?

She didn't think that was likely. Not when there was a chance some random employee might stumble across them. But still…what if?

Alyssa was still lost in thought when Zane came back. "There's an entrance to the offices around the corner, but it's covered by two security cameras. There's no way we'll ever be able to slip in that way without someone seeing us."

"It will take me a little while to get my team working on this," she said as they walked back up the ramp. "When it comes to doing searches, the department I work for isn't as constrained as most parts of the federal government, but it will still take time. They probably won't have anything useful until tonight, longer if Black Swan Enterprises is involved. With their money, they can hire people good at making the truth disappear."

Once outside, they headed to Zane's SUV parked four blocks away. He pulled out his phone and sent a quick text to someone. "I'll get mine on it right now. They can be hip deep in data within minutes."

She stopped walking, forcing him to do the same. "Without a warrant of any kind?"

Zane put his phone back in his pocket. "You don't have to be part of this if it makes you uncomfortable."

Something about the way he said the words made her think he genuinely wanted to protect her from this.

"I want to meet your teammates," she said. "I want to be there when they dig into Stefan's company."

She didn't know how putting herself firmly in the middle of Zane's illegal activities was going to make the situation any better, but she wanted to do it anyway. Maybe because she couldn't seem to think straight when she was around him. If she was thinking at all.

Zane was silent for so long she thought he might refuse, but then his phone buzzed. He dug it out and glanced at it, then nodded at her. "They're waiting for us at the motel we're staying at."

He started walking again, and Alyssa hurried to catch up. Trusting a trio of Dallas SWAT cops who probably weren't even human might not be the smart thing to do, but her instincts were telling her it was okay. That was enough for her.

—∿∿—

Alyssa already knew they weren't heading to Zane's room, so she was a little surprised when he didn't even bother to knock before slipping a key card into the scratched, dingy door of the charming, little no-name motel room and pushed his way in. Hell, he didn't even announce himself. Wasn't he afraid of getting shot? And getting shot in this place was a distinct possibility. It looked like the kind of motel Sam and Dean would only stay in when they were seriously short on cash. Or hiding from particularly scary demons.

"Hope you two have your clothes on because we have company," Zane said as they walked into the room.

The comment earned him synchronized snorts of amusement from the man and woman sitting on the shabby couch. She hadn't gotten a great look at them last night—it had been dark in the club and those flashing strobe lights hadn't helped—but there was no mistaking they were the people she'd seen follow Stefan out. Even sitting there clicking away at the keyboards of three different laptops spread out on the coffee table in front of them among all the fast-food containers, they projected the same barely contained animal grace and power as Zane.

"Diego Miguel Martinez and Rachel Bennett," Zane introduced. "Diego, Rachel—Alyssa Carson."

Diego stood and held out his hand. "Nice to meet you."

He wasn't as tall as Zane, but she could tell that, under his T-shirt, he had muscles on top of muscles. Heck, his forearms were so built she thought he might crush her hand. She almost pulled it back out of pure self-preservation. But then she met his kind, dark eyes and instinctively realized she wasn't in danger.

"Zane mentioned having dinner with you last night,

but I have to admit, you don't fit the description he gave us," Diego said.

She threw a confused glance in Zane's direction before turning to Diego. "How did he describe me?"

"Don't worry. He didn't say anything unflattering," Rachel said in a distinct southern twang as she got to her feet. "But after listening to him go on and on about you last night, we got the impression you'd be…I don't know…bigger."

Alyssa eyed the tall, athletic SWAT cop, wondering if she should be offended by that. She might not be as muscular as Rachel, but she was nearly as tall.

Rachel smiled and extended a hand in greeting. "I'd offer you something cold to drink, but there aren't any fridges in the rooms and the ice machine out front is broken."

As Zane told his teammates about how the meeting with Zoe and Chloe had gone, Alyssa looked around the room and decided she'd never again complain about the hotel per diem the FBI authorized for her. The places she stayed in were the Ritz compared to this dump. The carpets were stained and dirty, and the small bed in the corner looked like the most uncomfortable thing in the world to sleep on.

"But on the bright side," Diego said in his naturally husky voice, "there's an In-N-Out Burger right down the street. So, how about a warm soda, a side of fries, and some dirt on Curtis Unified Parking Services?"

Alyssa headed for the couch and sat down. "You had me at fries."

Diego laughed and took a seat on the other side of Rachel, reaching across her to hand Alyssa a little red-and-white cardboard tray filled with beautiful, greasy fries. As she picked one up and nibbled on its salty goodness, she threw a look in Zane's direction, silently telling him he had some explaining to do. She still wanted to know how he'd described her to his teammates but decided it could wait.

The hunky Brit gave her a subtle nod. Yeah, he knew he was in trouble.

Funny how she and Zane seemed to be able to communicate with each other without words, even though they'd only met last night. There were people in the bureau she'd worked with for over a year she still couldn't read as well.

Alyssa pushed the thought aside for later and turned her attention to the three laptops on the table. The ones on either side were opened to the Internet. Skype was up on the middle computer, and she found herself gazing at an attractive guy with dark-blond hair, blue eyes, and an amused expression on his face.

"So, you're Alyssa Carson—federal agent and all around badass," he said.

Alyssa smiled. "All around badass?"

"Hell yeah." He grinned. "Your personnel record kind of makes you out to be some kind of superhero."

"Ah," she breathed. "You must be the hacker Zane mentioned. Breaking into the FBI personnel system, huh? That's impressive. With those kinds of skills, you should be working for the feds."

He gave her an appraising look. "Zane told me there was something different about you. I see what he means. By the way, my name's Eric Becker. But everyone just calls me Becker."

Alyssa felt more than saw Zane move over to stand

beside her end of the couch. She was a little surprised he'd told his teammates such complimentary things about her. She hadn't thought dinner had gone that well last night. The urge to ask him what he'd said about her was difficult to suppress. It was crazy, but she wanted to know what he genuinely thought of her. He seemed to find her impressive, and for some reason, she liked the way that made her feel.

She bit into another fry and focused on the real reason she was there. "So, what do you have on Stefan and his garage?"

Becker shuffled papers around on the desk, looking for something while Rachel and Diego picked up small spiral notebooks from the coffee table, the kind police officers everywhere carried to write down info for an investigation. The two SWAT cops flipped through the pages, reviewing what they'd already written.

Zane sat on the arm of the couch, his hip brushing her sleeve. Alyssa closed her eyes for a moment. Crap, she could practically smell him. No…strike that. She could *definitely* smell him. The scent was so strong she had a hard time resisting the urge to turn and bury her face in the front of his shirt and breathe all of him in. She'd never ever wanted to do that to a guy before.

Get a frigging grip, girl.

"First off," Becker said, "there's definitely a connection between Curtis Unified and Black Swan Enterprises. It's buried in about a hundred layers of shell corporations and misleading legal paperwork, but it's there if you look hard enough."

"What kind of connections?" Zane asked from beside her, and she glanced over to see him leaning in close, his eyes focused on the Skype screen. Damn, he made intense look good.

"To start with, Black Swan Enterprises fronted the money for the construction of the parking garage," Becker said. "They went out of their way to hide it from casual observers, but at the same time, they made sure if anyone bothered to dig deep, they'd find a completely rational trail of investment decisions ending in a net profit. Maybe not enough to justify a worldwide conglomerate like Black Swan Enterprises wasting their time on something as trivial as a parking structure in downtown LA, but the numbers support their involvement. I think all that's a cover, though."

"A cover for what?" Alyssa asked.

"To hide the fact that Black Swan Enterprises wanted the parking garage built a very particular way."

"What do you mean?" Diego asked.

Becker shrugged. "I'm not an expert on building things, especially parking garages, but when I compared the costs for Stefan's garage with several others in LA, Black Swan Enterprises put a lot more money into the foundation work than other people—like more than they paid for the entire rest of the structure."

Alyssa almost gave herself a high five as the answer clicked in her head. "You think they put extra money into the foundation because there's more than just a foundation down there. Like maybe rooms to hide people they kidnapped?"

"The building plans filed with the county show a few small offices on the ground level for management purposes, then not much beyond maintenance and utility space below that," Becker said. "But unless Black Swan

Enterprises was using the construction costs as a way to launder money, you've got to think it's at least possible there's something else down there."

"Maybe even our illustrious police chief," Zane said.

That was a possibility, Alyssa thought. "This is all great supposition, but what are we going to do to confirm it? Zane and I already figured out there's no way to get into the offices on the lowest level without being seen. I doubt we'll have better luck trying to go in from the ground floor."

"We could set up a stakeout on the garage," Zane suggested. "Keep an eye on the place until we see something worth moving on."

Becker opened his mouth to say something, but a man called his name from somewhere behind him. "I have to go. We got a call—barricaded suspect in an apartment building. If you guys need anything else, let me know."

"So, how do you want to do this?" Rachel asked after Becker hung up. "It might look suspicious if we're parked by the curb across the street from the garage 24–7."

Alyssa considered that. "I have an FBI credit card. We could see if there's an office or apartment for rent nearby that'd give us a good visual on the entrance and exit of the garage."

Zane and his teammates agreed that sounded like a good plan. Alyssa stood to head out with Zane when Diego caught his eye.

"Before you guys leave, could I talk to you for a second?" he asked Zane. "Outside."

Alyssa pretended she didn't see the curious expression on Zane's face. Or the way he glanced at Rachel out of the corner of his eye. When he gave Alyssa a questioning look, she nodded and sat down on the couch again.

She didn't know them well at all, but it seemed obvious there was some kind of tension between the three SWAT cops. She'd thought Zane's joke about Rachel and Diego having their clothes on when they walked in was exactly that—a joke. Now, she wasn't so sure. Maybe the two of them had slept together and regretted it.

Alyssa knew it was absolutely none of her business, but she also knew what it was like being a woman in a male-oriented career field, so she figured it wouldn't hurt to ask if Rachel wanted to talk about it, but the SWAT cop spoke before she could get the question out.

"So, you have a federal credit card, huh?" Rachel asked, the smile on her face making Alyssa suspect the woman knew what she'd been thinking. "I bet it has a nice limit on it. Any chance you can use it to get us some rooms in a different hotel? Someplace that doesn't have bedbugs the size of poodles?"

Alyssa laughed. Rachel did, too. The sound was almost enough to make the lingering tension in the room fade away. That's when she realized Rachel didn't seem tense. She seemed…tired. As in really, really tired.

Maybe that's all that was going on. Maybe Rachel couldn't sleep well in this crappy motel from hell. Maybe that's what Diego wanted to talk to Zane about.

"I'll see what I can do," Alyssa said. "The team I'm on in the bureau has a lot of leeway when it comes to expenses, but a few extra hotel rooms in a city as pricey as LA are going to be noticed and raise questions. I'll probably need to wait until after I drop the bill on them for the place we're going to need for the stakeout. Once they finish crapping bricks over that, anything else will probably look like chump change."

Rachel laughed again and opened her mouth to say something, but then looked sharply at the door. "Zane and Diego are coming back."

Alyssa wasn't sure how Rachel could possibly know that, but before she could ask, the door opened and both men stepped into the room. Diego looked more relaxed than he had a few minutes ago, but now Zane seemed tense. Maybe this *was* about more than the rinky-dink, bedbug-ridden motel they were staying in.

"Do you mind if Diego goes with you to find that stakeout location instead?" Zane asked. "Something came up here I need to take care of."

She had no doubt the *something* that had come up was whatever was going on between Rachel and Diego. Well, good luck dealing with that.

"Yeah, sure," she said. "I'll call as soon as we find something, so we can come up with a duty roster." Alyssa glanced at Rachel as she headed for the door. "I'll get in contact with the credit card rep for my team, too. See if I can at least warm them up to the idea of paying for another hotel."

Rachel nodded. "Thanks."

Alyssa glanced at Diego. "Come on. Let's go spend some taxpayers' money before I change my mind."

Chapter 5

NEITHER ONE OF THEM SAID ANYTHING FOR A GOOD TEN minutes. Instead, Zane and Rachel polished off several burgers and two trays of fries. Being this close to In-N-Out Burger meant they were living on fast food. Which wasn't a hardship. He frigging loved American cheeseburgers. In fact, he could eat them every day for the rest of his life and not get bored.

"So, what happened with the twins?" Rachel finally asked. "How did they handle it when you told them they're werewolves?"

"Surprisingly well." He knew Rachel was purposely trying to get him on a topic of conversation that had nothing to do with why he was there. He told her about what happened to the twins' parents, then explained, "It turns out they came to LA looking for their alpha. Apparently, they're following some kind of homing instinct that tells them this is where they need to look. You ever heard of anything like that?"

Rachel shook her head.

"I mentioned that you and Diego would stop by their hotel soon," he said, "so they could see if either of you happen to be their alpha."

Another nod. Well, this talk was going well.

"What was Alyssa saying about paying for another hotel?" he finally asked after he'd finished chewing, figuring it was as good a way as any to get the conversation started. If Rachel let him.

Rachel picked up her can of Diet Coke. "I was joking when I asked her if she could get us rooms at a place that didn't have bedbugs, but I think she's actually going to try and find us another hotel. Which is pretty damn cool, not that I'm surprised. Something tells me she's special."

He chuckled. "*Special* would be a good word for her."

Rachel regarded him, a knowing look in her eyes. "How special?"

Zane cursed silently. His pack mate had just played him like a cheap instrument. "Not that special. And just so you know, I didn't stay behind to talk about me. I stayed so we could talk about you. Diego is worried about you."

Rachel grabbed another handful of fries, chewing slowly before washing everything down with a gulp of lukewarm soda. "Yeah, I know. But I figured before we get into my issue, we could get into yours."

"I don't have an issue."

"Cool." She shrugged. "Neither do I. Now you can tell Diego to stop worrying."

He sighed. He hadn't known Rachel very long, but he'd already figured out she was as stubborn as a stump. At least, that's what some of the other members of the Pack said. Personally, he wasn't sure how stubborn a stump was. Despite having an American mother and living in Dallas for years, he still didn't get a lot of the slang and metaphors he heard on a daily basis. He understood the ones with a southern bent to them even less. Sometimes it felt like that part of the country was a world all its own.

But he knew enough to realize Rachel wouldn't talk to him if she didn't want to. And after the stuff Diego had mentioned, Zane needed her to talk to him.

"Alyssa makes me feel kind of crazy," he finally

admitted softly. "My heart starts beating fast every time she gets close. And her scent? I've never smelled anything close to it. It's like she's a chocolate-covered cinnamon cake sitting on a bed of rose petals. Bloody hell, I'm drooling right now just thinking about it."

He couldn't believe he'd said all those things to a pack mate he wasn't even sure he trusted. He hadn't intended to share, but the moment he thought about the gorgeous blond FBI agent, his mouth wouldn't stop running. It was like he'd lost his bloody mind.

Regardless, he meant every word of it. And that scared the hell out of him.

"I'm sure you've already thought about this yourself," Rachel murmured, "but I have to ask. Do you think all this stuff you're feeling—combined with the way she smells—means she's *The One* for you?"

Zane opened his mouth to give the knee-jerk response. The one where he claimed there was no possible way Alyssa was his bloody soul mate. He was even ready to point out that the only reason he felt this way was all the drugs he'd been taking for his arm lately. But he couldn't, because he didn't believe any of that crap. He doubted Rachel would either.

"Becker told you what Alyssa does for the FBI, right?" he asked quietly.

Rachel nodded. "I know Becker thinks she tracks down werewolves for the federal government. I'm just not sure I believe it. Hell, you're the one who told us about what she did to help those two girls in the alley behind the club last night. Between that and meeting her in person, she doesn't come across as a coldhearted federal werewolf assassin."

"Federal werewolf assassin?" He let out a short laugh. "Bloody hell, you make her sound like a comic book hero."

"You think this is funny?" Rachel snapped. "I never really thought of you as a chucklefuck, but maybe I was wrong. It's been known to happen."

Chucklefuck. Another one of Rachel's favorite words, the precise meaning of which still eluded him. But he could pick up enough through context to understand what she was trying to say.

"No, I don't think this is funny." He picked up his can of soda and took a swig. "There's not a single part of me that wants to believe Alyssa could be the kind of woman who'd hunt down and kill a werewolf, especially since I have a hard time being around her without wanting to do something crazy and definitely inappropriate. But I can't afford to be naive about any of this, regardless of how she makes me feel. She very well might be *The One* for me. But she could also be a threat to me, you, Diego, and every other member of our pack. I can't overlook that, no matter how much I might want to. If the federal government knows about our kind, we have to be very careful. *I* have to be careful."

Rachel was silent for a long time. "So what are you going to do? How do you treat Alyssa like a threat and *The One* for you at the same time?"

"I have absolutely no idea," he admitted. "I'm kind of working this out as I go at the same time I'm focusing on finding Curtis and those missing girls Alyssa is looking for. After that, I'll play it by ear."

Rachel considered that. "Can I ask you a simple question?" When he nodded, she continued. "Do you believe a woman who might be *The One* for you could willingly hurt you or those you care about? I'm not asking you to answer with your head. I'm asking you to answer with your heart."

He knew what Rachel was asking. Simply put, she wanted him to stop thinking so damn much and go with his instincts. But the truth was, he didn't trust his instincts—human or werewolf. He hadn't for a long time. Not since he'd learned how terrible he was at knowing whom to put his faith and trust in.

"I wish I could answer your question, but I can't," he said. "My first inclination is to protect my pack. I can't see myself ever trusting her completely."

He grunted in pain as something suddenly twisted his guts into a knot, making sweat pop out on his forehead and tingles race down his spine. It was gone as quickly as it had appeared, but Rachel still looked at him in concern.

"You okay?" she asked.

"Just a twinge in my arm," he lied.

Zane could tell from the look on her face that she didn't believe him. But it wasn't like he could explain what the hell had just happened. He didn't know. He'd never felt anything like it before. It was like his inner wolf had just punished him for doubting his soul mate.

Rachel's eyes narrowed, a sure sign she was about to start digging, and he had no desire to go down that road. Time to get this discussion back to the real reason he'd stayed there instead of going with Alyssa.

"Now that we've talked about my issues, how about we talk about yours?" he said, cutting Rachel off as she opened her mouth. "Diego told me you've been having a hard time sleeping lately. He said you wake up in the middle of the night screaming from nightmares."

Rachel sighed, flopping back on the couch. "Are you effing kidding me? Diego promised he wouldn't tell you about that. He swore it."

Zane frowned. "He's worried about you. And it sounds like he has a good reason to be. How long have you been having these nightmares?"

Rachel didn't say anything. Instead, she rested her head back on the couch and stared up at the ceiling for a long time.

"I've been having them a few times a week since the night I went through my change, but they've gotten worse since we came out to LA," she finally said softly, lifting her head to look at him. "I'm lucky if I get more than an hour of sleep a night now. It's so bad I have to keep the light on even though I can see perfectly fine in the dark, which is driving Diego crazy. Though I don't think that bothers him nearly as much as my screams of terror."

Zane didn't know what was more disturbing—the brutal honesty in her response, the look of flat-out exhaustion in her eyes, or the fact that she and Diego had kept this from him.

"Dammit, Rachel," he growled, both angry and frustrated that a member of his pack was trying to deal with something like this on her own. "Why didn't you tell me what was going on?"

She leaned forward, resting her forearms on her thighs and staring down at the ugly carpet. "Because I didn't want to bother anyone with my problems. It's something I need to handle on my own."

Zane opened his mouth to tell her that she was a member of a pack now and that meant she didn't need to solve problems on her own anymore. But then he remembered he had no room to preach considering how hard he'd pushed his pack mates away after being shot by that hunter. He knew what it was like to let pride — and maybe more than a little shame — get in the way of letting people help.

"Gage never told any of us what happened to you the night of your change," he said slowly, trying to tread carefully. The events that flipped the gene and turned a person into a werewolf were always extremely traumatic. Rachel was clearly still working through hers and might not want to talk about it. "Not that he ever would," he added when Rachel looked at him suspiciously. He didn't want her thinking he and the rest of the Pack sat around talking about her. "Hell, I don't even know how long you've been a werewolf. But I'm assuming what happened to you was really bad if it's still affecting you now."

Rachel shot him a glare, her normally brown eyes flashing the vivid green of a female werewolf. He glanced at her hands to see that her claws were extended, too. No doubt about it — she was pissed. More often than not, getting angry could cause werewolves to lose control and partially shift.

"It happened about a year ago," she said, her claws retracting as she regained control. A moment later, her eyes returned to their normal brown. "And yeah, it's still affecting me. But it's nice to hear you're completely over the events that happened the night you changed. Gage mentioned you'd been in the war and lost some friends. I guess you put their deaths behind you with no problem, right?"

Zane flinched like she'd slapped him. Harry dying in his arms. Billy bleeding out all over the ground. Oliver begging to be left behind. No, he'd never be able to put those memories behind him. They might not be wrecking his sleep every night like they had in the beginning, but they were still there.

"Sorry," he muttered, feeling like a jackass. "That was a stupid thing for me to even say. I'm just…" He sighed. "Look, I'm trying to help here, okay? But I don't know how."

Her eyes flashed green again, but the anger faded more quickly this time. "I know you're trying to help, and I appreciate it. But let's face it—I can't even seem to help myself, so I'm not sure what you think you can do." She took a deep breath. "I'm starting to think that maybe I'm going crazy."

"You're not going crazy," he said firmly.

Damn, he wished Gage were there. Their commander was much better at dealing with stuff like this than Zane was. If Rachel needed help with how to breach a door or how to study for an exam to get promoted, that he could do. But Gage wasn't here, so he had to try.

"I'm starting to see and smell things that aren't there," Rachel said softly, her gaze fixed on the wall above the TV. "I think most people would agree that's a sign I'm going crazy."

Bloody hell. If Rachel was hallucinating, this was bad. As in way-the-fuck-over-his-head bad. But short of looking for a shrink in downtown LA who treated werewolves, he was on his own here.

"You mentioned it's been getting worse since coming out here," he said. "Is that when you started seeing and smelling stuff?"

Rachel opened her mouth, then she closed it again as

she thought about it. "Before, actually. I guess I didn't make the connection between that moment and what's been going on out here because it was kind of nice in the beginning."

"What do you mean, nice?" he prompted when she didn't continue.

"The morning after the hunters attacked us at the compound, I woke up from a great dream and noticed this seriously amazing scent. Only I didn't smell it in my apartment. I smelled it in my dream."

Zane had definitely never smelled anything when he dreamed. He hadn't even known it was possible. For werewolves, scents were simply a fact of life. They were surrounded by thousands of them every day. If a scent stood out—like Alyssa's did for him—it usually meant something significant.

"What kind of scent?" he asked.

Rachel blushed. "It was leather and gun oil." When he didn't say anything, she glared at him. "What? I'm a cop. I like the smell of well-worn leather and gun oil, okay? It's not like I can control what scents show up in my dreams, so don't you dare judge me. You can't tell any-body either. I haven't even told Diego about this part."

He held up his hands in surrender. He'd never thought Rachel would be the type to worry about what he—or anyone else—thought about her. If leather and gun oil did it for her, that was fine with him. "I'm not judging. And I won't tell a soul. I promise."

That must have satisfied her because she nodded.

"So it started with picking up the scent of leather and gun oil in your dreams. You said you're also seeing things. What exactly are you seeing?"

"This is the part that's harder to explain. And why I think I'm going insane." Her brow furrowed. "I keep catching sight of someone out of the corner of my eye, but when I turn to see who it is, there's no one there. Most of the time it's when I'm out of the room, but it's happened in here, too. Even when Diego is with me."

"And you think the smell and this person are connected?"

Zane had the feeling he knew where this was going—even if it was too insane to consider.

She considered that. "Yeah, I guess, since sometimes I pick up the scent and see the person out of the corner of my eye at the same time."

He took a deep breath, not sure how she'd take what he was going to say. "Don't get pissed at me, but do you think there's a chance the scent you smell and the person you see out of the corner of your eye might have something to do with the hunter you let get away at the compound?"

Rachel's face went blank, her heart rate kicking into high gear. Jumping up, she circled around the table to stand in front of it, her claws and fangs extended, her body tense, as if she was getting ready to attack—or respond to the attack she thought was coming her way.

Zane stayed where he was, holding up his hands in a placating gesture to show her she wasn't in danger. "Relax, Rachel. It's not like that. I'm not saying you let that guy get away on purpose or did anything to put the Pack at risk. I'm just asking if you think it's possible there's a connection."

Rachel stared at him for a long time before the green glow faded from her eyes and her fangs and claws retracted. She took a deep breath and let it out slowly. "Who told you?"

"Brooks," Zane said, naming his pack mate and best friend. "He said you had a clear shot at one of the hunters and didn't take it. He wasn't sure what your reasons were but decided he should give you the benefit of the doubt."

"It didn't keep him from telling you about it," she said flatly. "Is that why you've been so hesitant to trust me while we've been out here? Do you think I'm working with the hunters or something?"

He frowned. "What are you talking about? I trust you."

"Are you effing kidding me?" She snorted. "You think I haven't noticed that you won't let me do anything on my own. You make sure you or Diego are with me 24-7 and keep me away from any situation where either of you might have to depend on me."

He wanted to deny it, but that was hard to do when it was the truth. He'd have to suck it up and deal with it. "Okay. I guess I have been keeping an eye on you."

"*Keeping an eye on me.* Another way of saying you don't trust me," she shot back, her eyes swirling with green.

"You never answered my question," he said. "Do you think the person you keep seeing—and smelling—could be the hunter who got away?"

"Would you believe me if I told you?"

"Yes."

Sighing, she put her hands on her hips. "I suppose it could be the hunter I let get away. I don't know why I even think that, but it feels right."

He nodded. "Do you know why you let him get away? Or why you think you keep seeing him?"

"I don't know," she answered.

Zane had a pretty good idea why. After telling him Alyssa could be *The One* for him, he was stunned Rachel didn't see it too. But maybe some people couldn't see what was right in front of them. He knew a little something about that, and thinking a hunter might be your soul mate was disconcerting to say the least.

Rachel walked around the table to sit on the couch again. "Since we're getting all this out in the open, I should probably tell you about the part of the nightmare that makes me wake up screaming in the middle of the night and freaking the hell out of Diego."

"Okay."

"That's when the dreams started getting darker and I started dying in them." She swallowed hard. "And that person I see out of the corner of my eye now and then? He's covered in blood. And I'm pretty sure it's mine."

Zane didn't know what to say. He got chills just listening to the scene she described.

After a moment, Rachel got up and slipped into a light jacket like their conversation had never happened. "I'm going to run down to In-N-Out and pick up some more burgers and fries."

"I'll go with you," he said, then added, "I could use a walk."

Rachel looked like she didn't buy his BS, but she also looked a little relieved to have company.

Neither of them said anything as they made their way along the busted sidewalk. That was fine with Zane. He was too busy wondering how he was going to deal with everything. Not only did he have to determine if Stefan was hiding Curtis and help Alyssa locate those missing girls, but he also had to figure out if she was indeed

The One for him. On top of that, he had to keep Rachel from losing her mind and help Zoe and Chloe find their alpha. All while his bum arm left him little more than half a werewolf.

Bloody hell, he was in so far over his head.

⁓⁓

"You know, you could have ordered anything you want," Alyssa said to Zoe and Chloe, sitting on the other side of the table at the restaurant where she'd taken them to lunch. "It's on the FBI's dime. You didn't have to go with the cheapest thing on the menu."

Zoe and Chloe looked up from their ooey-gooey grilled cheese sandwiches and smiled at exactly the same time, with exactly the same smile.

"We ordered grilled cheese and potato chips because we both love them," Zoe said. "Not because they're cheap. After all the money you spent on us this afternoon, saving a few bucks is the last thing we'd be thinking about."

Alyssa smiled, satisfied the girls weren't depriving themselves out of some twisted sense of guilt. The whole purpose of this little shopping spree and late lunch had been to get the twins out of their hotel room and hopefully get their minds off their troubles for a little while. It wasn't like retail therapy would bring back their parents or make their nightmares go away, but if it helped for even a few minutes, it would be worth it.

"Thanks again for all the clothes," Chloe said softly. "But thanks even more for the personal hygiene stuff. Rinsing the one set of clothes we had in restroom sinks was getting old, but brushing without toothpaste was the absolute worst."

Alyssa laughed and munched another one of the fries that had come with her ginormous turkey club. "No problem at all. If you two decide you need anything else, call me and we'll go get it."

The girls nodded and spent a few minutes paying attention to their food. Alyssa had to admit they were holding up a lot better than she'd expected. Of course, having experienced something similar herself when she was about their age, she knew there was a good chance the girls were in denial at the moment, refusing to even think about what had happened to them, much less talk about it. She knew from experience that coping mechanism wouldn't work for long. But until the girls were ready to talk, there was little anyone could do.

"I want you guys to know that if you ever need to talk, I'll never be more than a phone call away," she said softly. "Even after we get this all taken care of and go our separate ways, you can always call me. Okay?"

Even though both girls nodded again, Chloe looked so timid right then that Alyssa knew she wouldn't be ready to talk for a while.

While the poor girls ate like they were starving, Alyssa couldn't eat all of her sandwich. Between the donuts this morning and the fries at the motel, she was still full. That was okay. Zoe and Chloe had no problem taking up her slack, splitting the remaining half sandwich and the rest of her fries, then practically inhaling them. They might be small, but they ate like Zane.

"Have you two thought about what you're going to do next?" Alyssa asked as they collected their shopping bags and headed out of the restaurant. "I know Zane mentioned you guys wanted to stay in LA for a while.

Are you just planning to sightsee and stuff, or is there someone out here you came to see?"

Chloe glanced at her curiously as they walked back to the car. "Zane didn't tell you why we wanted to stay?"

Alyssa shook her head. "No. I assumed it was something private."

"It was," Zoe agreed. "But we thought since you two were partners that he'd tell you anyway."

"Oh, we're not partners," she admitted with a laugh. "We just met the other night."

Zoe exchanged looks with her twin, as if they were somehow communicating with each other telepathically, then smiled at Alyssa. "That doesn't mean you won't become partners soon."

Alyssa almost laughed. She remembered what it was like to be that young and naive. Zane was definitely attractive, and even if they ended up in bed at some point—never mind overlooking the whole he-may-not-be-human thing—there was no way in hell the two of them would ever end up as partners. Not when they were worlds apart.

It wasn't until she dropped Zoe and Chloe off at their hotel that she realized the twins never did answer her question.

⁓⁓

"You changed your hair again," Alyssa said the moment she walked into Christine's tiny broom closet of a space at the FBI's LA field office. She'd curled her shoulder-length, dark-brown hair just enough so that it framed her face and softened her features. "Wasn't it straight when I saw you the other day?"

Her friend looked up from her computer with a smile. "I didn't really change it as much as left it up to fate to determine what it was going to look like today. Obviously, fate likes my hair to have some waves to it because this is what it looked like after I washed it."

Alyssa shook her head. Christine's hair looked better by accident than hers did on purpose. Alyssa could use a curling iron on her hair for an hour, and five minutes after walking outside, it was straight as a board and going wherever it wanted.

"Well, whatever you did or didn't do, it looks great."

Alyssa took a seat in one of the two chairs in front of Christine's desk. She couldn't help noticing her friend had added a few new pictures to the wall behind her desk since Alyssa had been there last. Anyone who'd ever met Christine figured out pretty quickly she was obsessed with photos. At least when it came to her family. Images of her husband, who was also in the FBI, pixie-size daughter, and goofy German shepherd, Klaus, covered every available wall and flat surface in the office. Not that Alyssa blamed her for putting them up all over the place. Her family was photogenic as hell. Great hair, an awesome family, and a cute dog.

If it wasn't for the fact that Christine was her best friend, Alyssa probably would have been jealous. She still didn't know how Christine was able to balance an incredibly stressful job with the perfect home life.

"How are our two girls doing?" Christine asked as she neatened up a stack of folders and moved them to the side, then sat back in her chair. No doubt they were more missing persons cases. Alyssa couldn't help but wonder how many of them were related to Stefan and whatever the hell he was involved in. "You took them shopping to get some clothes, right?"

"Yeah. They're doing okay for now," Alyssa said. "I only hope they find someone they trust to talk to soon before everything they're holding inside comes busting out."

Christine lifted a brow. "Maybe they'll talk to you."

She shrugged. "I made the offer, but I'm not sure if they'll take me up on it. Those two are so tight with each other it's going to take someone really amazing to get them to open up."

Christine smiled. "I don't know. You strike me as someone pretty amazing. If they're going to trust anyone, it'll be you."

Alyssa appreciated the compliment. Eight years older than Alyssa, Christine sometimes didn't realize how amazing *she* was, or the influence she had on the people around her. The woman had damn sure changed Alyssa's life. But she knew if she mentioned it, Christine would disagree. So instead, she focused on one of the reasons she'd come to see her friend. It was something that had popped into her head while she'd had lunch with the twins.

"Do you need help covering their hospital stay? Or the hotel room?"

Her friend had probably racked up some significant expenses helping her keep the two girls off the official FBI radar—costs she likely wouldn't be able to put on her bureau credit card.

Christine smiled. "Relax. I've been doing this for a little while, remember? I have arrangements with all the local hospitals, a dozen or so hotel chains, the bus lines, and even a few of the airlines. They help me take care of people I come across who need help without a lot of questions being asked. So I got this."

Alyssa snorted. "Of course you do. Why did I even bother asking?"

"No idea." Her friend leaned forward, resting her folded arms on the desk. "But if you're feeling generous, maybe you could fill me in on exactly what the hell you've gotten yourself involved in. Who tried to kidnap those girls, and what the hell did that hunk Zane have to do with it?"

Alyssa hesitated, not sure she wanted to get her friend involved in this mess. Because there was no way this wasn't going to get messy at some point. But Christine had stuck her neck out for her. She deserved a few answers. At least as many as Alyssa could give her.

So she told Christine about what had happened at the club last night and the parking garage today, filled her in on Stefan Curtis and Black Swan Enterprises, then she explained about Zane and the other two SWAT officers from Dallas. The only detail she kept to herself was her suspicion that Zane and his friends were some kind of supernatural creatures. That was something she couldn't share. Not that Christine would have believed her anyway.

When she was done, Christine got up to close the door of her office. When she sat down at her desk again, she had a worried expression on her face.

"You seriously think an organization as large as Black Swan Enterprises could be involved in this level of human trafficking?" she asked. "Why would they risk getting caught and going to prison? Besides money, of course, which they already have a hell of a lot of."

Alyssa shrugged. "I don't know, but my gut is telling me they're mixed up in all this somehow. That's why I just spent a buttload of FBI money to rent an office space across the street from that parking garage, so we can stake it out. Stefan is kidnapping people and making them disappear. We're going to figure out exactly what he's doing and hopefully find those people who've gone missing."

Christine looked at her like she thought Alyssa was crazy but finally nodded. "Okay, I guess I can understand your reasoning based on the evidence you've dug up so far. But seriously, four of you trying to go after an international corporation like Black Swan Enterprises? Even if you disregard the fact that your three SWAT cops have absolutely no jurisdiction here, it's still insane. Pulling full-time stakeout duty on a garage alone would probably take a dozen people. How are you going to do that?"

Earlier today, as she and Diego had hunted down a place for their stakeout, Alyssa had that same thought. There was no way the four of them could maintain a long-term stakeout on the garage and Stefan's home, not to mention follow Stefan and his Neanderthals when they went out to the clubs to look for more victims. But it wasn't like they had an option. She couldn't ask for more manpower to help out. It would take her whole team, and Nathan wouldn't go along with that until she had something more to go on than instincts.

"We'll figure it out," she said. "Somehow."

Christine regarded her thoughtfully. "You know, I could help you out. Off the books, of course. No one upstairs would have to know. There are some other agents who'd be willing to help, too. People I trust."

Alyssa's heart just about melted in her chest. Her

friend was too much. Of course, she couldn't take Christine up on the offer, but it was sweet as hell regardless. "Thanks, but no. I kind of need to keep the official exposure on this operation to a minimum."

Christine looked disappointed but nodded. "I get it. I know enough about what you've gotten yourself into over the past year to recognize you think there's weird crap involved—weird crap I'm not allowed to know anything about."

Alyssa tried to play it cool and keep the surprised look off her face but was pretty sure she failed. Obviously, Christine had figured out she wasn't doing normal FBI stuff anymore, since Alyssa had been the first person she'd called when that corpse had shown up drained of blood in the landfill. Alyssa only hoped her friend hadn't been digging around too much. She didn't imagine Nathan or his boss would be too thrilled to have someone poking around their little covert operation, even if it was a fellow FBI agent. It was something that could get Christine fired.

"You don't have to say anything, Aly. I know you can't talk about it, so I'm not going to push. But I want you to know that if you ever need help, all you have to do is call me and I'll be there, no questions asked."

Alyssa felt like crying. "Thanks. I can't tell you how much that means to me."

"Then don't try." Opening her desk drawer, Christine pulled out a thick manila folder with the familiar icon of the FBI Medical Examiner's Office on the cover and handed it to her. "I've been holding on to this for two days, waiting for a chance to show it to you. There's some stuff I know you're going to find interesting in there."

Alyssa set the folder down on the desk and opened it. She'd been waiting for the ME's final report on the body from the landfill since getting to LA and had been frustrated it was taking so long. She knew why, of course. Dead Jane Does with no one to claim them didn't get much priority.

She slowly flipped through the pages, looking at the photos of the woman's body in the condition it had been found in at the dump, then after she'd been taken to the morgue. Both versions made her want to cry. How did a young, pretty girl end up in a landfill?

"You know you could have scanned all this and emailed it to me, right?" Alyssa frowned as she tried to decipher the nearly illegible notes. It would take hours to figure out if there was anything in here she didn't already know. "You realize we do live in the twenty-first century."

"I know, but the ME made me promise I wouldn't make copies or let the original out of my hands. There's some stuff in there that he doesn't want getting out or associated with his name."

Alyssa looked up. "Okay, now I'm definitely interested. Spill. Because I know you read it."

Christine snorted. "It's scary how well you know me. But let's talk about that later because you're going to freak when I tell you blood loss isn't the official cause of death."

Alyssa stared. She did that a lot lately. She hoped it didn't make her look stupid. "How is that possible? The body was drained of every drop of blood. That has to be what killed the girl."

"You'd think." Christine shrugged. "But the ME discovered the true cause of death was heart failure. The blood was drained after the fact."

Alyssa tried to grasp the implications of that. After a few moments, she decided she couldn't. "How could she have died of heart failure? She was twenty-two years old and in good shape—at least superficially."

"You won't find this part in the report, but the ME thinks the girl had heart failure from being terrified for a sustained period of time."

Alyssa hadn't even known that was possible. "But the initial report stated there was no severe trauma, bruising, or other signs of torture."

Christine reached over and flipped through several pages in the report until she came to a form with the outline of a woman's body on it—half the page for the front and the other half for the back. The ME had drawn in little dots all over the place.

"The two puncture wounds in the neck were obvious, since that's where the killer drained all the blood from," Christine said. "But when the ME put the body under a black light, he found hundreds of small puncture wounds on the neck, wrists, forearms, shoulders, inner thighs, behind her knees, inside her ankles, stomach, hips, even her breasts. He thinks they stuck her with a large gauge needle, slowly draining her blood in small amounts at a time over the two-year period she was held, letting her heal up in between. Based on the number of puncture marks, he thinks they must have given her something to help her heal faster because it's the only way to explain how they were able to do it. When the girl's heart gave out, they drained the rest of the blood."

Alyssa felt the urge to throw up. Holy crap. The girl had been slowly tortured for two years, poked with needles over and over, her blood drained from her body.

Alyssa mentally reviewed everything she either knew personally about monsters, or had read, things she and her team had learned while dealing with creatures that went bump in the night. The only problem was lots of nasty things out there liked human blood. The thing that had tortured the girl could be anything.

Alyssa flipped through the rest of the ME's report, copying down a few notes here and there as she went. She was so caught up in what she was doing she barely noticed Christine studying her from the other side of the desk.

"What?" she asked when she finally couldn't ignore the pressure of her friend's gaze any longer. "Why are you staring at me like that?"

"Nothing." Christine's lips curved in a sly smile. "I was just going to ask how your dinner went last night."

"What dinner?" Alyssa asked, getting a sinking feeling she knew exactly where Christine was going with this.

The smile on her friend's face broadened. "The dinner at the diner with that devastatingly handsome SWAT cop from Dallas—the one with the sexy British accent. I can't imagine sitting through an entire dinner listening to a man that good-looking talk to me in that voice. I'd end up drooling on my plate."

Alyssa's jaw dropped. "Christine, you're married! You can't say stuff like that."

Her friend laughed. "I'm just messing with you. But seriously, the guy is hot. Just because I'm married doesn't mean I didn't notice that. You can't tell me you didn't notice, too."

She almost blushed as she remembered exactly how much she had noticed. Not to mention how good he'd smelled and how much she'd wanted him to kiss her in the diner parking lot.

"Yeah. I noticed. And yes, Zane is very attractive and easy to talk to. I'd be lying if I said he didn't intrigue me."

Because he's a supernatural creature that growls and throws people around like sandbags. And oh yeah, his eyes glow yellow sometimes. She did love the color yellow.

Alyssa pushed those thoughts aside and cleared her throat. "And dinner with him was nice. Okay, it was better than nice. It was also the first time in forever that I've sat across the table from a man I wasn't interrogating."

That earned her another laugh from Christine. "Do you think the two of you might get together?"

She shook her head. "No way."

Christine frowned. "Why not?"

It wasn't like Alyssa could tell her she thought Zane might not be human—or that he might be as dangerous as whoever or whatever had kidnapped and killed that poor girl and tossed her in a landfill. Instead, she went with a lie Christine would most likely believe.

"I'm here working a case. I don't have time to get involved with anyone."

Crap. That sounded lame even to her.

Christine gave her a look. "First off, I'm not saying you have to have a deep, meaningful, long-term relationship with the guy. There's nothing wrong with a roll in the hay to relieve a little stress. You're both adults. You can do that, you know."

Alyssa closed the folder, focusing all of her attention on her friend. "Okay, say Zane and I sleep together. What then?"

Her friend arched a brow. "Your love life must be really sad if you have to ask a question like that. But just in case you really are that socially challenged, let me lay out the two most likely possibilities when it comes to a man like Zane. One, the sex is amazing and you keep sleeping with him until the case is closed and you both go your separate ways. Or two, the sex is amazing, and you continue to see your hunky Brit long after the case is solved."

Alyssa snorted. "And what if the sex is horrible?"

Christine looked at her like she was insane. "I've seen the man, honey. Horrible sex isn't anything you have to worry about with him. I'm sure of that. It's simply a matter of whether you're looking for short-term pleasure or long-term gratification."

Both options worked for her, but unfortunately, the first was unlikely and the second a complete pipe dream.

"Long-term wouldn't work," she said. "I'm always on the road, and Zane's a cop in Dallas. Even if we worked at it, we'd never get to spend any time together. Why even bother?"

"I'll give you a good reason to bother," Christine said. "Having nothing in your life but your work sucks."

"I like my work," Alyssa insisted. "And I have friends."

Christine let out an impatient sigh. "I like my work, too, but that doesn't replace the human connection that comes with spending time with the person you're meant to be with. And as much as I appreciate you as a friend, it doesn't compare to my hunky husband serving me breakfast in bed after a night of serious lovemaking."

Alyssa had met Christine's husband—many times. While he was handsome, it was weird to think about him and her best friend having sex. "But you guys are married and work in the same field office. That's not like my situation at all."

"We weren't always married." Christine shrugged. "And we weren't always in the same field office, either. We had a long-distance thing for the first four years of our relationship, but we made it work because having a chance to be with him—even if it was only now and then—made everything else worthwhile. I'm not saying that's the way it would be with you and Zane. Heck, once you spend some time with him, you may discover that there's absolutely zero chemistry between you regardless of how incredible the sex is."

Alyssa let out a little snort. There was definitely some chemistry there.

"Look," Christine said. "I'm just saying you shouldn't let a few miles between the two of you deter you from even trying. You have to hang out with him anyway. Why not sit back and see where it leads? If there's a spark, go with it and have some fun. If there's more than a spark, maybe give that a chance, too."

Alyssa didn't mention the part where Zane might grow fangs and eat her for fun. Instead, she stood up. "Speaking of Zane, I have to get back to my hotel and clean up. We're pulling stakeout duty together tonight. I'll text you later. Give the hubby and kiddo a hug for me."

Christine came around her desk to walk Alyssa out. "I will, but promise me you'll give what I said about Zane some thought. And also promise me you'll be careful. If you're right and these disappearances are connected to Black Swan Enterprises, then this might be more dangerous than you think. They're big enough to make people like you and your SWAT cop friends disappear without a peep."

Alyssa had a sudden vision of Zane and his two friends dressed in Easter Peeps costumes calmly being led away to slaughter by Neanderthals in dark suits. The image didn't fly with her. She was pretty sure they'd make one hell of a peep.

She was almost out the door when a thought struck her. She turned to look at Christine. "You know those hotels you said you have an arrangement with? Any chance you could swing three expensive rooms for Zane and the two SWAT cops with him? They're staying in a fleabag with gigantic bedbugs. I was hoping to get them out of there."

"Three rooms?" Christine asked with a smile. "Sure you don't want to make that two, since Zane will be sleeping in your bed at the Westin?"

Alyssa didn't dignify that with a response, but instead gave her friend the stink eye and walked out.

Chapter 6

It was 10:00 p.m. by the time she and Zane arrived at the office space across from the parking garage to take over for Rachel and Diego. Normally, Alyssa would have driven herself over for their nighttime stakeout shift, but they wanted to limit the number of vehicles sitting in front of what was supposed to be an empty office complex, so Zane had driven them over in his SUV. She hadn't minded. Besides not having to deal with LA traffic—which sucked yellow lemon balls—he'd suggested stopping by In-N-Out Burger to pick up takeout for dinner. She'd never complain about eating more french fries. Besides, Zane made her laugh most of the drive over, telling her stories about growing up in London. She'd almost peed herself when he described the uniforms he'd worn for school. For some reason, she'd had visions of that guitar player from AC/DC. A young Zane must have looked so damn cute in his proper little shorts.

"Anything interesting happen today?" Zane asked his friends, motioning with his head toward the parking garage visible through the window.

The space they'd rented had a good view of the administrative offices and gated area where vehicles entered and exited the garage. Rachel and Diego had rearranged the furniture, placing a table and two chairs near the window, making it easy to keep an eye on the place. And since the building they were in had mirrored windows, no one outside would be able to see in, especially since they'd kept the lights low. There was also a comfy-looking couch that would come in handy if she or Zane needed to grab some shut-eye.

"Not really," Rachel said. "Two men and a woman in fancy clothes went into the administrative offices around three this afternoon, then came out about an hour later looking pissed."

"We got pictures of them." Diego slung a backpack over one shoulder. "I sent everything to Becker to see if he can ID them. I'll bet money they were from Black Swan Enterprises."

Rachel and Diego were halfway to the door when Alyssa remembered the folded piece of notebook paper in her back pocket. "Wait up. I've got something for you guys."

Rachel unfolded the paper, her brow furrowing as she read the address and two sets of numbers on it. "What's this?"

"Your new hotel," Alyssa said. "I couldn't get you into the Westin where I'm staying, but the Fairfield Inn and Suites on Sepulveda is close by and a hell of a lot better than the place you're in now. It's where Zoe and Chloe are staying. With the discount I was able to get, you'll have a two-room suite that's actually cheaper than the no-name you're in. Though I can still get you a separate room if you want."

Rachel shook her head. "A room with Diego is fine. I'd rather not be alone anyway. Thank you for this. I owe you."

Alyssa wondered what Rachel meant about not

wanting to be alone. She assumed it had something to do with the tension she'd picked up on earlier at their motel, but Zane was going out of his way not to look at her, so she couldn't tell.

She gave Rachel a smile. "Don't worry about it."

"We'll swing by Stefan's house to see if anything is going on there, then check out of the motel and move everything over to the Fairfield," Diego said, opening the door. "We'll grab your stuff, too, Zane."

"Thanks," Zane said as he took their burgers and fries out of the takeout bags and set them on the table.

Alyssa shrugged off the light jacket she was wearing and hung it on the back of one of the chairs, glancing out the window, then at the open laptop on the table. None of the cars she and Zane had marked with the tracking devices had moved all day.

"What was Rachel saying about not liking to be alone?" She took their drinks out of the cardboard carrier and set them down on the table beside the food. "I know she and Diego are pretending to be a couple, but something tells me that's not what she meant."

Zane didn't bother to take off the leather jacket he'd been wearing since she'd met him, and a part of her hoped he wouldn't. He looked so damn sexy in it, even if it wasn't needed in the temperature-controlled office space. In the dim light of the room, Alyssa could see the pensive expression on his face as he sat down and started to unwrap his cheeseburger. He looked tired—and worried.

"Rachel went through some stuff about a year ago, before she came to Dallas and joined our department," he said. "It was pretty rough, and she still has bad dreams about it. I think it helps knowing there's someone in the room with her. Someone she can trust."

Alyssa slipped into the chair across from him and started opening ketchup packs. That was the part she hated about eating takeout. How the hell was anyone supposed to eat fries with these tiny dribbles of ketchup? And whenever she asked for more, it was like they were handing out gold. It took twenty of the damn packs to even get a respectable-size puddle.

"It's not really any of my business, but if she's having nightmares, wouldn't it have been better for her to stay back in Dallas, so she could get some help?"

"If any of us knew she was having issues, then yes, but she's here now and she wants to see this through," he said. "And truthfully, I understand why she needs to. When our compound was attacked, Rachel was as much a target as the rest of us. She wants to get the man who tried to kill her teammates just as much as I do."

Alyssa never had a boss who'd tried to kill her, but she supposed she could see how that might drive someone to ignore everything else going on in their life until they caught the person. She'd pushed herself in the past to do her job. Rachel was obviously no different.

Other than the possibility of not being fully human.

They ate in silence for a while, keeping an eye on the parking garage at the same time. She was nibbling on a fry when she noticed Zane regarding her thoughtfully.

"What?" she asked, hoping she hadn't dribbled ketchup on herself.

"Nothing." He smiled. "It's just…I wanted to thank you for getting us other rooms. I could care less about where I sleep and I'm sure Diego is the same, but Rachel has had a bad few days. A nicer room will help a lot more than you might think. So, again…thank you."

She started to say it wasn't a big deal, but then she caught the genuine gratitude on Zane's face and realized that it was a big deal to him because Rachel was important to him. For all of a second, she felt a little twinge of something that might have been jealousy. But it disappeared just as quickly. While Rachel was obviously important to him, so was Diego and every other member of his SWAT team back in Dallas.

"Rachel and the other people on your team are like family, huh?" she asked, picking up her cheeseburger and biting into it. It was juicy and delicious. Not as good as the fries, because seriously, nothing was as good as french fries. Still, she could see becoming addicted to the things.

Zane didn't answer right away, his expression introspective. Like he was thinking hard about what she'd asked. Of course, it was also possible he hadn't replied because he didn't feel like talking to her about it. But then, his sensuous mouth curved.

"Yeah, they are my family."

She wasn't sure how it was possible, but he was even more attractive when that charming smile of his was mirrored in his dark eyes. When that happened, they seemed to almost sparkle. And when his dimples deepened, she almost jumped up and hugged him just for an excuse to bury his face in her breasts.

"You said you grew up near London, right?" she asked, mostly to get the image of his gorgeous face nestled between her boobs out of her head. "Are you still close with your family? Your blood family, I mean."

His smile faded, and Alyssa immediately regretted bringing up the subject.

"The FBI background check didn't cover that?" he asked, taking a big bite of his cheeseburger. Crap, he could put away food. Which probably explained why'd he'd bought enough to feed four people. "I'm not sure whether I should be thrilled or disappointed."

She laughed. "Truthfully, the file I saw didn't go that far back. I know you served in the British military, then came to the U.S. in late 2007. I know nothing about your family at all. But if you don't want to talk about it, that's okay. I didn't mean to pry."

Zane shrugged as he took a sip of his soda. "Not really much to talk about. I'm not close with my family. I haven't been in a long time."

There was something about the way he said the words that made her think he was trying to act like it didn't matter to him when it really did. "Did you and your family have a falling out? Is that why you left home and came to the States?"

He scarfed down the rest of the first burger and reached for the second. "We didn't exactly have a falling out, but there were a lot of arguments."

"What did you argue about?"

She knew she'd said she didn't want to pry, but she was shocked by how eager she was to know about Zane's past. She wasn't sure if he'd tell her about it, though. He didn't seem like the sharing type.

Across from her, his expression betrayed something painful, something long buried he'd probably prefer not digging into. "The men in my family have served in the British Army for generations, and there was never any doubt I'd serve, too. Hell, at one point, I thought I might make a career of it."

"But?" Alyssa prodded.

He tensed, his shoulders and chest visibly tightening up. Damn, maybe it had been a bad idea to bring this up.

"I was in Afghanistan with three other members of my special ops unit," he said, not looking at her. "We got involved in a rescue mission that went badly. The other guys—men I'd been friends with for years—didn't make it. I barely did myself."

All the air was sucked out of Alyssa's lungs at that announcement. It took everything in her not to start crying. She had no idea why, since she barely knew Zane and hadn't known any of his friends, but she could feel the pain he was carrying like it was her own.

Before she realized what she was doing, she reached across the table with her right hand, inviting him to take it. She expected him to offer his left hand since it was opposite hers, but instead, he used his right. It was a little awkward, but she was surprised he'd accepted the gesture at all, so she wasn't going to complain.

"I'm sorry," she said softly, squeezing his hand. "I can't even imagine what it's like going through something like that, but I hate that you had to."

He glanced down at her hand where it held his like he'd just now noticed it. He gave her a small smile, then slowly pulled his hand away. Alyssa immediately missed the warmth under her fingers.

"Thanks, but it was a long time ago," he said. "I don't even think about it now."

That was a lie if she'd ever heard one, but she didn't call him on it, deciding it was better to keep him talking.

"So I'm guessing your family freaked out when you got injured. Is that what you guys fought about? It must have been pretty serious to get you to leave the country and move all the way to Dallas."

"We fought about my injuries, just not the ones you're referring to." He spoke slowly, like it was painful to get the words out. "My physical injuries healed up surprisingly fast. Amazingly fast to be truthful. But the man who came back from Afghanistan wasn't the one they knew, and my family didn't handle that very well. They talked a lot about wanting me to get better, but what they really wanted was for me to go back to being the person I'd been before. When that didn't happen, they walked away from me."

"Wait a minute," she said, sure she'd missed something. "Are you telling me your family turned their backs on you because you were dealing with stuff that takes time to work out?"

She avoided saying *PTSD*. She'd known a lot of people who hated that acronym and all the negative connotations that came with it.

"It wasn't all on them." He looked out the window, his gaze focused on the garage. "It took me a while to accept it, but mostly, it was me. I knew I was changing, turning into some kind of monster. I could see it every night in the mirror when I woke up from the god-awful nightmares. But I didn't reach out to anyone for help. I guess it was easier to shove them all away—my parents, my brothers and sisters, even my fiancée."

Fiancée?

To say Alyssa was shocked as hell at that tidbit of information was an understatement.

"You were going to be married?" she asked in disbe-lief. "And she walked out on you?"

He gave her a shrug. "Like I said, I pretty much turned into a monster. That wasn't what Sienna had signed up for, and I've never held it against her."

Alyssa bit her tongue to keep from saying something she shouldn't. Zane was apparently a lot more forgiving than she was. If someone had walked out on her like that—someone who was supposed to be in love with her—she'd be royally pissed.

His fiancée might be well in the past, but that didn't mean Alyssa wanted to hear about her, so she changed the subject.

"How did you end up in Dallas?" she asked.

Zane snorted. "I'll admit, it wasn't exactly a well-thought-out plan. I'd been separated from the army, wasn't talking to my family, my fiancée walked out, and I had no real job prospects. Oh, and I had enough money in the bank to last me three weeks." He unwrapped his third burger of the night. "I was sitting on a bench in Hyde Park, wondering what the hell to do next, when this big American bloke sat down next to me and asked right out of the blue if I'd ever thought of becoming a cop. That man was Gage Dixon, the commander of the Dallas SWAT team. He was attending an Interpol conference in London and had gone for a walk when he found me."

Good thing her mouth was full of french fries; oth-erwise, it probably would have fallen open. "You're kidding, right? You meet a stranger on a park bench in London, and just like that, he offers you a job in Dallas? You didn't even know him."

Zane chuckled. "I know you've never met him, but

suffice to say Gage is an extremely persuasive man. And as strange as it might seem, we had a lot in common at the time. I truthfully couldn't have found Dallas on a map, but he had me convinced to move there within ten minutes."

"It's not really my area of expertise, but weren't there...I don't know...visa issues to deal with?"

"My mum is American, so I have dual citizenship. Moving to the States wasn't that complicated for me even though I'd never been here prior to that."

Alyssa couldn't believe Zane's family had abandoned him. How could parents turn their backs on a son like that? Yeah, Zane had said he'd pushed everyone away, but to Alyssa, who was from a close family, it seemed harsh.

"So you up and moved to Dallas completely on a whim and haven't spoken to your family since?" she asked. "Not even a call during the holidays?"

He picked up some fries and dunked them in mayo. "I've tried to call a few times. I've even gotten as far as picking up the phone and punching in the number. But I always hang up before it rings."

"Why?"

"Law of inertia, I guess," he murmured. "You know, an object at rest stays at rest. Every day that passed without me calling made it that much harder to pick up the phone and close the distance between us. After a while, it seemed easier to accept I'd waited too long to repair the damage."

She reached out her hand to take his again in support, not surprised when he chose to use his right instead of his left. Now that she thought about it, she realized he rarely used his left arm when he didn't have to. The fight in the alley behind the club, driving his SUV, even while eating—in almost all those cases, he used his right arm for everything while his left hung loosely at his side.

"How did you injure your arm?" Alyssa asked, closing her fingers around his and gently squeezing. "Did it happen in Afghanistan?"

He lifted his left arm and placed that hand over the one his right was already cupping. The movement didn't seem like it hurt, but she could tell he was moving carefully.

"No, it didn't happen in Afghanistan." He took a deep breath, then let it out. "It happened during a drive-by shooting back in November—people associated with my former chief of police. They were trying to kill a young woman simply because they thought she was different from them. I got hit in the back of my upper arm. There was a lot of damage and I'm still trying to overcome it."

Alyssa knew his injury and how he was dealing with it was none of her business, but that didn't stop her from caring.

"Is that why you always wear your jacket?" she asked. "So no one can see the scars?"

Zane returned her gaze, so many emotions flickering across his features that she found it hard to breathe. Self-loathing and doubt. Confusion and fear. Something else that almost seemed like longing. But then the mask that had started to slip was back and the emotions disappeared.

"Sometimes I forget you're a fed, trained to be observant." When she didn't say anything, he continued, "But yes. The scarring is pretty bad." He broke eye contact, gazing over at the parking garage again. "I wore a bandage wrapped around it for weeks, so I wouldn't even have to look at it. But the doctor said it was slowing down the healing process, so I just make sure to wear a jacket whenever I go out. Fortunately, the weather here is cool enough right now to do that. If it were the middle of summer, I'd be in trouble."

Alyssa couldn't help but shake her head. Up to now, she'd never seen Zane lack for confidence in anything. Not in the way he carried himself and not in the way he interacted with others. On the contrary, he filled any room he was in with an aura of calm masculinity. She'd never thought of him as anything other than self-assured and comfortable in his own skin. But when the topic of conversation turned to his injured arm, everything about him changed. It hurt like crazy to see him like that.

She knew a little something about scars, of course. Not the physical kind, but scars nonetheless. They had a way of getting thicker—rougher—if you didn't force yourself to go through the agony of breaking them down. But sometimes it was hard finding the courage to deal with them when you carried them on your own. Sometimes you needed help.

"Hiding yours scars makes them worse, Zane. Not physically, but in every other way. Especially emotionally. If you refuse to let people into your world, the scars take on a life of their own and you're all alone with them."

He looked at her. "Sounds like the voice of experience. Want to tell me about it?"

"It is." Zane was trying to get her to change the subject and she wasn't falling for it for a second. "And I'm willing to tell you about it. After we talk about you a little more."

"What do you want to talk about?" he asked, though she was pretty sure he already knew.

She motioned at his left arm. "Why don't we talk about exactly how you were injured, and more importantly, why you're working so hard to hide it behind a leather jacket?"

Zane snorted, like he'd been expecting something like that. "Maybe it would be easier if I showed you. One picture being worth a thousand words and all that."

Alyssa was a little surprised by the offer but nodded. "If you're comfortable with that…okay."

He locked eyes with her, a slight smile tugging at his lips. "I have to admit, normally I wouldn't be, but with you, I am."

Zane had no idea why he was shrugging out of his jacket so he could show Alyssa the god-awful injury he'd gotten from those hunters. But what she'd said about being alone with his scars because he wouldn't let people in made a lot of sense to him. His friend Brooks had said something similar to him back in Dallas about needing to stop using his injured arm as an excuse to push people away. He'd been pushing people away for so long, it seemed like all he knew how to do.

But he didn't feel like pushing Alyssa away. When he was alone with her like this, surrounded by her scent and mesmerized by the sound of her voice, he found himself having a difficult time remembering why he'd been fighting the connection they so clearly had. The idea that she was his soul mate still scared the hell out of him—especially since she was FBI—but at the same time, there was something about her that gave him the courage to take risks he thought were beyond him.

He got his leather jacket off his left shoulder, making sure not to move that arm any more than he had to. Contracting his triceps could cause anywhere from a slight twinge to a burning firebrand of pain. Since he never knew which he was going to get, he tried his best to avoid aggravating the shredded muscles as much as he could.

Alyssa stood and came around the table, her expression curious as he carefully pushed the sleeve of his T-shirt up higher. Something as simple as skimming his fingers over the scar tissue along the back of his arm could trigger a stinger of pain, so he definitely avoided doing that.

"It's difficult to explain," he said as Alyssa studied the long, ragged scar that ran along the back of his arm from an inch below his left shoulder all the way down to his elbow. Several places along it, horizontal slices had been made so the skin could be folded back, exposing the damaged tissue underneath. "But basically, the bullet I got shot with was filled with…well…poison, for lack of a better word. It destroyed most of the muscle and it had to be taken it out. That's why my arm looks so messed up."

He glanced at Alyssa out of the corner of his eye, waiting for her to look away from the ugly scar in disgust, but she didn't. He waited for her to ask the inevitable question about whether it hurt or not. That's what the few people who'd seen the wound usually started with. But instead, she reached up and gently rested the palm of her hand on the vertical scar. He instinctively held his breath, waiting for the wretched pain to come.

But it didn't.

In fact, as he slowly let the air ease out of his lungs, he realized Alyssa's touch felt unbelievably nice. It was hard to describe, but the contact was both soothing and exciting, calming the tremors that had been a near constant companion since the shooting, but also creating a pleasant tingle everywhere her fingers traced. He was once again thankful she didn't have a werewolf's hearing, or she would have picked up on the fact that his heart was racing.

Alyssa moved her fingers along the wide suture line of the main scar and the smaller lines radiating out from it, pressing and examining the injury, her expression curious and a little confused. "These cuts don't look like something a doctor would do with a scalpel. I don't mean to make this sound like a joke, but it looks like someone took a steak knife to you."

Zane snorted. "You're actually closer to being right than you might think. The poison in the bullet was fast acting, and there was no possibility of me making it to the nearest hospital alive if it spread. So one of the SWAT team medics had to remove the infected tissue with a pocket knife while transporting me in the back of an SUV."

Alyssa stood there with her hand resting on his damaged arm, staring up at him with a look that suggested she hoped he was messing with her. "That sounds extremely painful."

It had been. The mere mention of the shooting brought back memories that he tried to always keep tucked away. The pain of the wolfsbane poison spreading through his bloodstream had been unreal. Worse even than the feel of his teammate's knife cutting through his flesh. He vividly remembered asking one of his pack mates to cut off his arm and be done with it—or kill him.

That probably wasn't something he should tell Alyssa. So he shrugged with his right shoulder—he'd gotten good at doing that—and smiled. "It was bad, but I survived."

Now that Alyssa had heard the story and seen the scar, he expected her to pull her hand away and walk back over to her side of the table. There were still more fries to be devoured after all. But instead, she slid her hand farther up his left arm. Then she lifted the other and casually placed it on his chest.

Maybe the move was casual to her, but as her fingers slid under the edge of the sleeve of his T-shirt, lightly massaging the scar tissue as if trying to soothe it, his heart beat even faster. With her hand on his chest like that, there was no way she couldn't feel it thumping like mad.

His fangs slowly extended.

Bloody hell. He'd never lost control so much since he'd first gone through his change. And it was all from a simple touch.

"Does it hurt when I do this?" she murmured, interrupting the thoughts spinning through his head as she ran the tips of her fingers above the top of the scar, testing the muscles along his shoulder.

He tried to speak, wanting to tell her how amazing her fingers felt on his skin, how the hand on his chest was as warm as the sun right then. But there was no way he could open his mouth and say a thing, not without letting the growl bubbling up in his throat escape. So instead, he shook his head, hoping she'd get the message and keep going.

It was crazy. He'd slept with women over the years since everything had fallen apart with Sienna. But not a single kiss or touch from any of them had felt as intimate as the simple contact of Alyssa's hand on the bare skin of his arm. It felt like the first time a woman had touched him in nearly forever. Hell, who was he kidding? He'd *never* been touched like this. It made him want things he'd been telling himself he shouldn't want. Things he couldn't have.

"Is there anything the doctors can do?" she asked, running her fingers tenderly from his shoulder and along his triceps. "Some kind of surgery maybe?"

He shook his head but felt he needed to answer. "The doctor has me on a few different experimental drug protocols trying to encourage new muscle growth. So far, it's not working. Truthfully, I think he's running out of options."

Alyssa gazed up at him, eyes filled with concern as she gently pressed the palm of her hand against the scar. Her heart was racing as fast as his. "You can't give up, okay? Something is going to work. You have to keep trying until it does."

He opened his mouth to reply when a scent so overwhelming and intoxicating surrounded him that he didn't even stop to think before bending his head to softly brush his lips against hers. Even that slight touch was electric, but he forced himself to hesitate, wanting to give Alyssa a chance to pull back.

But it didn't seem like pulling back was something Alyssa was interested in. Instead, she wrapped her hand around the back of his neck and tugged him down farther, her mouth urgent and demanding on his. Zane was more than willing to meet those demands, slipping his tongue between her lips, tangling and teasing as a growl rumbled out. She tasted even better than she smelled.

He moved a hand down to her waist, intending to tug her closer, when the sound of squawking tires from the direction of the garage caught his attention. His inner wolf told him to ignore the noise and keep snogging, but his human side got in the way, forcing him to lift his head and glance at the window.

Alyssa stepped back a bit, looking slightly embarrassed. His inner wolf, on the other hand, was pissed off—and turned on.

Shoving his arousal to a small, dark corner of his mind, Zane leaned over to look out the window. He immediately caught sight of a vehicle spiraling up one level of the garage to the next, moving fast enough to squeal the tires.

"They're heading up, not down to the lower levels," Alyssa pointed out, moving up beside him, her delicious scent almost making him drool. "That probably means they're not involved with Stefan."

Zane would have agreed if he had been capable of forming coherent words at the moment. But he wasn't, because he'd finally recognized what it was about Alyssa's scent that was so mesmerizing.

She was aroused, too.

He curled his fingers in as he felt his claws partially extend...then his fangs...then his cock. Bloody hell, it was like a werewolf hard-on trifecta. He fought for control, but it was nearly impossible. She smelled like chocolate buttercream frosting. And damn, did he want to lick her off a spoon right then.

"They stopped on the fifth level and turned off their lights, but they're not getting out of the car," she added. "What the hell are they up to?"

Zane forced his gaze away from Alyssa and looked across the street, finding the car easily in the darkness. Yeah, werewolves had excellent night vision.

He saw movement inside the front seat of the car, then even more movement as the two occupants of the vehicle climbed into the back seats. It didn't take too long after that to figure out what they were up to.

He chuckled. "They're shagging."

Alyssa laughed as she moved around the table and sat down on her side. "Sex in a parking garage. O-kay. But I guess we should take that as a sign and pay attention to what's going on across the street. If those two hadn't been in such a hurry for a quickie, we never would have heard them pull in. We could miss Stefan just as easily."

He sighed with disappointment and dropped into his own chair. "You're right. It wasn't very professional of us to let ourselves get distracted."

"No, it wasn't." She picked up the last few fries she'd spilled out on her burger wrapper earlier. "But it sure was fun."

Alyssa said that last part so softly she probably thought he wouldn't hear. But he'd heard all right. That's when his inner werewolf told his human side to get lost. The animal inside him wanted her, risk be damned.

Chapter 7

"I DON'T HAVE ANY TEA, BUT DO YOU WANT TO COME IN FOR coffee?" Alyssa asked when they pulled into the parking lot of her hotel the next morning. Zane had admitted he preferred Earl Grey over java, but they'd both consumed copious amounts of Starbucks dark roast during their late-night shift, so she knew he drank it sometimes. All that coffee was probably the reason she wasn't aching to crawl straight into bed even though she'd been awake for well over twenty-four hours. "I have a couple of boxes of Pop-Tarts I'd be willing to share, too. I know it's not much, but I feel badly I still haven't bought you breakfast. And since you paid for dinner last night, that's two meals I owe you."

Zane gave her an appraising look as he parked the SUV. She'd caught him doing that several times last night. Like she was a puzzle he was trying to figure out. Then again, he might simply be wondering if she had an ulterior motive for asking him in. She didn't. She'd had a good time last night and was hoping the fun didn't have to end just because their shift was over.

It was sad to admit, but that stakeout had been the most fun she'd had with a guy in years. That pretty much defined her love life, didn't it? A twelve-hour stakeout on the graveyard shift with a guy who might not be totally human was the best date she'd been on in years. Christine had been right—her love life was pathetic.

"What kind of Pop-Tarts are we talking about here?" Zane asked, clearly intrigued by the offer, but not shutting off the engine yet. "Please tell me you don't eat those unfrosted fruit-filled things? If so, forget it. You couldn't pay me enough."

She laughed. "Nope, I'm old-school. Chocolate fudge and brown sugar cinnamon."

He flashed her a grin. "You had me at chocolate. But I won't turn up my nose at the brown sugar cinnamon, either."

Killing the engine, Zane climbed out and fell into step beside her as they walked into her hotel. As they rode up in the elevator, Alyssa knew she'd be lying if she said the possibility of getting another kiss out of him didn't make her giddy with anticipation. They'd only kissed once, but damn, it had been a doozy. She was seriously hoping for another one, even if it meant bribing him with toaster pastries.

"Do you always drag your own coffeemaker with you when you stay in a hotel?" he asked as Alyssa made a fresh pot at the counter in her room's kitchenette. "What's wrong with the one they have?"

Alyssa made an *ick* face as she dumped fresh grounds in the filter of her eight-cup machine. "Are you kidding? Those things are nasty. It's a known fact that most hotels never clean them. I shudder to think about the freaky crap people probably pour in there. And if that's not enough, the coffee that comes out of those contraptions tastes like pond scum. With all the time I spend in hotels, it makes more sense to bring my own."

While the coffee dripped, she dug through the cabinet above the sink and pulled out two boxes of Pop-Tarts, one of each flavor. The chocolate felt a little light and she could foresee a scenario where she might have to fight Zane for the last one in the box. If so, she wasn't sure if she could take him. It would be worth the tussle, though. She couldn't imagine anyone she'd rather wrestle with more than Zane.

"Speaking of hotels," he murmured, following her over to the small table, "are you ever going to tell me what the FBI has you running all around the country doing? And before you answer, I noticed the way you avoided talking about yourself the entire night."

Alyssa sighed. Even though they'd talked the whole night, she'd managed to avoid telling him almost anything personal. Instead, they'd spent the time talking about what it was like growing up in London, his family, his time in the British SAS, and especially his SWAT teammates. Zane had told her so many crazy stories about his friends back in Dallas she almost felt like she knew them.

Was it really fair of her not to give him a look inside her own life? As long as she made sure not to say anything she shouldn't.

She pulled the single silver package of the chocolate flavor out of the box and shook it in his direction, "Only two left. You okay with sharing?"

Zane seemed to consider that. "Normally, I'd say Sauron does not share. But in this case, I think I can be persuaded."

Alyssa snorted at the *Lord of the Rings* reference, tearing open the foil package and handing one of the frosted toaster treats across the table to him.

"When I first joined the FBI, I worked in the Sacramento field office for four years," she said in answer to his earlier question. "But for the past year and a half, the FBI has been paying me to fly around the country and investigate cases that either haven't shown up on anyone's radar yet—like the kidnappings here in LA—or ones that seem destined for the cold-case stack. They run the gamut from murders and kidnappings to missing persons, assaults, and rapes."

That was a shockingly good synopsis of her job—if you left out the weird, supernatural stuff and the fact that none of her cases ever made it to a trial. Well, a normal trial at least.

Zane didn't say anything as he walked over to get their coffee. He fixed her cup exactly the way she liked it, then came back over to the table with mugs in hand, sat down, and picked up his Pop-Tart.

She liked a man who ate his Pop-Tarts cold. It was damn sexy in her opinion.

"The FBI sends you out on all these cases by yourself?" He eyed her. "Isn't that kind of crazy?"

She shrugged and sipped her coffee, wondering why it tasted better when Zane made it than when she did even though they both added the same amount of cream and sugar. "I work better on my own."

That earned her another look that was hard to interpret. "Everyone needs backup now and then, no matter how good they are."

"I call in backup when I need it. Admittedly, it can take a little while since the rest of my team is spread out all across the country, but if it's important, my boss in DC will get people to me."

Alyssa realized how horrible that arrangement sounded the moment the words were out of her mouth.

But it was the truth, and at least in this particular area, she didn't feel the need to make up a lie.

Zane regarded her silently, his expression still unreadable. "I won't bother to point out how incredibly stupid that scheme is. In the past year or so that you've been part of this team, how many times have you called and asked for backup?"

Alyssa knew Zane wasn't going to like the answer. "Technically, I've called for backup twice. But in both of those situations, I only needed them for cleanup. I'd already handled the situation."

He only grunted and swigged his coffee. He took his with cream, no sugar.

In reality, she handled all her cases on her own even though Nathan told her time and again to pull back and wait for help. But she simply wasn't wired that way. Charging ahead and doing what was right regardless of if it meant going it alone had always been her thing.

"Why did you become an FBI agent?" Zane asked.

The question caught her off guard. She'd expected him to keep pushing on the subject of working alone, especially when the rest of the Bureau was a team-focused, rule-obsessed bureaucracy.

"Did you always want to be a fed, or did you just end up there?" he prompted when she didn't answer right away. "Kind of like me and the Dallas SWAT team."

Alyssa smiled, wanting to point out it was unlikely anyone in the world had a career path quite as convoluted as his. But then she remembered exactly why she'd gone into the bureau and the smile faded from her face.

"When I was seventeen, my friend Amanda and I were kidnapped on our way to see a movie," she said softly, her face mostly hidden by her mug as she slowly inhaled the aroma of her coffee, letting it soothe her. She very carefully avoided looking in Zane's direction, not wanting to see the expression on his face.

"It was in Tampa, where I grew up, and it was during summer break between our junior and senior years in high school. We were young, naive, and just plain stupid when it came to protecting ourselves. We foolishly parked in the darkest part of the lot at the movie theater and didn't even notice the van following us as Amanda looked for a space. Hell, we wouldn't have thought twice even if we had."

"They grabbed you when you got out of the car?" Zane asked, his voice tight.

"Yeah." She swallowed hard, reliving that moment as if it had been yesterday. "They pulled up beside us as we were walking toward the movie theater and rolled down the window like they wanted to ask us a question. Amanda and I walked right up to them without even thinking about it. Before we knew what was happening, two guys jumped out, dragged us into the back, and the van sped away. We tried to fight, but there were four of the assholes, and they'd done this enough times to be good at it."

She set down her mug and finally looked at Zane to see him sitting there with a stunned expression on his face. "They'd grabbed several other girls over the previous few weeks, including the daughter of a foreign diplomat who'd been in town on vacation. That's why the FBI got involved so fast."

Alyssa fell silent, dark thoughts and memories overtaking her. She gave herself a little mental shake.

"They chloroformed Amanda and me, but for some

reason, it wore off faster on me than it did on her. When they stopped the van, they left us alone for a few seconds and I was able to escape. I tried to take Amanda, but she was completely out of it and I knew I could never carry her. So I bolted, praying I could get away and find help."

She popped open the box of frosted brown sugar Pop-Tarts to give herself something to do with her hands, hating the way they were shaking all of a sudden. Opening the silver wrapper, she offered one of the pastries to Zane. He took it without comment.

"It was dark, and we were way out in the swamps." She set down her Pop-Tart and broke off a piece but didn't eat it. "The kidnappers realized fairly quickly that I'd escaped and came after me. All I remember is a lot of falling and running into tree branches and thickets. They shot at me a few times and I'm pretty sure there was a gator in there somewhere, but after running for what felt like forever, I finally made it to the highway, where someone stopped for me."

It seemed as if Zane was right there in her nightmare with her, his chest rising and falling so fast it seemed like he was almost hyperventilating—kind of like what she was doing. She abruptly realized how similar what had happened to her was to the twins she and Zane had rescued the other night. The kidnapping part of the story anyway. Maybe that's why she was so concerned about them.

"Unfortunately, I ran for hours through the swamps without a clue where I was going, so when the FBI tried to talk to me, I was a complete mess," she said. "The agent in charge of the case decided I was a lost cause and that I didn't have any information to help find Amanda and the other girls they'd kidnapped. I overheard him saying to the other agents that my escape almost certainly meant Amanda and the other girls were dead."

The guilt she'd felt at that moment was something she'd never forget.

Zane cursed. "What happened?"

She gave him a small smile. "Christine happened. She came into my room and asked me bizarre questions, like what movie Amanda and I had been going to see, whether we were going to get popcorn or candy, even if we liked to sit in the center of the row at the movie theater or on the end. I didn't have a clue why she was asking me all that stuff, but I answered her anyway. So she kept it up. For hours. Then when I thought she couldn't possibly ask me anything else, she wanted to know what the van smelled like, whether I remembered driving over any bridges or gravel roads, what the kidnappers had said while they were chasing me, whether the moon was in front of me or behind me as I ran. And even though I couldn't recall any of those things before the two of us talked, I started to."

Alyssa nibbled on the piece of pastry she was still holding. She remembered thinking that all of those questions had been a waste of time—or maybe simply a way to distract her from the fact that Amanda and the other girls were already dead and it was her fault. But at the same time, Alyssa remembered latching on to Christine's sure, confident style, believing her when she'd said that it was all going to be okay.

"The next morning, Christine brought me out to the swamps, believing I should be able to work my way backward along the path I'd taken to escape. I thought she was absolutely insane, but…"

"But?"

"But we did," Alyssa said. "We found this ugly, little cabin in the middle of the swamp with the van parked beside it covered with a military-style camo net. Christine called in for backup, and when the cavalry arrived, she led the way in and saved Amanda and three other girls. They're all alive today because one junior FBI agent figured out how to get that information out of me."

"And that's when you decided you wanted to be just like her." Zane grinned. "That's why you went into the FBI."

"Pretty much," Alyssa admitted. "But I couldn't have done it without Christine's help. She's the one who helped me figure out the best college to go to and what degrees to get. My poor parents weren't thrilled with my career choice. They wanted me to do something less dangerous, like become an accountant. Even after getting a bachelor's in criminology and a master's in criminal psychology, they still thought I'd change my mind. It wasn't until after I completed my training at Quantico that they realized I was serious about becoming an FBI agent."

"They're okay with it now then?"

She nodded. "Uh-huh. I mean, they still worry about me, but they're cool with it. They just want me to be happy."

"Are you?" he asked. "Happy being an FBI agent, I mean."

"Yeah." She smiled. "The pay isn't the greatest and I practically live in hotels, but I love what I do."

"That's what's important." Zane leaned forward, resting his forearms on the table. "I am curious how you find time for anything resembling a social life since you're never in one place very long."

She snorted, remembering how Christine had ragged on her about this same subject. "Social life. What's that? As far as I'm concerned, if the FBI wanted me to have a social life, they'd issue me one, like my sidearm and badge."

Zane lifted a brow. "Are you saying that a woman as beautiful as you hasn't gone on a date with anyone in a year and half?"

Coming from anyone but Zane, that question might have irritated her. But for whatever reason, it didn't. She especially liked the compliment. "While I'm not going to come out and put an exact time frame on it, I'll admit it's been a while. But if we're going to discuss our social lives, how about you? Don't tell me a big, good-looking man like you isn't involved with someone."

Zane's gaze turned molten in the sun coming through the window and she felt her stomach do that funny flutter thing that had only started happening after they'd met. "If I were involved with someone, do you think I would have kissed you like I did last night?"

"I don't know," she said. "Would you?"

He lifted his mug and took a long, slow sip of coffee. "No, I wouldn't have. I've dated a few women since moving to Dallas. Probably more than a few, I guess. But it never felt right with any of them, and after a while, it didn't seem worth the effort. Then I met you and everything felt different. That's why I kissed you."

She'd just been messing with him about kissing her if he was involved with someone. His response was a lot more real than she'd expected. The part about why he'd kissed her made her warm all over. But the stuff about him not connecting with anyone since leaving London hurt more than she would have thought possible.

"You broke up with your fiancée a long time ago," she pointed out. "Are you saying that in all that time, you never met anyone you could see yourself falling for?"

He didn't answer at first, pausing to slowly chew his Pop-Tart. When he did finally answer her question, he kept his gaze fixed on the mug in front of him. "This probably won't make much sense, but for people like me, it can be difficult finding that perfect person we're supposed to be with. Some might even say it's impossible." The words were so soft she had to lean forward to hear them. "When the woman I thought was the right one for me walked out, I didn't think it could happen again. But since meeting you, I've started thinking maybe I gave up too soon."

Alyssa didn't know what to say. It wasn't a declaration of love or anything, but still...

Picking up her mug, she got up and poured herself more coffee. She held the pot up in Zane's direction, but he shook his head. She didn't necessarily want a refill, but it gave her a chance to think about everything he'd said. The guy had just unleashed a lot. It would take a while to absorb it all.

Like those three simple but significant words: *people like me*. Just that fast, the big, sexy Brit had confirmed he was different. Surprisingly, that acknowledgment didn't bother her as much as she thought it might. While she'd discounted the possibility of him using some kind of spell on her, part of her wondered if Zane was putting out some kind of supernatural pheromone to attract his victims with and make them easier to subdue. But one look at him sitting at the table chewing thoughtfully on his frosted brown sugar Pop-Tart made her toss that ridiculous idea right out of her head. Zane didn't need to put out any pheromones to lure her in. All he had to do was look at her.

She shook her head. One smile from him and she was ready to throw caution to the wind. Was she really that easy?

Alyssa walked back over to the table with her coffee, thinking about the other stuff Zane had said—especially the part where he'd confessed he'd given up on the idea of finding someone until meeting her. She'd never thought of herself as the kind of woman who cared about romantic drivel, but when Zane said those words, she had to admit there'd been some serious feels going on. Part of her wanted to wrap her arms around him and hug him. The other part wanted to throw him on the floor and bang him like a cheap screen door—but that part was only making noise because it had been so long since she'd gotten laid.

"So," she said, ignoring her chair and instead sitting on the edge of the table right in front of Zane. "I'm guessing you think I might be this perfect someone you'd given up hope of ever finding? Do you mind if I ask what makes you think that?"

Zane pushed his chair back a bit to make room for her, his dark eyes meeting hers. "You're not going to like this answer, but…it's complicated."

He was right. She didn't like it. "You're going to have to do better than that."

"Let's just say the first time I saw you at that club, taking down Stefan's goon, I knew you were someone special. And even though I'm still not sure if I'm comfortable with the idea—actually, I'm downright terrified—I'm also sure you're *The One* for me."

That sounded so romance-bookish Alyssa almost laughed out loud. The serious expression on Zane's face was the only thing that stopped her. It might be crazy as heck, but the big, sexy hunk seemed to genuinely believe it.

They sat there looking at each other, Alyssa cupping both hands around her mug, breathing in the warm coffee while Zane seemed to be holding his breath like he thought she might bolt for the door at any second. Which was crazy since this was her room.

"Okay," she said, setting her mug on the table. "Assuming you're right and I'm *The One* for you, what do we do now?"

Zane grinned. "Kissing would be nice, yes?"

His big hands were coming up to wrap around her hips, tugging her forward off the table and onto the chair with him until she was straddling his thighs. As sexy as that position might be, Alyssa couldn't help laughing. "Seriously? That's the movie line you're going with to get into my panties?"

Zane buried his fingers in her hair, tugging her mouth closer to his. Just before their lips met, he flashed her that thousand-watt smile, which made her pulse skip a beat. "I don't know," he murmured, his coffee-scented breath warm on her skin. "Did it work?"

Alyssa hadn't realized exactly what she'd said—about getting into her panties—until right then. But as she gazed down at Zane and his beautiful smile, she decided letting him have his way with her unmentionables sounded like a really good idea. After that, who knew what she might let him get into?

She didn't bother to answer his question. Instead, she lowered her mouth to his and kissed him hard enough to pull a growl out of him. And what an interesting growl it was, rumbling up through his chest and straight into her open mouth, making little tingles and shivers dance all over her body.

Apparently, she was into guys who growled. That was new.

When Zane's fingers tightened more firmly in her hair, Alyssa responded and deepened the kiss, her tongue tangling with his, tasting him as her hands came up to slip inside the top of his leather jacket to get a firm grip on his broad shoulders. She massaged them, digging her fingers into the tense muscles there until another growl of pleasure slipped past their joined lips. That only encouraged her to do it even harder. Soon, she was rocking back and forth on his lap, kissing him hard enough to leave a smile on his face for the next week.

Alyssa was so caught up in the sensations she barely noticed when one of his hands came down to rest on her hip—until he slid her higher up his lap, so the junction of her thighs was resting right on his hard-on.

She moaned as she found something firm and inviting to wiggle herself against. Damn, it really had been a long time. But just like riding a bike, her hips remembered the rhythm she'd always enjoyed, grinding in tight, little circles until her clit began to tingle like mad in her jeans. She sighed against Zane's mouth, positive her panties were already getting wet.

The sensations only got more intense when his other

hand slipped out of her hair and teased its way under the hem of her T-shirt, warm fingertips tracing up and down her back, toying with the strap of her bra when they weren't moving along the ridges of her spine and shoulder blades. Then, just when she thought she might go mad from how good those simple touches felt, Zane moved his right hand around to her front, pulling her shirt up to tease those magical fingers along her belly button, her ribs, and her stomach.

She was practically hyperventilating by the time he reached her breasts, her nipples screaming for attention, even with the soft material of her bra in the way. Zane didn't disappoint. His strong fingers found her already-hardened nipple and squeezed it to an even stiffer point.

"You have no idea how good that feels," she said hoarsely, breaking their kiss to bury her face in the curve of his neck, breathing in the combination of Zane's masculine scent mixed with the leather of his jacket.

He chuckled as he tweaked her nipple even harder before moving over to its neighbor and doing the same. "If the scent you're putting off right now is any indication, I'm guessing it feels nearly orgasmic."

Before she could ask what the hell he'd meant by that, she realized he was right. All this grinding and teasing had her on the edge of coming. He was so hot she was ready to explode before she even got her clothes off.

She closed her eyes, grinding her hips even harder, pushing herself those last few inches toward the precipice, when Zane suddenly stood, making her yelp in alarm and completely ruining her chances to come. Her legs went around his hips out of pure survival instinct, even as she felt his right hand come down and cup her ass protectively to make sure she didn't fall as he carried her toward the bed.

"You do realize I was close to something kind of important there, right?" she complained against his chest as he walked.

Zane laughed softly, the sound making her shiver in a completely different way than his growls had. "I was aware. But the first time you fall apart for me, I'd prefer if you were completely naked. I'm kind of visual that way."

She started to respond, but her mouth snapped closed as Zane's words finally filtered through. *The first time you fall apart for me.* Multiple orgasms were on the menu? Yes, please!

Alyssa was about to ask him how many climaxes he planned on giving her—purely out of academic interest, of course—when Zane dumped her onto the cushy bed, distracting her. By the time she got her head working again, her shoes, jeans, and T-shirt were already halfway across the room and the sexy man in front of her was working fast to get himself naked, too.

She lay back in her bra and panties, taking in the scene as he slipped out of his leather jacket and T-shirt, then shoved his jeans down and kicked them aside. *Daaaaammn!* His chest was the stuff of fantasies. It was all she could do not to jump up and run her hands all over those lusciously sculpted muscles. Then there were his rock-hard abs. Seriously, she could wash her clothes on them—if she was interested in washing her clothes at that moment, which she wasn't.

She lifted her gaze to his chest again, paying more attention to the tattoo on his left pec that she'd barely glanced at before. Although, now she was focused on it, she didn't know how she'd missed it. The head of a fierce-looking wolf with *S.W.A.T.* in bold letters above it, the ink was truly a work of art.

Some part of her wondered if the wolf was the team's mascot or whether there was more significance to it than that. She'd figure that out later...much later. When they weren't naked. Or nearly naked.

Alyssa bit her lower lip as he reached for the waistband of his underwear. She should probably be getting her own undies off right then, but she couldn't. She was too focused on the big reveal. And if the sizable bulge in his underwear was any indication, the big reveal was definitely going to be...*big*.

"This is probably the absolute worst time to mention this," he said, hesitating with his fingers hooked in his boxer briefs. "But I'm not carrying any condoms on me. I'm praying you have some?"

Alyssa smiled and pointed at the inside of her left upper arm. "Long-term birth control implant. Between my lack of social life and FBI-mandated semiannual physicals, I can promise I'm clean. You?"

He returned her smile as he pointed at his injured arm. "The doc has been testing my blood nonstop for months. I'm very clean."

She considered that for a moment, going with her instincts on this one before motioning down toward his midsection and everything he was hiding down there. "Given our recent histories and my birth-control implant, I think we're safe. So, please, feel free to carry on with what you were doing."

The smolder he threw her way was enough to make her panties sticky—if they weren't already. Then he slowly pushed his briefs down over his hard-on, dropping them to the floor and leaving her feeling like she'd won the lottery. She did her best not to stare and completely failed. His cock was as well built and mouthwateringly perfect as the rest of him.

Alyssa was up on her knees and wiggling toward the edge of the bed before she took another breath, eager to get her hands on all of him…not just his cock. She wasn't that shallow. As he approached the bed, a rational part of her mind attempted to point out there were about a million and one reasons she shouldn't be doing this. But the nonrational part of her mind—the one being run by her sex drive—decided to disregard all that.

Zane pulled her into his arms when he got close enough, and she moaned at the feeling of all that warm skin next to hers. He let out a groan as her hand sought out his cock and she wrapped her fingers around it. That part of his body was warm, too. Not to mention firm…and throbbing.

She was so caught up in masculine yumminess she barely noticed when her bra dropped away. But then his palms cupped her breasts and she couldn't help noticing he had big hands. She shuddered as his strong fingertips began to roll and tweak her nipples at the same time his mouth moved down to her neck to lick and nibble at the sensitive skin there.

"Harder," she whispered, almost embarrassed when she realized she'd said the words out loud.

Zane chuckled against her neck, a spectacular sensation on its own "Do what harder? Squeeze or bite?"

"Yes," she whimpered, too far gone to care about minor details like that.

He let out another warm laugh against her neck, but

then gave her exactly what she asked for, his fingertips squeezing her nipples so firmly she hissed out loud…but in a good way. Then his teeth closed down on the skin of her neck. Not hard enough to leave a mark but definitely hard enough to feel it.

Oh yeah, she really liked that.

Alyssa wasn't sure how it happened—magic maybe—but she ended up on her back with Zane nibbling and licking his way down her body, paying special attention to every tingly erogenous zone along his travels south. And while her nipples were definitely two of those tingly spots, she was shocked at how many others he found. It turned out the crease right under each of her breasts was incredibly sensitive, especially when a man with a tongue as sinful as his traced warm, wet lines back and forth along each.

There were more nibbles and bites as he worked his way down her abs, and she couldn't stop herself from reaching down to weave her fingers in his dark, silky hair to stop him when he reached her belly button. "Oh, yes. Right there!"

Zane chuckled, his lips soft against the ticklish skin of her stomach, and she realized how much she loved the sound of his laugh. In a crazy way, it was as arousing as his growls…or even his love bites.

"You like that, huh?" he murmured, his words nearly indistinct as his tongue dipped and teased a place that nobody else had ever touched.

How it was possible for her to be a belly-button virgin was a mystery. Why had no one ever done this to her before? Why had she never demanded it? Hell, she should have made it a requirement.

"I like," she sighed.

After she'd achieved an acceptable number of belly-button orgasms—she'd have to check Google to see if that was a thing—Zane continued his journey south. As he neared the place she'd wanted him to get to for the past fifteen minutes, all Alyssa could think about was how good he was with that tongue. If he made her squirm when he'd licked her belly button, what the hell was she going to do when he reached her pussy?

He teased her, of course, his teeth closing down lightly on the tender skin of her inner thighs, making the muscles there spasm and tremble and dragging deep moans from her throat.

"That feels so amazing," she breathed. "I never imagined…"

Alyssa had been about to tell him that she'd never imagined enjoying the sensation of a man's teeth sinking into her skin like that, but then Zane's mouth moved up to the juncture of her thighs, his tongue tracing a line right up the center of her folds, and coherent words abandoned her.

She started panting when she felt two fingers slip inside her, teasing, searching. Zane touched those sensitive places inside her like he had a road map for them. Then his mouth came down on her clit and Alyssa lost it.

At least she had enough presence of mind to remember there were probably guests in the rooms next to hers, grabbing a pillow and shoving the corner of it in her mouth as Zane flicked his tongue rapidly over her happy place. His eyes caught hers and a brow arched.

"Hotel rooms," she murmured around the pillow. "Really thin walls."

It was almost embarrassing how easily he made her

come. It was like he could read her mind, or rather, her body, his tongue and fingers knowing the perfect places to touch her to take her to the precipice quickly. Then he shoved her right over the edge into one long, continuous wave of pleasure that had her writhing on the bed, her thighs clenching tightly around him.

She'd never been able to make herself climax this fast, even with the assistance of modern technology.

His tongue continued to move on her clit while his fingers massaged her G-spot, making Alyssa scream into the pillow until she thought she might pull something. Like an orgasm muscle maybe.

Just when the sensation started to be too much, Zane pulled back, licking and nibbling on her inner thighs again. The feel of his sharp teeth was the perfect sensation to pull Alyssa out of the orgasm-induced haze threatening to pull her down into a mushy slumber. He kept his fingers inside her a little longer, coaxing a few more tremors of bliss from her core when she'd sworn her body was too worn-out to even move.

Alyssa tried to speak and realized she still had a mouth full of crisp, white cotton pillowcase. Spitting it out wasn't exactly the sexiest thing she'd ever done, but at least she was able to do it without sounding like a cat with a fur ball. Okay, maybe she did sound like that—a little bit.

"You okay up there?" Zane asked, gazing up from between her widespread legs. His chin glistened from her wetness and it had to be just about the sexiest thing she'd ever seen on a man.

"I'm good," she whispered, the smolder in his eyes making her tummy quiver all over again as she remembered what Zane had said to her earlier about multiple orgasms.

Mouth quirking, he climbed up from between her thighs, his movements animalistic as he stalked his way up the bed and over her body. As his lips hovered above hers, she felt his hard shaft nudging and sliding along her wetness, making that part of her anatomy hum.

"Oh, you're very good," he whispered, his lips coming down to cover hers, her essence mixing with his masculine taste as he kissed her long and slow.

She gave herself over completely to the kiss, tracing her hands up his forearms, then higher, the fingers of one hand lightly caressing the scars there. She had no idea why she did it, beyond the inherent need to show him in some real way that there was nothing about him she didn't enjoy. Even those parts he tried to keep hidden.

He growled softly at her touch, his full weight pressing her into the mattress. "That feels so damn good. I didn't know that could be possible. But it does...when you do it."

She had no idea if Zane had meant that to be as meaningful as it sounded. She pushed the thought aside and turned her attention back to the muscular hunk resting his weight between her thighs.

"You can stop teasing," she whispered. "I'm ready."

"I'm not teasing." He pulled back so he could look at her, his eyes molten with arousal. "I'm waiting for you to tell me what you want."

She didn't hesitate. "I want you inside of me—now."

Zane slowly slid in, gaze locked on hers the whole time. The sensation as he filled her took Alyssa's breath away. There was a better-than-even chance she had a tiny orgasm from his initial thrust. And if how good he felt going in didn't do it for her, the look of pure rapture on his face would have.

As he bent his head to kiss her lightly, she couldn't help but noticing a slight golden glow emanating from behind his eyes. It should have freaked her out— especially knowing what she knew about the world—but for some reason, she wasn't concerned with the color of his eyes at the moment. Maybe it was the sun streaming through the windows. Yeah, that was it.

He slowly began to move his hips, sliding almost all the way out, then back in. Within seconds, her butt was bouncing off the mattress as he picked up the pace. She wrapped her legs around his waist and held on tightly. The tingle deep inside her spread outward, making it feel like her whole body was on fire.

"Yes!" she shouted. "Just like that."

Zane lifted his head to give her a wicked smile, all the while pumping into her. "What was that you said earlier about thin walls? Maybe you should keep the shouting to a minimum."

She tried to snort, but it came out more as a moan. "This from the man about to make the bed smash through the wall. If you break the bed, you're paying for it."

That earned her a little nip on the neck from his sharp teeth and a round of serious pounding, yanking gasps, moans, and cries of pleasure from her—to hell with the thin walls. She was probably going to be a little sore tomorrow, but she wasn't complaining. She'd never been with a man like him in her life.

As the first waves of her second orgasm of the day rolled over her, Alyssa wondered if sex with Zane was this good because he really was some kind of supernatural being. Then the crest of the wave smashed into her at the same time her hunky lover growled and poured his warmth inside her, and she decided maybe some paranormal creatures weren't bad after all.

Chapter 8

ZANE WOKE UP WITH HIS FACE BURIED IN A SILKY TANGLE OF blond hair, the scent so delicious he couldn't find the strength to move, even if it meant he couldn't breathe very well. Instead, he lay there with his arms wrapped around Alyssa, taking in her scent and replaying the best twenty-four hours of his entire life. While that might sound like hyperbole, it was true. Nothing he'd experienced from the day he rolled over in his crib and discovered his toes until this very moment could compare to the joy he felt when he was with her.

Alyssa let out a soft whimper when he pulled her scrumptious body closer to his, and he had to bite his tongue to keep from groaning as his semi-erect cock nestled comfortably against her warm, perfect ass. That small amount of contact—not to mention the sexy sound she'd made—was enough to get him going all over again. Despite the number of times they'd made love, he still wanted her again.

He moved his hips back a little, taking a few deep breaths in an effort to get control of himself. He glanced at the clock on the nightstand and saw that it was a little after 2300 hours—aka 11:00 p.m. They'd need to get up soon so they could shower and dress in time to get over to Stefan's parking garage for their next shift.

His gaze drifted back to Alyssa, his heart squeezing

at how beautiful she was—even after hours of shagging and a serious case of bedhead.

Zane hadn't expected Alyssa's invitation to come in for coffee this morning to end with the two of them in bed together, but he sure as hell wasn't sorry about it. There was something about Alyssa that made her impossible to resist and he had no idea what it was.

Okay, that was a lie. The truth was he knew exactly why he was so attracted to her. He'd even said the words out loud last night, though he doubted Alyssa had noticed. Even if she had, there was no way she'd realized the significance of those two words.

The One.

Bloody hell, he couldn't believe he'd actually said that out loud. But he had, and now he had no idea what the hell he was going to do about it.

Zane didn't doubt the connection between him and Alyssa, not after everything that happened last night and today. He'd slept with women before, and it had never been like this with any of them, not even with Sienna. But just because the link with Alyssa was real didn't mean the whole world had suddenly turned into rainbows and unicorns. At some point, either she'd figure out he was a werewolf, or he'd have to tell her. And soul mate or not, she wasn't going to handle it well.

He couldn't imagine how badly she was going to freak when she realized she'd slept with a monster. Worse, because she'd been on long-term birth control, she'd been okay with him not using a condom. When she finally learned what he was, she was going to hate him. Maybe even try and kill him. Hell, she might even succeed.

Even though it was hard as hell to do, Zane slowly

pulled away from her. But the moment he slid his arm from her, she moaned in complaint and darted a hand out to stop him, gently holding onto his left arm, tucking it around her like a protective blanket.

He considered trying to tug away again, until one of her hands came up and wrapped around his upper arm, her fingers gently caressing the scar along the back. Any contact—even that tender—should have hurt like hell, but it was far from painful. On the contrary, it was pleasurable. It was almost scary to realize it was yet another indication of how strong the connection was between them.

A few moments later, Alyssa slowly opened her eyes, like she'd somehow been able to pick up on the distress buzzing through his head right then.

"Hey there," she murmured, turning her head a little so she could look at him, her voice rough and sexy with sleep…and sexual satisfaction.

Zane couldn't resist leaning in to kiss her. Of course, that only ended up pressing his hard cock against her ass. Alyssa's expression went from fuzzy to sultry in a heartbeat.

"I know it's dark outside," she said, her words pure liquid smoke as she arched a brow at him, "but is that morning wood I feel?"

"Maybe I'm just happy to see you," he answered, unable to stop from grinding his rapidly hardening erection against her, grinning despite his earlier thoughts of concern. When she looked at him like she did now, there was only one thought that popped into his head.

Alyssa reached back, making enough room to fit her hand in between them and wrapping her fingers around his shaft.

"Doesn't this big guy ever get satisfied?" she asked. "We made love for hours."

Zane chuckled, peppering soft kisses and nibbles along her jawline as he slowly eased inside her. "If you're asking whether I'll ever get enough of you, I think the answer is obvious."

Alyssa was just letting out a long, husky moan of pleasure when Zane's mobile phone rang. He really wanted to ignore the damn thing, but he couldn't.

She must have realized the same thing because she reached over to pick up his mobile from the night table, handing it to him over her shoulder without comment. She didn't pull away from him though, so he couldn't really complain.

He glanced at the screen to see Diego's name. He thumbed the green button and put it to his ear. "Kendrick."

"Hey," his pack mate said. "About an hour ago, a single car left the garage and went straight to the Black Swan headquarters off Figueroa. It came back twenty minutes later with passengers and disappeared into the garage. Five minutes after that, Stefan and four sedans full of knuckleheads took off. They're heading north toward the Downtown area. Whatever they're up to, it must be big."

Alyssa must have heard enough to realize something important was going on because she started easing away from him. Zane stopped her with a hand on her hip, then held a finger to his lips, silently telling her to be quiet.

"I'll pick up Alyssa and head that way," he said. "Text me with an address as soon as you figure out where they're going."

"Sounds like a plan," Diego said.

Zane hung up and reached over to toss his mobile on the night table. "You heard all that?"

She nodded. "Yeah. No need to put him on speakerphone. He has one hell of a deep voice."

Alyssa started to move, but he held her in place. Getting a firm grip on her hip, he rocked slowly in and out of her, barely able to contain the growl that wanted to slip out at how good she felt around him.

"You know we're going to need to shower before we leave, right?" she asked, her body automatically moving in time with his.

"I can shower and be ready in five minutes," he whispered against the curve of her neck, fighting the urge to bite her there. "How about you?"

"The same," she said softly. "But that doesn't give us a lot of time."

"Two minutes is all the time I need to make you fall apart again," he told her, thrusting faster even as he slid his hand between her legs to caress her clit.

Alyssa didn't reply. Instead, she reached back and tangled her fingers in his hair, silently urging him to take her harder.

"You guys got here fast," Rachel said as he and Alyssa met up with her and Diego at the entrance to an alley off Third Street.

Zane looked around, wondering what they were all doing there. The area was dark and relatively deserted, which was surprising considering Downtown LA was full of clubs, restaurants, shops, and tourist traps. But when he'd plugged it into the map app on his mobile phone, he hadn't seen anything of interest around there.

"I thought for sure you'd get stuck in traffic," Rachel added. "You must have gotten dressed and out the door in thirty seconds flat to make it here this soon."

Zane threw a glance in Alyssa's direction, seeing the quick grin that slipped across her face. No, they hadn't gotten dressed and out the door in thirty seconds—not even close.

The look Rachel and Diego shared spoke volumes. They smelled Alyssa on him and him on her. Diego looked surprised while Rachel looked extremely satisfied. To their credit, neither of them said anything, though they looked like they wanted to.

"We were lucky. Traffic was light," he said. "What are we doing here in an alley at midnight? It doesn't seem like a place where Stefan can nab his next victims."

Diego jerked his chin at the area farther down the alley.

Zane didn't see anything at first, but then he spotted a couple in dressy clothes walking toward them. Halfway in the alley, they turned and headed down a set of steps, disappearing underneath one of the buildings. He picked up bits and pieces of their conversation, then the distinct clank of a heavy, metal door. Thirty seconds later, three women hurried into the alley, teetering on their high heels and laughing. They vanished down the same stairs.

Obviously, there was a club down there.

Zane looked around. Other than a piece of red neon attached to the wall near the steps, there was nothing to tell anyone the place was there. Even the neon—a stylized cat with back arched—didn't exactly scream nightclub.

Maybe it was an invitation-only kind of place.

"I thought for sure we'd lost Stefan when we got here. They parked in a lot nearby, so we followed their scent and it led us to this place," Diego said as four guys jogged down the steps, joking with each other about who was buying the first round of drinks. "Oh, and I should probably mention, some of the people with Stefan reek of mud and stale blood. The stench was nasty as hell."

Zane threw a glance Alyssa's way, knowing there was no way she could have missed that whole thing about Diego and Rachel tracking Stefan's scent. But Alyssa didn't even bat an eye. Maybe she hadn't been paying attention?

He seriously needed to have a talk with his pack mate about keeping a low profile regarding the werewolf stuff.

"How long have Stefan and his buddies been down there?" Zane asked, not caring if Stefan's friends stunk. The guy was a wanker. It wasn't shocking the people he hung out with smelled crappy. "And is there a back way out of the club?"

"About twenty minutes," Rachel said. "And there's a loading dock on the far side of the block that seems to be connected to this side. I wouldn't be surprised if it's a labyrinth of interconnected rooms and corridors down there. If Stefan and his chucklefucks grab someone, that's probably the way they'll get them out."

"We need to get down there," Alyssa said. "They might already have drugged someone by now. Twenty minutes is a long time."

As they headed toward the stairs, Diego slipped ahead to fall into step beside Alyssa while Rachel hung back with Zane. "You and Alyssa, huh? Wow. Who saw that coming?"

He gave her a sidelong glance. "If you say I told you so, I'll bite you."

"You won't hear it from me," she promised. "I'm only glad you figured it out. You two are good together."

"We haven't figured out anything." He sighed. "Part of me is sitting back, waiting for the other shoe to drop."

Rachel frowned. "It doesn't always have to go that way, you know? Just because there have been some crappy moments in your life, it doesn't mean this time can't be better. Sometimes, it's all right to believe things are going to turn out okay."

Zane would have told her that was a naive view of the world and that his experiences indicated things really could go from bad to worse to horrible damn fast, but they'd reached the stairs to find Alyssa and Diego already waiting for them.

The big, dark-haired guy with tattoos on both arms at the bottom of the steps barely looked at them, but the petite girl with pin-straight, cobalt-blue hair standing beside the bouncer stared at them like she'd seen a ghost. The girl looked eighteen at the most and too young to be working at a place like this.

"Wow," she breathed, her lavender eyes going wide. "We don't usually get your kind here. Now it's like Grand Central Station."

Zane was still trying to figure out what kind of people she meant when the girl motioned with her head toward the metal door. The tattooed bouncer opened it without a word and waved all four of them in.

"Okay," Diego murmured as they descended another set of steps, illuminated only by small, red, neon cats lining the walls. "Is it just me or was that girl weird as hell?"

"She smelled funny, too," Rachel said.

Zane ignored the curious look Alyssa threw his teammate's way, praying she wouldn't ask what Rachel meant.

As for the girl with the blue hair smelling odd, he hadn't gotten a good sniff of her, mostly because he'd been too busy trying to understand why she was the one in charge and not the mountain of muscles beside her. Now that he thought about it, there was something off about her. Besides the fact that she didn't seem to possess a filter when it came to knowing what to say to potential customers, her eyes seemed way too old for someone her age.

They were about halfway down the steps when he felt the bass beat of the club's music vibrating through his boots. But it wasn't until he got to the bottom of the stairs that he realized the music wasn't merely loud. It was bloody deafening. The moment he pulled open the set of heavy double doors, the thumping techno beat smacked him in the face and hundreds of strobe lights did their very best to blind him.

As if that wasn't enough, a dozen bizarre scents he didn't recognize hit him all at once, making his eyes water. He glanced at Rachel and Diego to see it was affecting them the same way. Rachel actually used the back of her hand to block her nose.

"What the hell am I smelling?" Diego asked.

No need to worry about Alyssa overhearing anything they said in there. Zane could barely hear himself think.

"I don't know," he told Diego. "Forget about that for now. We need to find Stefan and his crew and figure out what they're up to."

Alyssa glanced over her shoulder at him. "This place is a complete madhouse. Should we split up and search?"

Madhouse was one way to describe it. Complete bedlam was another. Then again, that could just be the effect of the strobes. The flashing lights made the club's patrons look like they were moving at half speed and fast-forward at the same time. It was disturbing as hell.

Zane tried to ignore the annoying lights and survey the club. Rachel had been right. The place wasn't one big space. Instead, it seemed to be a series of individual rooms on different levels, all connected by archways and tunnels. This level had a gigantic bar along the back wall and a dance floor packed with partying people.

"You two take the left side. Alyssa and I will go right," he said to Rachel and Diego. He reached into his pocket and pulled out his wireless earpiece, slipping it into place, then clipped the mic to his shirt. "If we see anything, we'll let you know. You do the same. And remember, watch yourselves. We don't have a clue what Stefan and his crew are up to yet, but we know they're dangerous."

"Will do," Diego said.

He and Alyssa slowly worked their way through the crowd, searching for Stefan, but the damn strobe lights made it nearly impossible to get a good look at anyone very clearly. He tried to use his nose to see if he could pick up anything, hoping maybe one of the guys he'd fought in the alley the other night had come with Stefan, but the strange odors in the air were messing with his head. He couldn't seem to focus on anything but them. A few of the scents were almost werewolf like, but not quite right. Definitely not like any alpha, beta, or omega he'd ever smelled. At least whatever it was smelled vaguely like an animal, which was comforting for some reason.

The other scents worried him. Because there were at least three or four of them, including that weird mud-and-stale-blood stench Diego had mentioned that made the hair on the back of his neck stand on end. At first, he thought he might be picking up the odor of something decaying in the walls or the air vents of the club. He could only imagine how many rats a place like this might have. But the scents moved around too much for that. Whatever was putting off those odors was wandering around the club.

Things that smelled like dead rats walking around an underground nightclub—nothing bizarre about that.

Zane was still trying to pinpoint the source of the scents—relatively sure one or two of them were out on the dance floor—when Alyssa dragged his attention back to the real reason they were there.

"I don't see Stefan or anyone who looks like his Neanderthals in here," she said, raising her voice to be heard over the loud music. "I think we should move to another part of the club."

He nodded and motioned toward one of the archways that led into another room. She headed that way without comment, and he fell in directly behind her, so he could keep both an eye on her and where they were going. When they stepped through the archway, Alyssa halted midstep, surveying a room that was even bigger than the one they'd just left.

"How the hell did they fit this all in here?" Alyssa asked.

Zane had to agree. Maybe there was some kind of TARDIS magic going on and it was bigger on the inside than the outside. If he didn't know better, he'd think they'd stepped onto the third level of the Dallas Galleria and were looking down at the ice-skating rink they set up in the main atrium of the mall during the winter season. Except this version of the Galleria was painted pitch-black, lit with more of those bloody strobe lights and neon cats, and had a multilevel dance floor instead of an ice rink, complete with at least a hundred half-drunk, barely dressed people grinding together.

As he and Alyssa made their way through the crowd, he realized it was going to be damn tough finding Stefan in here thanks to the dark alcoves all along the walls. Even with the improved night vision that came with being a werewolf, he still couldn't see very far into them. Stefan could be ten feet away from them right now and they'd walk right past him.

Zane slowed as a strobe light spun around and almost blinded him. By the time his eyes cleared, Alyssa was a good ten feet ahead of him and he had to hurry to catch up to her. He was moving so fast he didn't see the dark-haired woman standing at the railing overlooking the dance floor until he bumped into her. He stopped to apologize when the woman's scent hit him. She smelled a little like a werewolf but different at the same time.

Eyes flashing bright green, she let out a low-pitched yowl. When that wasn't enough to immediately scare him away, she lifted her hand, revealing petite, curved claws, then hissed at him, exposing a delicate pair of fangs.

Bloody hell. She was some kind of werecat!

He put up his hands in surrender. "Sorry, I didn't mean to bump you."

Catwoman—yeah, he was going there—glared at him, letting out another hiss. "Stay the hell away from me. I don't know what you're doing here, but I'm not getting involved in your crap."

Baring her teeth at him again, she hurried away, disappearing into the crowd, leaving Zane to wonder if they were pumping psychedelic drugs into the club's air system. Because there was no way in hell he'd seen what he thought he'd seen.

"I don't know what the crowd looks like on your side of the club," Diego's voice in his earpiece jerked him out of the minor mental breakdown he was currently experiencing, "but there's some weird shit going on in this place."

"You have no idea," Zane muttered. "I think some kind of werecat just threatened to rip my face off. She had glowing eyes, fangs, and claws, but she definitely wasn't one of us."

He expected an immediate barrage of questions—and maybe a few comments about how insane he sounded—but he got neither.

"This is going to sound crazy, but when we ran into this guy who didn't smell like any human I've ever come across, he freaked out and took off through the crowd," Rachel said. "We followed him to a small alcove, and when we tried to tell him we only wanted to talk, he ran through a wall to get away from us."

Zane did a double take, sure he'd heard that last part wrong. Finally, he forced the words out. "He did what?"

"He ran through the damn wall," Diego said. "As

in he disappeared through reinforced concrete without leaving a mark on it."

Zane was still letting that sink in when Alyssa walked up and stopped in front of him. She must have realized he wasn't behind her and circled back. "What's up? Did you see Stefan?"

"Not yet. Let's do a lap around this level, then head down to the second floor."

As they moved through the crowd, he kept a hand on her lower back this time, so they wouldn't get separated again. They stuck close to the rail, keeping an eye out for Stefan, but between the swirling lights, hidden alcoves, and ridiculous number of people in the club, it was impossible.

"Anything yet?" he asked Rachel and Diego.

"Negative," Diego replied.

"But we just walked by a girl who didn't have a heartbeat," Rachel added. "She actually had the audacity to look at us like we were something she'd only seen in the off-limits part of the local petting zoo."

Zane didn't know what kind of animals were off-limits in a petting zoo but was afraid to ask. This night was bizarre enough as it was.

They were heading toward the stairs to the second level when he picked up a scent he immediately recognized. An alpha werewolf. It was difficult to pinpoint exactly where the guy was in the sea of humanity, but he was close by. The comment about Grand Central Station from that girl with the blue hair out front suddenly made a lot more sense. Another werewolf must have slipped in there just minutes before they had.

Zane wasn't sure if they found the other werewolf or

he found them, but five minutes later, they ran into him. Alyssa didn't realize what the tall, broad-shouldered Asian American guy was, so she stepped to the side to slip around him but stopped when she noticed Zane wasn't following her.

"Man, am I glad to see you," the werewolf said, relief clear on his face as he extended his hand. "Jake Huang."

Zane automatically shook his hand. "Zane Kendrick. This is Alyssa Carson."

Jake gave her a nod in greeting as he shook her hand. "I'm looking for two betas. Identical twin girls about eighteen-years old. Tall, platinum-blond hair, blue eyes—you can't miss them. They're in trouble, and if you're willing, I could use help finding them."

Out of the corner of his eye, Zane caught Alyssa looking at Jake in confusion, and he wasn't sure what was crazier about this situation—that the other alpha had said something like that in front of a human or that he'd just described Zoe and Chloe to a tee.

Then it hit him. This guy was the twins' alpha. And based on the racing heartbeat and waves of anxiety rolling off Jake, it was obvious he knew his betas were in danger. It must be so bad he'd simply stopped caring about the normal rules of werewolf behavior—like not letting random strangers know werewolves existed.

Zane would have preferred not to have this conversation in front of Alyssa, but asking her to wander off on her own for a few minutes so he could chat with Jake wasn't going to work. "I know who you're talking about and you can relax. The girls are okay. They're safe in a hotel room halfway across town."

Jake stared at him in confusion. "No, they aren't. I

tracked their scent in through the front entrance not more than ten minutes ago, but there are so many strange odors in here I can't find them now. Every instinct I have is telling me they're in serious trouble and that I have to help them even though I've never actually met them."

Alyssa was standing there looking baffled as hell, but Zane ignored her. "How could you describe them if you've never met them?"

"Because I saw them on a security camera last week." Jake ran his hand through his hair and blew out a breath as he added, "I'm a cop in Santa Fe. After my shift, I stopped at a diner to grab something to eat before I went home, and the moment I walked in, I smelled them. They must have been there right before I was." He shook his head. "I can't explain it, but something told me they were in trouble. I got the manager to show me the security footage and as soon as I saw them on camera, I knew I had to find them. I took emergency leave and have been tracking them ever since. The sensation they're in trouble has gotten stronger every day. They're in here now…and they're in danger."

"You're saying Zoe and Chloe are here in this club?" Alyssa asked.

She might not have a clue what was going on, but she was picking up speed fast.

"I think we would have seen Zoe and Chloe if they were up here," Zane said. "Let's check the next level down."

They were heading downstairs when Zane spotted a woman with cobalt-blue hair running up the stairs, nearly shoving people aside in her haste to get past. For half a second, he thought it was the girl from the front entrance, but then just as quickly realized that while she was almost assuredly related to her, she was twice the girl's age. Her mother maybe?

The woman's lavender eyes filled with panic as she skidded to a stop in front of them. She ignored Alyssa, instead focusing all of her attention on him and Jake. "You can't be here. My daughter should never have let you in. You need to leave—now. Before anyone sees you. I'll take you out the back way."

"What are you talking about?" Alyssa said. "Why can't we be here? We're not breaking the law."

The woman flipped her long hair over her shoulder and turned her gaze on Alyssa, looking at her like she was an idiot. "I'm not saying you can't be in here. I'm talking about them." She jerked her thumb at him and Jake. "It's a death sentence for those two."

Zane opened his mouth to ask what she meant by that, but Jake cut him off.

"Holy shit. There they are."

Zane followed his gaze to see Zoe and Chloe working their way through the packed dance floor. Bloody hell, the twins were there. The strobe lights bounced off their platinum hair and pale skin, making it seem like they were glowing. Dammit, he'd told them to stay at the hotel!

The woman with the cobalt hair cursed. "There are more of you? What the hell was my idiot daughter thinking letting you all in at the same time *they* decided to pay me a visit?"

Zane couldn't miss the emphasis on the word *they*. He suddenly got a sinking feeling in the pit of his stomach that the woman with the blue hair, the twins, the weird smells, and Stefan's presence here was all connected. How, he wasn't sure yet.

"Oh crap," Alyssa muttered. "Stefan's on the far side of the dance floor and he's locked on Zoe and Chloe."

Zane scanned the lower level until he found Stefan. The wanker was flanked by a crew of oversize security goons.

"Rachel. Diego. Get your asses back to the main room we first walked into," he said urgently into his mic, his gut telling him this situation was about to go to hell in a carpetbag fast. "You'll find an archway near the back of the dance floor. And hurry up. Stefan's found his next targets, and they're Zoe and Chloe. It's about to get ugly."

He and Alyssa brushed past the woman with the blue hair and were already starting down the stairs after Jake when a stench so overwhelming hit him that he almost gagged. It was a combination of old blood and dirt mixed with the odor of something long dead. He swung his gaze around the dance floor, trying to see where the horrible smell was coming from even as the woman with the unusual lavender eyes shouted something about damn werewolves getting them all killed.

Zane ignored her, still searching for the source of the odor. It was coming from three of the men with Stefan. They were standing so far back in the shadows behind Stefan that Zane wouldn't have seen them if he didn't have such keen vision. Dressed all in black, they weren't heavily muscled, but they were tall and put off a vibe that made anyone who wasn't in Stefan's immediate group steer clear of them. Despite how crowded the club was, there wasn't a person within five paces of them. Even as he watched, people stumbled over themselves in an effort to keep their distance.

The tallest of the three men moved forward to stand beside Stefan, and Zane did a double take as he stepped out of the shadows. His eyes were so black and lifeless they seemed to swallow the light. They reminded Zane of a shark—or a corpse.

Lifeless gaze locked on the twin werewolves in the middle of the dance floor, the man nodded.

As one, Stefan's crew waded into the crowd, some of them pulling their weapons out as they began shoving people aside in order to reach their targets.

Zoe and Chloe must have realized they were in trouble because they latched on to each other's hands and backed away. But there wasn't anywhere for them to go on the crowded dance floor.

Before he realized what he was doing, Zane gripped the railing with his good arm, intending to vault over it, when a deep growl ripped through the air, followed by a shout of pain as Jake engaged with one of Stefan's men on the floor below. The sounds were loud enough to be heard over the blaring techno music, and for a fraction of a second, everyone froze. Then the shooting started, and the club lost its collective mind as the crowd below erupted and people started crawling over each other in an attempt to get away.

Zane felt the muscles in his legs and arms twist and spasm as his body began to partially shift. At the same time, his claws and fangs extended, the tangy taste of blood filling his mouth as the bones of his jaw cracked to make room for all the long, sharp teeth. He knew it was a terrible idea to shift in a room full of people, but he couldn't stop it. Alyssa was already on the dance floor, inundated by the tidal wave of terrified people and cold-blooded killers. If she didn't get shot by Stefan's men, she'd be trampled by the crowd.

Fear tore through Zane at the thought. He tightened his grip on the railing and vaulted over it. He had to save her, even if it meant revealing what he was.

Chapter 9

ALYSSA TRIED TO TELL HERSELF SHE'D IMAGINED THE TER-rifying growl she'd heard right before everything went to hell in a shopping cart. Maybe she'd heard someone shout and mistaken it for a growl. But as more of the sounds echoed around the dance floor, making the hair on the back of her neck stand on end, she was forced to admit she hadn't imagined anything. There was something scary out there on the dance floor, and everyone in the club knew it.

She was reminded of that fact when a big guy with long, curly hair slammed into her on the way to the exit, nearly knocking her down. She spun out of his way just in time, but then barely avoided the next panicked person shoving past. Okay, in retrospect, maybe venturing into the middle of the dance floor hadn't been the best idea. But it wasn't like she'd had an option. When she'd seen the terror on the twins' faces as Stefan's Neanderthals closed in on them, she knew she had to do something. So, she followed her instincts and charged into danger. As crazy as it sounded, that was what she did for a living.

Alyssa directed people to the stairs even as she tried to work her way toward the last place on the floor she'd seen Zoe and Chloe. Why the hell hadn't they stayed at the hotel like they were supposed to?

She pulled up short as one of the Neanderthals

stepped in front of her. She had a split second to realize he was one of the guys from the other night in the
alley before he lifted his weapon and pointed it at her.
Alyssa's training kicked in and she darted to the side,
lifting her gun at the same time. But she already knew
it was too late. She wouldn't be able to get her shot off
before he did.

Another one of those deep growls reverberated in
the air as someone flew from above, smashing the man
with the gun to the floor. More growls followed, and she
caught a glimpse of impossibly long fangs and claws as
her rescuer straightened to his full height and tossed the
man's broken body aside like a toy.

Alyssa blinked, recognizing Zane from the way his
injured arm hung at his side even before he turned to look
at her. The strobe lights made it difficult to see his face
clearly, but it was hard to miss the sharp fangs extending
beyond his lower lip or the glowing, yellow-gold eyes.

Chest tight, she opened her mouth to say something—
though she wasn't sure what—but he was moving again,
fighting his way through the rapidly thinning crowd to
take on another one of Stefan's men. She stared after
him, not sure if she wanted to consider the possibilities
of what she'd just seen. But then the sounds of fighting pierced the fog surrounding her, forcing her to stop
thinking and go after Zane.

She'd barely taken two steps before realizing Zane
had followed Jake to help protect the twins, but it
already seemed too late. Some of Stefan's men had the
girls corralled and were herding them toward the far end
of the dance floor, violently shoving aside anyone who
got in their way. The rest of his Neanderthals forced

Zane and Jake back in Alyssa's direction. One of the assholes lifted his .45 and pulled the trigger. There was a bright muzzle flash and a deafening boom. Zane staggered back a step.

Alyssa's heart seized in her chest. Even though she couldn't tell exactly where Zane had been hit, she knew it was bad. Any wound from a weapon of that caliber would be. Eyes filling with tears, she ran across the now-empty floor toward him, only to halt in her tracks when Zane let out a terrifying snarl. She watched in disbelief as he grabbed the wrist of the man with the .45 and snapped it like a twig, then quickly slashed the guy's throat with his claws, cutting off any sound he might have made.

The man hadn't even hit the floor before Zane was moving again, this time into the middle of the remaining Neanderthals, snarling, punching, and tearing apart anyone unfortunate enough to be close to him. Jake fell in beside him, claws and fangs flashing. Together, the two of them were more violent and unrelenting than anything Alyssa had ever witnessed—or even imagined.

If there'd been time, she might have been terrified by what Zane was doing and how he was doing it, but then one of Stefan's men rushed at her. She lifted her weapon and fired, not thinking anymore as the man went down and another took his place.

Alyssa started to pull the trigger again, but then hesitated when she realized the second man wasn't carrying a weapon. Hair as dark as pitch and skin unnaturally pale, he wasn't dressed in a suit like Stefan's other muscle. Instead, he wore dress slacks and an expensive silk button-down. He walked toward her almost casually, his expression amused. Even though he didn't look like he posed a threat, something told her he was far more dangerous than the armed Neanderthal she'd just shot. She'd seen enough weird over the past year to make her tighten her grip on her gun and aim for the center of the man's chest.

"Don't come another step closer or I will shoot you!" she shouted.

The man didn't slow. Flat, dark eyes locked on her, his lips pulling up in a snarl, revealing two long fangs. A shiver of fear ran down her back, leaving her short of breath. Forcing herself to ignore it, she focused her attention on the sights of her weapon and squeezed the trigger before the damn thing got any closer to her.

The first 9 mm round tagged the man in the left shoulder but didn't slow him down. Worse, it didn't even knock that creepy snarl off his face. Instead, the damn freak's mouth opened even wider, exposing an entire mouth of razor-sharp teeth. Shaking in revulsion, she put five more rounds directly through the center of the thing's chest.

The silk shirt he wore shredded as each bullet hit, yet he still kept coming.

Alyssa emptied the rest of her magazine into the man from less than five feet away, then quickly backpedaled, trying to give herself room to reload, even though she knew it wasn't going to help. She'd dropped an entire mag in the thing from point-blank range, and it hadn't even fazed him.

She slammed her second clip home and thumbed the slide release, bringing the weapon up for a head shot when a blur of movement crossed her vision and someone fast and growly kicked the bullet-ridden thing with fangs squarely in the chest, sending him flying a good fifteen feet across the dance floor. Zane had come to her rescue again. He was still all fangs, claws, and animal snarls, but it was him.

Before Alyssa had a chance to sigh in relief, another man in dress slacks and a silk shirt appeared from the darkness and charged forward. Zane slashed the thing across the throat with his claws, causing horrific damage, but the creature barely slowed as the wounds immediately healed, leaving behind little more than dark-red smears.

Alyssa brought up her weapon, intending to shoot the thing in the head, only to freeze when it let out a high-pitch screech. The primitive sound tore through the club, turning her muscles to jelly.

Before she could squeeze the trigger, the thing leaped at Zane. The creature was faster, inflicting five wounds for every one that Zane got in. But Zane was more powerful. When he landed a blow, it was devastating.

But then, without warning, the thing lunged forward, going for Zane's exposed neck with its sharp teeth.

Zane grunted in pain as he got his left arm up to protect himself, and while Alyssa knew it had hurt him to move his injured arm, that was nothing compared to the howl he let out when the creature's fangs sank into his forearm.

She held her breath, expecting the monster to go for Zane's throat again, but instead, it immediately released him, shrieking in pain as it fell to the floor. The skin around its mouth and along its jaw bubbled and hissed, like someone had thrown acid on it.

Alyssa didn't hesitate this time. Lifting her weapon, she took aim and shot the thing in the head.

The creature paid no attention to the hole in the center of its forehead, but instead frantically wiped at its half-melted face, and Alyssa watched in shock as the bullet wound slowly healed itself.

"You can't kill vampires that way!" someone shouted from the floor above them. Alyssa snapped her head around to see the woman who'd accosted them earlier on the stairs. "You have to rip out their hearts or tear off their heads!"

Vampires?

Time staggered to a standstill as Alyssa's mind attempted to process the word she'd just heard. In the past year and half, she'd dealt with dozens of horrible creatures, including several that drank human blood. But none of them had come close to fitting the stereotypical vampire image that Bram Stoker and Hollywood had put into the collective human mind. Hell, most of them hadn't even looked human. Which was why she'd come to accept that the whole vampire mythology was nothing more than a grain or two of truth mixed in with an overactive imagination.

Apparently, she'd been wrong.

She barely saw Zane move he was so fast. One second, he seemed as stunned as she was, and the next, he was on top of the vampire, right arm around the monster's head. The vampire let out another one of those screeches as Zane ripped its head off.

All at once, the blaring techno music stopped, and the lights came on. The harsh glow was unexpected and overwhelming, and it took a few moments before Alyssa could see anything at all. When she finally was able, she wasn't sure she wanted to because it was an image she knew she'd never be able to forget.

Zane stood in front of her, almost unrecognizable in his current form. The muscles of his shoulders, chest, arms, and legs had twisted, somehow becoming larger and thicker than they'd been before. Two-inch-long claws tipped each finger, blood dripping off them onto the floor. She knew he'd killed those vampires to protect her and everyone else in the club. Still, it was difficult not to heave at the evidence of the violence he was capable of.

She lifted her gaze to his face, flinching when she saw that his nose was pushed outward a little, making his features seem more animal-like. His upper and lower jaw were wider, too, and the fangs hanging down over his lower lip had to be as long as her fingers and razor sharp.

But it wasn't until Alyssa saw his eyes that she finally realized how different Zane had become. They were striking, glowing yellow gold even in the bright light of the club. But the eyes staring at her then didn't seem to possess any of the humanity she'd seen when they'd glinted earlier while they'd been making love. Those eyes had been filled with hunger and desire. Now, they seemed to be filled with rage and loathing.

Alyssa was vaguely aware of Jake saying the twins were missing, and Rachel and Diego announcing that Stefan, some of his guards, and one of the vampires had gotten away, but she paid no attention. Unable to take the contempt in Zane's eyes anymore, she looked away. She needed to get some space to think—and breathe.

Out of the corner of her eye, she saw the woman with the blue hair hurrying down the steps, yelling about never letting werewolves in her club again and that they'd never get the place cleaned up before the police showed.

Werewolves?

Oh God. She'd known Zane was different before tonight but a werewolf?

That's when Alyssa started to hyperventilate.

———

Zane could tell that Alyssa was freaking out, and the urge to comfort her was overwhelming. But all it took was one look at her face for him to realize there was no way she was going to let him get anywhere near her. He'd known she'd find out at some point, but even so, something inside him died then because he realized whatever had been between them was over.

Confusion, anger, disappointment, regret, disgust, revulsion—it seemed like dozens of emotions flitted across her face in those agonizing moments before she turned away from him. It was eerie how closely Alyssa's expression resembled Sienna's the night his former fiancée had walked out of his life. It was something Zane never thought he'd have to experience even once in his life. Now, it had happened for the second time. Only this time, it hurt even more. It felt like someone was ripping his guts out with a piece of razor wire.

He wished he could think of something to say to her to get her to understand how incredibly sorry he was for not telling her the truth sooner. But he couldn't. She might be *The One* for him, but she was going to walk away from him anyway, and there wasn't a damn thing he could say or do to stop her. He locked eyes with her for a moment, but as he opened his mouth to say something—anything—that would explain what she'd just seen, Diego ran toward them from one of the side entrances.

"Stefan took the twins. Rachel and that other alpha are still chasing after them, but I knew we'd need help if there are any more of those things outside." Diego was breathing as hard as if he'd run a marathon, and blood dripped from a dozen lacerations across his chest and arms. "They were heading for the back loading dock when I left to come find you."

Cursing, Zane threw a quick glance at Alyssa before following his pack mate into the darkened corridors of the club, the stench of those things easy to track. Alyssa wordlessly followed, her heart pounding like a drum. He wished there was time to stop and talk to her, but there simply wasn't. They couldn't let Stefan and those vampires get away with Zoe and Chloe. The thought of what those wankers might do to the twins worried the hell out of Zane.

He moved after Diego quickly, zigging and zagging through the club's twisting passageways and dimly lit storerooms. They ran into a handful of terrified people along the way, crouching behind boxes and hiding in dark corners. He couldn't imagine what they were thinking after what they'd seen tonight.

Vampires.

He didn't want to believe the creatures were possible. That was silly, considering he was a werewolf. He was bloody living proof of the existence of the supernatural. But in the end, he couldn't deny what he'd seen. That thing he'd fought had smelled like a grave, and though it had made a mess when he'd pulled its head off, the lack of blood spray made it obvious the creature wasn't alive—at least not in the normal sense. He guessed that made it a vampire.

The moment they got to the loading dock, Zane knew it was too late. The vampires were nowhere in sight, and Rachel and Jake were standing there staring into the darkness, scowls on their faces.

Alyssa cursed and took off running in the direction of the rental car. No doubt, she was going for her laptop and the GPS tracking app. It was hard as hell letting her out of his sight even for a minute, but the car was parked just around the corner. Besides, Stefan and his monsters were long gone.

"We were fast, but not fast enough," Rachel said softly. Her jacket and jeans were ripped in several places and she had bloody scratches on her neck. "We didn't even see which direction they went."

"We have to go after them," Jake snarled, turning to look at Zane, his expression a combination of utter devastation and barely suppressed rage. His fangs were still fully extended, and it was obvious he was barely holding it together. "We can't let those creatures have them."

Jake's reaction didn't surprise Zane. Even though Jake had never actually met Zoe and Chloe, he still felt the overwhelming need to keep them safe. That's what it meant to be an alpha. They were genetically coded to protect betas. Jake had already bonded with the twins as their pack alpha.

"I want to go after them as much as you do," Zane said. "But it's not like we can go driving around LA without a clue where we're going. We have GPS trackers on their vehicles. As soon as Alyssa comes back with her laptop, we'll go after them."

That seemed to calm Jake down a little, but when Alyssa came running around the corner without her laptop Zane knew something was wrong.

"The signals from the trackers are gone," she said. "The vampires must have found them somehow and destroyed them."

Jake's growl was loud enough to echo off the surrounding buildings, but even that wasn't enough to cover the sound of approaching sirens. They were about to have a lot of company.

"What about the parking garage?" Diego asked. "Do you think Stefan would have taken the girls there?"

Jake snapped his head around to look at Diego before turning back to Zane, his eyes filled with hope. "Stefan. You said his name in the club. That he was targeting Zoe and Chloe. If that's true, we should go check out this garage of his, right?"

Zane was fully aware that Jake didn't have a clue who Stefan Curtis was, but also recognized the alpha was more than ready to go after a man he'd never heard of on even the slimmest chance it would lead him to his betas. The man was grasping at any straw offered to him, anything to make him believe those girls were safe and that he'd be able to get them back.

Zane's instincts told him heading to the garage wasn't a good idea, though he couldn't say why. But after seeing his doubts mirrored on both Rachel's and Alyssa's faces, he was sure of it regardless.

"As far as we know, Stefan's normal MO is to troll a club with a small group of his goons until he sees a victim or two that catches his eye. Then he drops a roofie in their drinks and his men slip them out without causing a scene." Zane shook his head. "But what happened in there earlier was something completely different."

"It was the first time any of us have seen him with those vampires," Alyssa said softly. "I'm not sure what was going on, but I'm willing to bet their presence changed everything."

"Did it seem like they were working for Stefan? Or the other way around?" Rachel asked. "If the vampires are in charge, it'd make sense they'd take the girls to wherever those vampires live. If *living* is the right word for it."

Their discussion only seemed to piss Jake off more than he already was and he snarled as he looked back and forth between the three of them. "So, where the hell does that leave us? Where do we go, if not the garage?"

Zane hesitated, knowing Jake wasn't going to like what he was about to say. "I don't think we go anywhere, not until we know more about what we're up against. We need to talk to someone who can tell us more about these vampires."

That earned him a growl "I don't think this is something you can just Google on your phone. Where the hell do we find someone like that?"

"That woman in the club with the blue hair seemed to know a lot about vampires," Alyssa murmured, voicing the same thing Zane had been thinking. "She knew they were here, knew how to kill them, and implied werewolves and vampires don't mix well. She even tried to warn us to get out."

Jake didn't look thrilled at the idea of taking the time

to talk to anyone, but when Rachel and Diego nodded in agreement, it wasn't like he had a lot of choice. The fact that the sirens headed their way were getting louder by the second probably had something to do with him going along with the plan, too.

"If we're going back into the club, we'd better hurry," Rachel said. "The cops are going to be crawling all over this place in a minute."

"Okay, you said you had questions, so ask." Davina DeMirci glared at Zane as she flipped her long, blue hair over her shoulder and sat back in the leather chair behind the big ornate desk in her office above the club. Unlike the rest of the place, the room had an old-world feel to it with lots of heavy antique furniture, hand-painted murals of mythical beasts and fantastical landscapes covering the walls, and shelves packed with exotic sculptures and art pieces. No neon cats here, either. Just a big, fluffy gray one who regarded Zane and his friends imperiously from atop the desk. "The sooner I answer them, the sooner I can get the lot of you out of my club. Hopefully before the cops figure out you're up here."

Davina had been seriously pissed when Zane and the rest of them had come back into the club and interrupted her efforts to clean up the mess they'd made during the fight. She'd muttered something about the cops being there any second and how she'd never be able to explain any of this if the five of them were standing there covered in blood.

Zane remembered thinking that five slightly disheveled people with a little blood on them was the least of

Davina's problems. He'd personally be more worried about Stefan's dead goons on the dance floor, not to mention the two vampires missing their heads. About the only good thing he could say regarding the shooting in the club was that no one else had been killed. That in itself was a bloody miracle.

"We're just here to get answers to some questions," Zane had told her. "Then we'll get out of here and you'll never have to see us again."

Davina seemed thrilled at the idea of never seeing them again, but not quite as happy about answering their questions, at least until her daughter had come running to let them know the cops had arrived. That's when Davina had finally relented and led them to her office, leaving her daughter to handle the cops.

"How is it possible my pack and I have never run into vampires before tonight?" Zane asked now. "Up until a few hours ago, we didn't even know they existed."

It wasn't the question he wanted to start with. He'd much rather ask the woman where the vampires had taken Zoe and Chloe and how many of those things they'd have to go through to get the girls back. But something told him Davina didn't want to talk about vampires right then. Probably because she didn't want to get on the bloodsuckers' bad side.

Davina snorted. "You do see the irony of a werewolf not believing vampires exist, right? What, did you really think you were the only supernatural creatures in the world?"

"I guess I did." He shrugged and crossed his arms over his chest. "We all did."

"Well, sorry to burst your bubble, sunshine, but the world is a lot more complex than you thought. There're all kinds of things that go bump in the night. Vampires just happen to be one of the nastier ones." Davina regarded him for a moment before studying each of the others in turn. Her gaze lingered on Alyssa who sat in one of the two wingback chairs by the low coffee table on the far side of the room before she finally looked at him again. "To answer your question, vampires avoid werewolves like the plague. Werewolves—alphas in particular—are the only thing in the supernatural world that can take down a vampire. That's why they spend so much of their money employing hunters to take out your kind."

Zane frowned as the implication of Davina's words filtered through him. He quickly looked at Rachel and Diego. They seemed as stunned as he was. "Hunters work for the vampires?"

Davina looked at him like he was stupid. "Of course. Vamps want werewolves gone, but they're not willing to do battle with you. They've been around a lot longer than you and are way too smart for that. Instead, they hide away in their covens along the East and West coasts, sending the hunters into the central part of the country to keep the werewolf population in check. If they had their way, vampires would wipe out every last one of you."

"So, Stefan is a hunter working for the vampires too?" Zane asked.

Davina sighed, leaning forward in her chair to caress the gray cat's fur. "It's a bit more complicated than that in Stefan's case. None of those men you saw downstairs were hunters, especially not Stefan. While there are a few trusted hunters allowed within the confines of the coven itself, most are viewed as little more than hired killers. The men you fought tonight are private security who work directly for Stefan, the scion of the Curtis family and the LA coven. The big vampire who got away is Dario Casteel, the ruler of the coven. He essentially runs this town—the supernatural part of it at least."

"Scion?" Rachel asked from the other wingback chair. "I thought Stefan was the redheaded stepchild of the family who got stuck doing all the menial dirty work for Black Swan Enterprises while the rest of the family got the cushy office jobs."

Davina let out a short laugh. "Hardly. The title of scion means he's the favored son. As far as the coven is concerned, it's the other members of the Curtis family who are the menials. All they do is bring in the money. Stefan is the one trusted to protect the coven, bring them food, and hire the hunters. At some point, once the Coven feels he's done enough for them, they may even turn him so he can be one of them. No one else in the Curtis family will ever be given that kind of honor, no matter how much money they bring in."

Jake pushed away from the bookcase he'd been leaning against with a snarl. "I'm sure this is all very interesting, but what the hell does any of it have to do with getting Zoe and Chloe back? Those vampires left with them twenty minutes ago and we're just sitting here talking about the coven's organizational structure. We don't even know why they took the girls, or what they plan to do with them."

Davina's lavender gaze softened at that, looking sympathetic to their situation for the first time tonight. "That's not something any of you want the answer to."

Jake's eyes flashed yellow gold. "Yeah, I do."

Davina exchanged glances with the gray cat before

answering. "It all depends on whether the vamps realize those girls are werewolves. If they do, they'll make an example out of them to discourage any more werewolves from coming to LA."

Jake cursed, his fangs extending. Davina didn't react, but out of the corner of his eye, Zane saw Alyssa flinch a little.

"I think Zoe and Chloe just started going through their change recently. What if they're not far enough along for the vamps to figure out the girls are werewolves?" Jake asked. "Would that be better for them?"

"Unfortunately, no. If they took the girls simply because they're attractive young women, the vamps will almost certainly enthrall them and bleed them slowly over time. Normally, that would never work with a werewolf." Davina looked at Zane. "You saw what happened to that vampire downstairs when he tried to bite you. Your blood is like acid to them. But if Zoe and Chloe are just starting to go through the change, I have no idea what will happen."

No one said anything for a long time. No doubt they were all thinking the same horrible thoughts Zane was.

It was Alyssa who finally broke the silence. "You said, 'enthrall them.' What does that mean?"

"When a vampire bites a person, two chemicals are passed into the victim's bloodstream along with the vamp's saliva," Davina explained. "One helps heal the wound, so their victim won't bleed out from the bite. The other is a form of sedative that makes the person docile. If a person's willpower is strong enough, they can fight the drug, but that's rare. After a time, the victim will not only gladly let a vampire feed on them day after day for years, but they'll actually become protective of the creatures. They'll die for them if necessary." She shrugged. "Again, I have no idea if that will work on a brand-new werewolf. It's terrifying to think about a vampire getting complete control over one of your kind that way."

If the room had been quiet before, now it was so silent you could have heard a pin drop. Zane couldn't help thinking of that girl Alyssa had told him about—the one they'd found in the landfill. With the way her blood had been drained, it could only mean that the vampires had killed her. He didn't want to think what that would be like. And he sure as bloody hell didn't want to think about it happening to Zoe and Chloe.

Jake started for the door. "We have to go. We can't let either of those things happen to the girls."

Zane caught his arm. "Like I said before, I want to get Zoe and Chloe back as much as you do—we all do. But we still don't know where they are."

Jake snarled, but Zane refused to let him go. Out of the corner of his eye, he saw Rachel and Diego move closer, ready to be backup. Zane didn't blame them. Jake looked like he was on the verge of losing it.

"What about that parking garage Diego mentioned?" Jake demanded. "If we don't have a better option, let's go look there."

"You mean the Curtis Unified Garage?" Davina asked.

Zane nodded. "Yes."

She waved her free hand. "Don't bother wasting your time. If Stefan had been on his own, he might have taken them there, but with Dario along, it's almost a certainty they took the girls straight to the coven nest for sure. Especially after you killed two of their kind.

Dario is going to want to talk to the elders and decide how they're going to respond."

"Do you know where this nest is?" Zane asked.

Davina tensed, her hand stilling on the cat's fur. "Look, I don't want those two girls getting hurt any more than you do, but this club has survived as long as it has because I don't take sides. If the vamps found out I told you anything, they wouldn't just kill me, they'd kill my daughter and everyone who works here."

Zane ground his jaw. "They won't hear anything from us. We'll go in and rescue the twins, then deal with the vampires. They'll be no risk to you or your club."

"No risk?" She snorted. "You're planning to attack a vampire nest as large as the one here in LA with four werewolves and a human, and you think you'll actually accomplish anything. Now that I think about it, I don't know why I'm worrying any of it will come back on me. You'll all get yourselves killed in the first five minutes, so there won't be anyone for the vampires to question about how you found their nest."

Jake jerked his arm away from Zane to glare at her. "We dealt with the vampires downstairs easily enough. We'll do the same with the ones in the nest."

Davina muttered a curse under her breath. "That was three vamps, and even with Dario being one of them, it's nothing compared to what you'll face if you walk right into their nest. I have no idea exactly how many vampires live there, but it's at least thirty—maybe as many as fifty. It would be a suicide mission, and that's before you even get around to dealing with all the guards and enthralled people there."

Zane wasn't the only one to let out a growl of

frustration at that. Davina was right. Going in would be a suicide mission. The four of them had gotten slashed up pretty good dealing with the small group of vamps and their human guards. While he and the others were healing up fine now, he didn't want to think about how much worse it would be facing a whole nest of those things. There was no way they could do this on their own.

"I'll call my pack alpha and tell him we need as much help as they can send," Zane said, then glanced at Jake. "I know you don't want to wait, but if we go in there without enough backup, it won't help Zoe and Chloe at all."

Davina considered that for a moment before letting out a sigh. "Okay, if you get more help from your pack, I'll tell you where the nest is. Though I still think you'll need more reinforcements than that."

Rachel looked at Alyssa. "Do you think the task force might be willing to help?"

Alyssa opened her mouth to answer, but Zane cut her off with a snarl. The idea of Alyssa going anywhere near Dario and the other vampires sent a stab of fear right through his core.

"I don't want her involved."

Alyssa shot him a glare but didn't say anything. If looks could kill… The expression on her face made his stomach clench so tightly he almost doubled over. But even that wasn't nearly as painful as the idea of her going into a building full of those damn vampires.

Diego cleared his throat. "If Davina will sneak Rachel and I out of here so the cops don't see us, we'll call Gage and let him know what's going on. Maybe you two should stay here and clear the air."

Zane shook his head along with Alyssa, but Rachel cut them off. "He's right. We need both of y'all to get your head in the game. And if Alyssa could get us some outside help, we'd be stupid to turn up our noses at it."

Everyone walked out, with Rachel leading the way and Davina bringing up the rear with her cat in her arm, closing the door quietly behind them and leaving Zane and Alyssa staring at each other.

Bloody hell.

He didn't have a clue what to say.

Chapter 10

NEITHER OF THEM SAID A WORD, AND THE LONGER THE silence stretched out, the more painful it became. But Alyssa couldn't seem to come up with something to say right then. Her head was spinning too fast. After the past year and a half, she thought she'd be immune to shock and surprise, but she'd been wrong.

Alyssa darted a glance at Zane, watching out of the corner of her eye as he walked over to stand in front of one of the ancient-looking wall murals, studying it as if he were interested in every small detail. His back and shoulders were stiff, his jaw clenched tight. Just another indication of how pissed he was at her.

When she couldn't take the silence—and the way he was ignoring her—any longer, she forced herself to say the first thing that popped into her head. "So, you're a...?"

"Monster?" Zane finished for her when she hesitated. "Yeah, pretty much."

"I was going to say werewolf," she snapped.

What the hell was his problem? She supposed he was mad she knew his little werewolf secret, but that didn't explain the disgust dripping from his words or the way he looked at her like she was something on his shoe he'd prefer to scrape off with a stick. Seeing him regard her that way made her feel physically ill. She honestly felt like she was going to throw up every time he glanced her way—when he bothered looking at her at all.

"Yes, I'm a werewolf." Zane glanced at her briefly before turning back to the wall mural. "Does it make you feel better to hear me say it out loud?"

She refused to respond to his sarcasm, letting it wash over her without allowing it to seep into the cracks of the wall that had already formed around her heart. But it hurt all the same, even if she didn't want it to. As she sat in the comfortable leather chair, she tried to understand why his sharp tone bothered her as much as it did. He didn't think much of her, that was obvious. Why couldn't she feel the same about him?

"Were you bitten?" she asked. "Is that how you became a werewolf?"

Zane turned to look at her sharply. "You're telling me you've been traveling all over the globe investigating werewolf murders for over a year and you don't know how we're created?"

It took Alyssa several moments to realize what Zane was talking about, but when everything finally clicked into place, a lot of confusing cases she'd worked suddenly made a lot more sense.

"Not all those cases involved werewolves. In fact, most of them didn't. But now that I know about werewolves—and hunters—some of the cases we couldn't solve make a lot more sense."

Zane's eyes narrowed in suspicion. Finally, he turned back to the mural. "We thought you were on the trail of the hunters—or working with them."

The accusation, even delivered as casually as it was, felt like a punch in the stomach. "You really think I'd be involved with scumbags who track down and execute people like you because they're different?"

He didn't look at her. "I've realized I don't really know anything about you. I could hear your heart beating as that vampire came at you with his fangs and claws out, ready to tear you apart. You were as calm as if you were taking a walk in the park. So don't try telling me this is the first time you've faced monsters—or the first time you killed them."

The accusation tore the breath from her lungs. But this one hit closer to home, because there was a grain of truth to it.

"Yes," she ground out through clenched teeth. "There have been occasions where I've had to deal with things that most other people will never have to even know about, much less see. Not werewolves or vampires, but things that leave me with nightmares. But no matter how scary they were, I've never killed anything that wasn't trying to kill me first. As a cop, you should understand that."

Zane glanced at her, his expression softening. "I do understand. I apologize."

That made her feel a little better, at least. Alyssa knew she should say something else while he might be willing to listen to her, but no words would come. She was terrified of opening her mouth and shoving her foot in it again.

"I didn't become a werewolf by getting bitten," he said suddenly, catching her off guard. "It doesn't work that way. So you don't have to worry about it happening to you even though I nipped you when we were…together."

Her breath hitched. To tell the truth, she hadn't even thought about that, but now that he mentioned it, she couldn't help remembering the love bites he'd given her neck and shoulders when they'd made love. She supposed it was good that she didn't need to worry about turning into a werewolf even as part of her wondered if it would be all that bad.

She shook that crazy thought off, waiting for him to tell her the rest of the story. When he didn't, she realized she needed to nudge him a little. But gently.

"If a bite doesn't do it, how does it work?"

He took a deep breath, then moved away from the wall mural, coming over to lean back against the desk, arms folded. Alyssa saw the doubt on his face as he stared down at the floor, like he was hesitant to tell her anything about his kind for fear of where that information would end up.

"Nothing you tell me will ever reach the people I work for," she assured him. "You have my word on that—if that's worth anything to you."

Zane's expression was hard to read, but after a moment, he seemed to have finally made up his mind. "People who become werewolves are born with a genetic marker in their DNA. If they go through a traumatic event, the gene flips on and they become a werewolf. It can't be passed on any other way. Every werewolf is born in violence and pain."

The thought of Zane going through something so awful made her heart hurt. Knowing what she already did about him, it wasn't difficult figuring out exactly what that event had been.

"The battle in Afghanistan," she murmured. "When you told me you'd come back as a monster, that's what you meant. What you went through over there turned you into a werewolf."

He nodded, his eyes a little distant. "I didn't realize it at first, of course. I just thought I was dealing with survivor's guilt or PTSD. Hell, for a while I thought it was brain damage from all the concussions I'd suffered. But it takes a while for the werewolf traits to come out. I'd been having nightmares from day one, but it wasn't until a month after I got back that I started waking up in the middle of the night growling and tearing the bed apart with my claws. A little while after that, my fangs showed up. Sienna left shortly after that. The rest you know. Gage found me and brought me back to Dallas and put me on his SWAT team, and now I'm in LA fighting vampires."

"Are the claws and the fangs all there is?"

"Isn't that enough?"

That small gain she'd thought was there after the apology was gone again, and she hated the way he refused to look at her. It was hard to believe that only a little while ago they'd been in each other's arms, making love and trusting each other. How could things change so fast?

"I just wondered if it went further than that," she said after a moment. "If some werewolves could shift all the way. You know, like in some of the movies when they turn into wolves?"

She realized how stupid that sounded the second the words were out of her mouth, but then noticed Zane wasn't laughing.

"The simple answer to your question is yes," he said, finally looking at her. "Some alphas can shift completely into wolf form—four legs, bushy tail, and the big, long snout."

She tried to keep her mouth from hanging open and failed. "Seriously? You can turn into a wolf? You're an alpha, right?"

"I'm an alpha, but I can't shift any further than what

you saw earlier," Zane said. "And before you ask, the basic theory is that only alphas who are—I guess the best way to put it would be—comfortable in their own skin can handle a full shift. As you can probably imagine, that's not really how anyone would describe me."

All Alyssa had to think about was how many times Zane had called himself a monster to understand what he was getting at. It was too bad. She had a sudden image of him with a thick wolf coat and a bushy tail and realized she would have loved to see that. The tattoo she'd seen on his chest made a lot more sense now, that was for sure.

"Is there anything else you want to know about werewolves?" he asked, his mouth curving slightly, as if he could tell what she was thinking.

She thought about the injury they'd spent so much time talking about the night before. "Was the damage to your arm caused by a silver bullet?"

Zane chuckled a little at that. She considered that show of amusement another step forward. Okay, maybe half a step.

"You really do watch too much TV, don't you?" he quipped. She was embarrassed at how even that lukewarm response made a wave of pleasure blossom inside her. "No, it wasn't silver they shot me with. In fact, silver doesn't hurt any worse than lead does, though neither is fun to get shot with. In the case of my arm, the hunters developed a concentrated form of synthetic poisonous wolfsbane they put in their bullets. They knew what they were doing when they made it. Just a flesh wound in the arm nearly killed me. The doctor had to put me into a medically induced coma until he could come up with an antidote."

She tried to hide it, but Alyssa knew Zane noticed her hyperventilating a little at the thought of him lying in a hospital bed, cocooned with tubes and wires, little boxes beeping and blinking in the background.

"Now that you know all of my secrets, what about you?" he murmured.

Alyssa forced herself to slow her breathing. "I don't think my secrets compare to yours. There's nothing special about me. I don't have claws or fangs. I can't fight a vampire hand-to-hand or track a bad guy by scent."

"I wasn't looking for a competition. Tell me about the stuff you hid from me before. Like how you ended up hunting monsters for the FBI."

Monsters.

She hated how often he used that word. She'd never thought of it as being a loaded term until he said it. The fact that he used it interchangeably for both the things she'd been forced to kill and when referring to himself bothered her the most.

"It started when I was assigned to the Sacramento field office." Crap, she was violating so many rules by doing this, but she was going to do it anyway. Outside of her boss, no one knew this story, not even Christine. "I was assigned to a serial killer task force looking for a guy they called the 'Sacramento Hunter.' He liked to grab his victims, hold them for a couple days, then let them go so he could chase them on foot and kill them. The guy was vicious as hell, too. He tore his victims to shreds."

"He was a supernatural creature?"

She shook her head, remembering that exciting yet terrifying case. "I don't know. Actually, I never even

saw the killer until he was dead. The supernatural creature I saw was the agent sent in from the Department
of Homeland Security. The moment I saw him, I knew
there was something different about him. He did things
a person shouldn't be able to do. He ran way too fast,
seemed to be able to see in the dark, and could track the
killer by scent. When he finally caught the killer, the
guy was torn to pieces the same as the killer's victims."

Alyssa saw wheels spinning in Zane's head as he
thought about that. "Do you think the guy from DHS
was a werewolf?"

She nodded. "I didn't realize it at the time. I just
thought he was different. But knowing what I know
about you now, yeah, I think maybe he was a werewolf."

"What happened?" he asked, genuinely curious.

"Being the dutiful and conscientious FBI agent I was at
the time, I put all my thoughts and suspicions in my official report, suggesting the FBI investigate the DHS agent."

Zane winced.

"Yeah, not the brightest thing I've ever done," she
agreed. "As you can imagine, I got a visit from some
extremely senior agents who bluntly told me if I didn't
change my report, I'd be destroying my career. When I
stood firm, they put my entire report through a shred-
der right in front of me, then politely escorted me to
the airport and put me on a plane for DC. Several other
very polite agents met me at the gate, then took me to
meet my new team leader—Nathan McKay. That was
the night I learned there are all kinds of things that go
bump in the night and that I'd been assigned to a joint
FBI and CIA team called the Special Threat Assessment
Team. Though to be honest, most of the people I work

with have unofficially replaced the word *Special* with *Supernatural* because of all the strange things we end up dealing with."

"You mean, like the *X-Files*?" Zane arched a brow. "You're not making this up, are you?"

She shook her head. "Nope, I'm not making it up. It's what I've been doing for the past year or so. Investigating cases involving things the regular cops can't—or won't—handle."

"Like vampires and werewolves?"

Alyssa nodded. "I can't honestly say I've ever had to deal with something quite this extreme, but yes, you get the basic idea."

"Whatever happened to the guy in DHS?" Zane asked.

"Nathan told me there were lots of bigger problems in the world to deal with than a supernatural working for Homeland and that the guy was on our side," she said. "He told me to drop it. Unless I wanted the people in black SUVs to show up at my apartment one day and make me disappear."

Zane was silent for a while after that, obviously lost in thought. Alyssa was working up the courage to ask him why he didn't want her help to find Zoe and Chloe when he spoke.

"Do you regret sleeping with me?"

The question was so completely out of left field that Alyssa gasped. "Why the hell would you ask something like that?"

He shrugged. "I saw the way you looked at me after the fight downstairs. After you saw the fangs and the claws, after you saw what I really am. I've been on the receiving end of that same look before. I'll never be able to forget the disgust and revulsion. After seeing me like that, can you truthfully tell me you don't regret sleeping with me?"

Alyssa was out of the chair and standing in front of him before she even realized she'd moved. Her heart was thumping a hundred miles an hour and she was half a second away from ripping into him like a complete psycho when the rational part of her reasserted itself and pointed out that screaming wouldn't help anything.

"I'm not Sienna," she said as calmly as she possibly could.

Those three words seemed to crack through the shell he'd put up around himself and he snapped his gaze up to look at her.

"I'm not the woman who walked away because you weren't the man she thought," she continued softly. "If you saw anything in my eyes, it was the confusion of a woman who'd just found herself in a world along with vampires and werewolves, coming to terms with the realization that she'd slept with one of those creatures. It didn't mean I was disgusted or revolted. It meant I needed a moment to process that."

He started to say something, but she cut him off.

"Yeah, I'm pissed you didn't mention you were a werewolf earlier. Right from the very beginning would have been best, especially since you told me you wouldn't lie to me. But I recognize it would have been a somewhat difficult subject to work into most of our recent conversations, so I'm willing to deal with it. At the same time, I realize I don't have room to talk since I never bothered to tell you I investigate crimes involving supernatural creatures."

He opened his mouth again. This time, she silenced him with a glare.

"Look, I'll admit I don't have a clue what the hell is going on between us, but there's something real and powerful pulling us together. I can't explain it, but I feel ill simply at the thought of you being shot over in Afghanistan or injured by those hunters. And the idea of you going up against another one of those vampires by yourself is enough to make me go insane with fear." She sighed. "I don't understand what I'm feeling, and it scares me a little, but I'm not going anywhere, no matter how hard you try and push me away."

Alyssa expected him to scoff at every point she'd made, but after gazing at her for a long moment, he nodded and slipped around her to admire the same mural again. Maybe she'd stunned him speechless. She couldn't blame him. She'd stunned herself. Until the words had come out of her mouth, she hadn't known what the hell she was going to say.

"It's called *The One*," he said, eyes locked still on that damn mural.

"The one what?" she asked, confused. "What are you talking about, Zane?"

"This sensation you're experiencing," he explained. "Being worried about me, feeling a connection that couldn't possibly exist this soon. It's caused by a soul mate bond called *The One*. At least, that's what were-wolves call it."

Zane turned to look at her, and for the life of her, Alyssa couldn't say whether his expression was one of hope or contrition.

"Soul mate?" she repeated.

They'd met a few days ago and now they were *soul mates*?

———

"Yes, Nathan. You heard me right," Alyssa said as she stepped into the alley outside the club, turning a little away so she'd avoid the worst of the cold wind whipping down Third Street. "LA is home to a coven of vampires, and they kidnapped two teenage werewolves. As soon as I get a location on their nest, I'm going to raid it with four alpha werewolves. And I could seriously use all the help you can send me because these things are hard as hell to kill."

There was silence on the other end of the line, then she heard a heavy sigh. "And you're okay working with this group of werewolves?"

Alyssa thought about Zane still waiting up in Davina's office, tense but okay with her stepping out for a few minutes to get some air—and a little perspective.

"Yeah, I'm okay working with them," she said. "I trust them."

Her boss asked a few more questions, which she answered, then hung up, promising to get her as much help as he could. After that, she stood there for a few seconds, wondering what the hell she was going to do now.

The whole soul mate thing had definitely thrown her for a loop. It wasn't that she didn't feel anything for Zane because God knew she did. But hearing him say the two of them had some kind of magical bond that meant they were going to be connected forever was a little insane. It should have been totally insane, but seeing as she now believed in werewolves and vampires, her definition of *insane* was currently being recalibrated.

The really scary thing was there was a part of her that knew Zane wasn't making up that stuff about the soul-mate bond. The moment she'd walked out of the office to head outside, she'd felt the pull on her insides, like her body was trying to tell her she shouldn't be separated from him right then. Even now, standing out there in the cool night air, it was harder to breathe than it should be.

Zane was a werewolf and there was something between them, maybe something she couldn't even fight. Crap, it was like she was trapped in some psychotic version of *Beauty and the Beast*, and she didn't have a clue what she was supposed to do about it. Hell, she wasn't even sure how she felt about the situation.

Needing to talk to someone, she took out her cell phone again and pulled up the number for her go-to therapy girl, knowing her friend would be asleep at this late—early—hour but that Christine wouldn't even think to complain.

"Aly, it's almost four o'clock in the frigging morning." Her friend's voice was rough with sleep. "This had better be life or death or I'm hanging up."

"Not exactly life or death," she admitted. "Okay, maybe it might be. I've had a really crazy night, and I just needed to talk to someone. And you're my dedicated someone for stuff like this."

She heard movement on the other end of the line, like Christine had gotten out of bed and was heading to the bathroom to talk so she wouldn't wake up her husband.

"Okay, what's the situation?" Christine asked.

Alyssa knew she'd been right about her friend going into the bathroom because her voice echoed on the other end of the line.

"I got involved in a crazy kidnapping at a club down-town," she said without preamble. "It won't make the news or anything, but there was a ton of shooting and a lot of dead bodies."

"Are you okay?" Christine asked urgently. "You aren't hurt, are you?"

Alyssa could envision her friend sitting on the edge of the garden tub in the master bathroom, biting her perfect nails and completely freaking out.

A car drove past on Third, slowing a little as if who-ever was in it wanted to look down the alley she was in. Alyssa had no idea why. The entire place was empty now and as dark and quiet as a cemetery.

"No, I didn't get hurt," she answered, pulling her thin coat a little tighter around her as a gust of wind swirled past, kicking up some street dust. "Zane pretty much saved my bacon, though."

"Is that why you're calling?" Christine asked. "Because you got a little shook up in the shoot-out? Or is it because Zane was the one to save you? You have a thing against big, sexy guys with British accents saving your bacon?"

Alyssa was silent for a moment. Damn, she wished she'd brought a heavier coat with her. She'd never expected it to be this cold down in LA. The temperature felt like it had dropped five degrees in the few minutes she'd been out here.

"No, it wasn't the shoot-out that has me reeling. Or Zane rescuing me. It's the fact that I think I'm falling for a man I've known for less than a week even though I just found out he's been keeping a really big secret from me the whole time."

Christine sighed. "This really big secret wouldn't involve him being married, would it? Or that he's only attracted to people who use the same bathroom as him? Or that he's not a U.S. citizen and only wants to marry you for purposes of gaining citizenship?"

This was why she could always depend on Christine—the woman was guaranteed to make her lighten up no matter what was going on in her life.

"To answer those questions in order—no, no, and no."

"Okay, now that we have the big issues out of the way, I guess the next thing I need to know is whether this secret you mentioned is something you can get over or whether it's a deal killer?"

Alyssa thought about that for a moment, trying to decide if she would be okay being in a relationship with Zane now, knowing what she knew about him. The problem was, she was kind of worried this soul-mate-bond crap was messing up her perspective on the whole thing. She needed an unbiased opinion from someone she trusted.

"Christine, this is going to sound bizarre, but I'm going to come out and say it anyway." She paused for a second, then blurted it all out as fast as she could. "Zane's a werewolf and I think I'm in love with him."

Alyssa supposed she should have mentioned the soul mate thing but decided at the last second to hold back that part. This conversation was pushing the boundaries of what she could expect her friend to deal with already.

The silence on the other end of the line lasted so long Alyssa pulled the phone away from her ear to look and make sure they still had a connection. After seeing they did, she put it back to her ear.

"Since you mentioned you were in a club, my first instinct is to ask whether you're drunk. Or high," Christine finally said. "But considering the mysterious nature of the work you do for the FBI, I'm going to make the leap and assume you aren't speaking about werewolves in the metaphorical sense."

"No, I'm not," Alyssa said. "This is all real."

More silence.

"Wow. Well, thanks for springing all this on me at once," her friend eventually said. "But okay. Werewolves exist, and you have the hots for one. I've seen the man, so I know for a fact he's definitely not hard to look at. And you just told me he saved your life. So what's the problem?"

"What part of *he's a werewolf* are you missing?" Alyssa said. "Don't you think something like that might make a relationship kind of difficult?"

She wasn't sure what she expected, but a long, amused laugh wasn't on the list. "First, you slept with him, then, you're falling for him, and now, you're worried about the long-term relationship possibilities? I think the fact that he's a werewolf is the least of your concerns. I'd be more worried about finding a place to hold the reception before the weekend."

"I'm being serious, Christine!" Alyssa snapped. "He's got frigging claws and fangs and can hear my heart beating from across the room. I'm freaking out and I don't know what to do."

"Yeah, you do," her friend said calmly. "You've always had good instincts and you're following them now. You're simply looking for someone to tell you it's the right thing to do. The answer is yes. If your heart is telling you to go after this guy, stop thinking so much and do it."

"I've never associated my instincts with my heart," Alyssa muttered. "I always assumed they were two different things."

"Nah. Instincts are instincts. They all come from the same place," Christine said. "You knew what you wanted to do before you even called me. You were just doubting yourself. So, I'm asking you again. Is the fact that Zane is a werewolf a deal killer?"

Alyssa took a deep breath. This was the real reason she'd called Christine. Her friend had the unique ability to simplify the most complex situation. In this case, now that everything was out in the open, the question seemed almost childish. Could Alyssa handle the fact that Zane was so different? Not that he hadn't told her what he was, but if she could be with a man like him.

Zane was a werewolf. There was every reason in the world that should not only freak her out, but it should also scare her away. Yet, if she was being honest with herself, it didn't. She'd slept with him, but more than that, she knew who he was beyond the claws and fangs. He was a man who intrigued and excited her. And yeah, he was also a man who seemed to feel something for her—likely the same thing she felt for him.

"Okay, it's not a deal killer," she finally admitted. "It might complicate the relationship a bit, but nothing we couldn't work through."

"Excellent," Christine said. "That leaves the final and most important question: Is he any good in the sack? I'm assuming he must be amazing, because it was barely more than twenty-four hours ago that you were completely disinterested in having anything to do with the man. Now you're calling me at a stupid time of the morning to tell me you're falling in love with him. A turnaround that extreme usually involves multiple orgasms—plus oral."

Alyssa laughed so hard she didn't hear the footsteps behind her until whoever it was got right on her. She spun around, her right hand reaching for the weapon behind her back out of pure muscle memory.

But she never got a chance to pull her gun. Fingers as hard as stone captured her right hand while Dario Casteel's other hand wrapped around her neck, jerking her off her feet. She got out a little squeak before her air supply was completely cut off. She dropped her phone, vaguely hearing it fall to the ground. She thought she heard Christine shouting her name, but her friend's voice was getting hard to hear as everything started going fuzzy.

Alyssa jerked at the hand holding her weapon secure, punching at the thing's face with her other hand even as she kicked like crazy. But nothing she did seemed to hurt Dario at all, not even when she caught him with a solid blow to the crotch. All the monster did was tilt his head sideways, stare at her with those lifeless, black eyes, and grin at her as if she were an interesting toy.

He was still smiling as she passed out.

Chapter 11

Zane wasn't sure how long he sat on the couch in Davina's office after Alyssa left. The twisting sensation in his gut had gotten worse as the minutes passed, and it was all he could do not to howl in pain. It felt like something inside him had torn when she'd walked out. He shouldn't have let her leave. But he hadn't had a choice. There was no way he could make her stay—or feel something she didn't.

The reminder that Alyssa didn't feel the bond between them like he did made him gasp for breath. He rested his forearms on his spread thighs and dropped his head into his hands. It felt like he was bloody drowning. He'd felt this same way after Sienna had left him. Only this time it was a hundred times more wretched.

Zane was so lost in his own misery he didn't realize Rachel had come into the room until she stood directly in front of him. He lifted his head to find her gazing down at him.

"Diego and I talked to Gage," she said. "He was as shocked as we were when we told him that vampires are real and that they're the ones who hired the hunters. He'll be on the next plane along with Brooks and some of the other guys. With the time change between LA and Dallas, they should get here before eight o'clock this morning."

Zane nodded, but didn't say anything. That meant

they'd be able to move against the vampires in four hours.

"What happened?" Rachel asked. "I'm guessing from the look on your face that your conversation with Alyssa didn't go as well as you'd hoped?"

Zane flopped back on the couch with a snort. "That's one way to put it. Another way would be to say it was a complete disaster that ended with her walking out. She said she needed to get some air, but I think that was an excuse to get away from me."

He didn't blame her. He didn't want to be around himself right now.

Rachel sat down beside him. "I'm sure it's not as bad as you think, but then again, it's possible you could have screwed up and said something stupid. In fact, given that you're a guy, it's almost a certainty. So, spill. What did you say to upset her?"

"I didn't say anything," he protested. "I told her how I became a werewolf, and she told me how she ended up hunting supernatural creatures for the FBI. Then I asked her if she regretted sleeping with a monster and she insisted she didn't. When she said she felt a connection between us, I told her about the legend of *The One* and how she's my soul mate. Then she walked out, taking a chunk of my soul with her."

Rachel regarded him in silence for a moment, then shook her head. "Wow. You said all that and you're surprised she bailed on you? Hell, I'm your pack mate and I want to walk out, too."

Zane frowned. "What did I say that was so terrible?"

Rachel sighed. "How long did it take you to come to grips with being a werewolf? Weeks…months…years?"

He shrugged. "It's probably not a stretch to say it's still a work in progress."

"Exactly," Rachel said. "Now imagine what it's like for Alyssa. She's known you for a few days and just learned you're a werewolf. Her head is probably spinning. And that was before you sprung the stuff about her being *The One* for you. I'm surprised she didn't pass out—or shoot you. Regardless, you need to give her some time to process all of this. It's a lot to take in."

Zane didn't say anything. He'd always considered himself a patient person, but the idea of waiting for Alyssa to wrap her head around everything made him nearly insane.

"Do you really think of yourself as a monster?" Rachel asked quietly.

He gave her a sidelong glance. "It's what I am."

"Then that must make Diego, me, and everyone else in the Pack monsters too, huh? That's bullshit. I'm not a monster and neither is anyone else in our pack, including you."

He bit back a growl, forcing his claws back in when they tried to slip out. "I never said my pack mates were monsters."

Rachel glared at him. "Well, then stop throwing that word around when you're referring to yourself. If you can't accept what you are, how the hell will Alyssa ever be able to do it?"

Zane suppressed another growl, this one out of anguish. How could any woman accept him for what he was, especially someone as perfect as Alyssa?

He was still wallowing in that when Diego and Jake ran into the room. Diego had a mobile phone in his hand

and his face was pale. Jake didn't look much better. Which was scary as hell, since that didn't usually happen to werewolves unless half their blood had been spilled.

Zane stood, his inner wolf on high alert. Beside him, Rachel did the same.

"What's wrong?" he asked.

Before either could say anything, a terrified female voice shouted unintelligible words over the mobile. Diego held it out to him.

"You need to hear this," his pack mate said.

Frowning, Zane took it and held it to his ear. His gut clenched all over again as he picked up Alyssa's scent on the phone. "Who is this?"

"Zane?" Christine said urgently. "Is that you? It has to be you. Nobody has an accent like that. Where the hell is Alyssa? I heard her drop the phone, but when I called back someone named Diego answered. He wouldn't tell me a damn thing and I'm starting to freak out."

Alyssa is in trouble. Bloody hell, he knew he shouldn't have let her leave.

"After Rachel came up here, Jake and I went outside to grab something out of the car when we found Alyssa's phone in the alley," Diego said. "Dario's scent was all over the area. I think he grabbed her."

Zane's heart seized in his chest. "Christine," he said into the mobile phone. "I'm going to have to call you back."

<hr />

The first thing Alyssa noticed was the splitting headache. Then she felt a throbbing in her neck that made her think it had been crushed to the diameter of a drinking straw. On the bright side, since she could feel pain, that meant she wasn't dead.

Memories of that asshole vampire choking her came back in a rush, and she instinctively gasped for air, hoping to assure herself that breathing was still possible. Her throat spasmed at the sudden intake of oxygen, closing off her airway and making unconsciousness seem like a much better way to spend the time.

Alyssa had no idea how long she lay there, gasping for air like a carp out of water, but it was long enough for her to figure out that whatever was underneath her was harder than a box of rocks and cold as hell. Despite her jeans and light jacket, her body was numb. Was she outside?

Praying Dario had left her in the alley behind the club, she took a shallow breath and pushed herself up on her elbow. Unfortunately, she wasn't in the alley. The dimly lit space she was in didn't look like she was inside a building either. Maybe the vampire had dumped her in a cave and left her for dead. It took half a second for her to realize that was a stupid thought. There probably weren't a lot of caves in the city of LA.

Taking another breath—deeper this time—she sat up and looked around. As her eyes adjusted to the near darkness, she took in the bare concrete walls and matching floor and realized she was in a basement. Then, Alyssa saw the steel bars surrounding her and her stomach plummeted. Crap, she was in a prison of some kind. She didn't need a PhD in vampire lore to know this was probably where the monsters held their victims until they got around to draining them dry.

She scrambled around for her cell phone but couldn't find it. Not that she thought she would, but still… A quick glance at her watch told her it was nearly eight o'clock in the morning. At least she hoped it was still morning. If so, then it had been about four hours since Dario had kidnapped her. Four hours for Christine to have figured out someone had grabbed her. Four hours for her friend to do something about it. But what? Christine didn't know about vampires and she didn't have Zane's cell phone number.

Zane.

He knew she'd gone out to get some air and clear her head because she'd needed to process. When she hadn't come back, there was a good chance he'd thought she walked away from him. How would she know Dario had come back for her? Even if they realized she was missing, how would they know where to look?

Oh hell. This was bad.

"Alyssa, are you okay?" a soft, familiar voice asked from somewhere to her right.

Alyssa turned her head slowly to keep from getting dizzy and found Zoe leaning up against the bars separating their cells, concern clear on the girl's face even in the darkness. Her twin, Chloe—still the more timid of the two—hung back a few feet.

"I'm a little roughed up," Alyssa admitted, afraid to talk too loud with her bruised throat. Carefully getting to her feet, she walked over to them. "How about you guys?"

Zoe shrugged even as Chloe moved closer to blink at her through the darkness with those big, expressive eyes of hers. "The same. We got a few bruises when those things manhandled us out of the club and into a car, but nothing too bad."

Alyssa breathed a sigh of relief. That was something

at least. After the horror story Davina had told them, she'd been worried the vampires had already killed the twins—or worse.

"What's his name?" Chloe asked suddenly, her voice a barely audible whisper. "The other werewolf who tried to help us at the club?"

Alyssa glanced at Zoe before turning back to the quieter of the two girls. "His name is Jake Huang. He's a cop from Santa Fe. He told us he'd picked up your scents in a diner there and somehow knew the two of you were in trouble. He got a look at you on the diner's surveillance camera and followed you out here. He couldn't explain why he did it, but his gut told him he had to. He freaked out after the vampires grabbed you. We had to almost physically restrain him from taking off and scouring the city, hoping to come across your scents."

Zoe exchanged looks with her sister, who kneeled there with a blatant *I told you so* expression on her face. Alyssa was about to ask if the vampires had told them what they had in store for them when a woman cleared her throat from somewhere to her left. She spun around to see two more cells on that side.

Alyssa moved over to the woman huddled close to the bars, relief coursing through her when she recognized Lindsay Carr, one of the missing girls she'd come to LA to find. Behind Lindsey, in the deeper shadows of the cell, two more women lay on the floor. Alyssa tried not to let herself hope too much, but every instinct inside her screamed they were Stacie Bryant and Georgie Sparks, the other girls who'd gone missing.

She'd found them, and they were alive!

Alive, yes, but not in the best of shape.

Lindsey looked pale and tired. Her dark hair was limp around her shoulders, her feet were bare, and her dress was dirty and torn in a few places. Worse, she seemed emotionally beaten down. A quick glance at her arms revealed bruises and several barely visible scars similar to the puncture wounds Alyssa had seen in those pictures of the dead woman from the landfill.

"Please tell me someone knows you were kidnapped." Lindsey reached through the bars and desperately grabbed Alyssa's hand. "That someone will come looking for you."

Alyssa almost said no one knew and that, while she'd be missed, it might not be for a while. That wasn't what these girls needed to hear though. "Yes, Lindsey. Someone knows I was kidnapped. And they'll rescue us. Soon."

Lindsey blinked at her in confusion. "You know my name?"

Behind Lindsey, one of the other girls pushed to her feet and shuffled over to them. It was Georgie Sparks. If possible, the blond looked even more beaten down than Lindsay.

"Are you a cop?" Georgie asked, her voice as hollow as the dark rings under her eyes.

"Yes," Alyssa said. "I'm an FBI agent, and the people I work with are going to get all of us out of here."

Hope began to shine a little brighter on the girls' faces at her words. Seeing their expressions change was enough to make Alyssa know she'd done the right thing telling them that. She only prayed it turned out to be true—that Zane and his friends would figure out where she was and they'd be able to get all these girls to safety.

Alyssa was still in the process of trying to convince herself that surviving this situation was actually possible when she realized Stacie Bryant hadn't moved since Alyssa had first looked in her direction. Lindsay must have seen the expression on her face because she turned to eye her friend with concern. Alyssa couldn't make out much in the darkness other than a pair of glassy eyes staring into the distance and pale, nearly translucent skin, but it was enough to scare her.

"Stacie isn't doing well," Lindsey said, turning back to Alyssa. "I don't know what the things are who kidnapped us, but they drink our blood. For some reason, they seem to be more interested in Stacie than they are in us. They feed on her more and whisper things in her ear sometimes, too. I don't know what they say to her, but it's making her act strange. When she looks at us, it's like she's not really there. She won't even talk to us anymore. She'll only talk to them."

"Another three or four days and there won't be anything left of her to recognize," a man said from the cell beyond the one the girls were in.

They were talking about the enthralling thing Davina had told them about, Alyssa realized. When she'd described it, the whole thing had sounded almost clinical, but seeing the effects firsthand made it much more real.

"Will she get better?" Alyssa asked, pitching her voice louder so the man in the far cell would know she was talking to him. "If we get her away from them, will she recover?"

The man slowly got to his feet and shambled over to the bars. He was somewhere in his mid-to-late fifties, wearing dark dress pants, a gray shirt, and leather shoes, all of which appeared to have seen better days. Brown stains covered the edges of his rolled-up sleeves. The vampires had been feeding on this guy, too.

When he moved into the light, Alyssa blinked. *Crap*. It was Randy Curtis. The former chief of police looked nearly as bad as the three girls. Davina had obviously been right about what the vampire coven would think of the man's failure in Dallas. They were treating him no better than the people they'd captured for food.

"You're Randy Curtis," she said flatly.

The man nodded, not surprised she recognized him— or not caring.

"What'd you do to get tossed in here with the rest of us?" she asked.

"I failed to deliver Dallas to them as the next city for them to build a coven like I was sent there to do. This is my punishment. As far as the girl, it's possible she'll get better. From what I understand, it's like detoxing from the worst drug addiction ever. But it supposedly can happen. Truthfully, she'd be better off dead."

Behind her, Lindsey and Georgie both choked back sobs.

Alyssa glared at him. She could understand why Zane and his teammates had traveled halfway across the country to hunt this bastard down. She'd just met this jerk and she wanted to kill him. "What the hell is wrong with you?"

"Nothing is wrong with me. I used to be one of them, so I know how this works," Randy Curtis snapped. "No one is coming to rescue you because no one knows where you are. Even if they did, the entrances to the nest are guarded by what amounts to an army of highly motivated killers masquerading as guards. On the off chance, your fellow FBI agents somehow make it past the guards and the vampires and manage to reach these cells, they'd find your friend, Stacie, fighting them tooth and nail to stay. How much more difficult do you think that will make saving the rest of you, if you have to drag her kicking and screaming every inch of the way?"

Alyssa didn't bother arguing with him. Partly because what he said was probably true and partly because Lindsey and Georgie had freaked out at the mention of vampires. Ignoring Randy Curtis, she turned her attention to the two women, reassuring them that it was going to be okay, that help was coming, and that they'd get Stacie out of here, too—vampires or no vampires.

Randy Curtis snorted at that and walked back to sit down in his dark corner.

Alyssa turned to talk to the twins when the dim lights hanging above their cells brightened. She squinted, her head throbbing even more than it had before. At the sound of heavy footsteps, she forced herself to ignore the discomfort and turn to face the approaching threat, her heart racing. A moment later, Dario walked into the room, followed by Stefan. The man's stride was quick. Like he was someone with lots of things on his to-do list. They were accompanied by eight armed men. She wondered if the vampires were there to exact their revenge against her now that she was conscious. The thought made her shudder, though she refused to show it. She might be terrified, but she'd never let them know that.

Coming to a stop in front of Alyssa's cell, Dario unlocked the door and stepped inside, Stefan at his heels. Alyssa took a step back automatically in a defensive stance, ready to fight for her life.

For all the good it did her.

One moment, Dario was near the door; the next, he was nothing but a blur. She didn't have a chance to even take a swing at him before his hand was around her neck again. Lifting her off the floor, he slammed her against the wall hard enough to knock the oxygen out of her lungs. Cold air seemed to pour off him in waves, making her numb. She fought him with everything she had, punching, kicking, and scratching. The results were no better than the first time she'd tried it in the alley. It was like hitting at a brick wall.

As her vision began to dim, it occurred to Alyssa he might actually choke her to death and be done with it. But then he grabbed her left wrist and yanked her arm toward him, forcing her to watch in horror as his fangs slowly extended and he bit her.

Alyssa swore the damn creature was doing everything at half speed simply so she'd have to deal with the torture of those fangs sinking into the soft flesh of her inner wrist longer. It felt like they were going all the way down to the bone. It was even more painful when he began to feed on her blood, his lips tugging on her skin as he sucked it into his mouth.

Screams echoed off the stone walls as the twin werewolves and the three girls begged Dario to let her go. Alyssa would have screamed, too, if she could have made a sound.

When Dario finally released her, she hit the floor hard, her head swimming like she'd just downed two Long Island iced teas—fast. Her vision went dark as shudders ran through her body. As much as she wanted to get up and protect herself, her mind was telling her to remain where she was.

But staying down had never been her thing.

She shoved to her feet and lunged at Dario, swinging the hardest punch she could. It landed—a solid round-house to the jaw that made her whole arm go numb, leaving her hand throbbing badly enough to make her think she might have broken something.

Unfortunately, Dario barely seemed to have felt the blow. He merely stepped back with a superior smile, licking traces of her blood off his lips.

"You're a fighter, I see," he said. "That makes you even more perfect for the ritual."

The words chilled Alyssa to the bone. She threw a quick glance at her wrist to see the two puncture wounds still trickling a tiny bit of blood, but not nearly as much as she'd expected.

"What ritual?" she demanded.

Dario grinned at her. "We have a ceremony planned for this morning, one you'll play a very important part in." He gestured to the younger Curtis. "We've decided to make Stefan one of us in appreciation for the faithful service he has provided the coven. The five oldest members of the coven will drain your friends, then they'll turn him."

Alyssa glanced at the three women on her left and the two werewolves on her right to see their eyes fill with terror.

"Stefan will be ravenous for blood after that and will need to quench that thirst," Dario continued, seeming to relish the panic he was causing all around as he focused his cold, black eyes on Alyssa. "That's where you come in. While I'm tempted to keep you for myself, I will honor my promise and allow Stefan to feed on you to complete his transformation."

Alyssa felt the blood drain from her face, fear making her feel weaker than she already was.

Stefan glanced at his uncle. "Don't think for a second this gets you out of the frying pan. You're still going to die. It's just a matter of how." Stefan looked at Dario. "Maybe we could give him to the younger members of the coven that don't normally get to feed during the ritual."

Dario considered that. "Perhaps."

When Randy Curtis didn't say anything, Stefan let out a snort.

"You don't know how glad I am that I get to feed on that fucking werewolf's mate instead of you, old man," he said to his uncle. "At least she'll be fresh."

That got a rise out of Randy. Eyes suddenly sharp, he got to his feet and hurried over to the bars. "Werewolf? There's a werewolf in LA?"

Stefan casually strolled over to stand in front of his uncle's cell. "Actually, there are several werewolves dumb enough to not only show up in town, but also to attempt to stand against us."

Randy gripped the bars. "And you're sure she's mated to one of them."

"I'm sure," Dario said. "I heard her talking about sleeping with one of the mongrels on the phone right before I grabbed her. That's part of the reason I *did* grab her. Stefan might be thrilled to have someone young and pretty to feed on for the ritual, but I'm more interested in using her dead body to lure her mate. That was an added bonus too good to pass up."

Alyssa started hyperventilating at the thought of being used as bait to hurt Zane. It was crazy. She'd be dead long before these monsters got around to even attempting to hurt Zane, but that didn't stop her from being afraid. As the fear welled up from her stomach and into her chest to wrap its icy fingers around her heart, she was sure she was going to pass out.

"Are you insane?" Randy demanded. "Doing the ritual with a group of werewolves around—especially if she's mated to one—is suicidal."

Stefan only laughed at that.

Dario remained expressionless.

"I'm warning you not to underestimate them," Randy ground out in frustration. "I know it's been decades since the coven has gone up against a pack of werewolves directly. They're far more dangerous than you can imagine. You won't need to lure them anywhere because they'll come for her. You have no idea what they can do when you threaten the people they care for."

Alyssa stared in shock.

While Randy had been dismissive when he thought there were some FBI agents out there to worry about, now that he knew werewolves were involved, he was far more worried—which was strange considering his nephew had just offered to serve him up as a sippy cup to the younger vampires in the coven.

Dario chuckled. "Forgive me if I don't put much stock in your opinion when it comes to werewolves. But given your dramatic failure in Dallas, I think you can understand my reasoning. That city was supposed to be supporting a thriving coven colony already, and instead, you had a pack of fucking werewolves in your own department. How blind and stupid can you be?"

"I admit I made mistakes, Stefan." Ignoring the vampire, Randy reached through the bars, extending his hand like he thought his nephew would take it. "But I'm not wrong about this. They'll come for her and they'll come gunning. You could use my help when that happens."

"They won't come for her," Stefan scoffed. "There are four of them at the most. None of them would be foolish enough to step foot in this place even if they know where we are. It would be a death sentence. Even a werewolf—as stupid as those mutts are—would know that."

Randy opened his mouth to say something, but the ringing of a phone interrupted him. Dario scowled in irritation and reached into the pocket of his slacks to pull out a cell.

"Yes," he said into the phone. Whatever the caller said must have pleased him because his mouth curved. "I'm on my way."

Hanging up, Dario looked at the muscle he'd brought with him. "Move them to the main gathering area. Heavy guards all around the amphitheater and the main entrances to the nest. I don't want any surprises."

Then he and Stefan were gone, taking two guards with them. The ones who were left looked uneasy, glancing furtively into the shadows around the holding area as if expecting a werewolf to jump out any second. Maybe they'd heard of the damage Zane and the were-wolves had done at the club and didn't want to be on the receiving end of that carnage.

One of the guards came into Alyssa's cell and grabbed her arm, shoving her out while his buddies did the same to the other captives. She automatically moved closer to Zoe and Chloe, hoping to provide at least a little moral support. Knowing what was coming, the girls had to be freaking out about now. Alyssa sure as hell was.

"Don't be scared," Chloe told her softly. "It's going to be okay. Jake is on the way. And Zane is with him. They're close. I feel it."

Chloe might have been trying to make her feel better, but hearing Zane was close to this horrible place—even if there was no way the girl could know something like that—made her stomach twist itself into knots. She didn't want him anywhere near there. It hit her then that as much as she didn't want to die, she was way more concerned that Zane would. The thought of him coming here to save her and getting killed in the process was tearing her soul out.

Alyssa prayed Chloe was wrong and that Zane would stay as far away from there as possible.

Chapter 12

ZANE STRODE ACROSS THE CROWDED, GLEAMING MARBLE lobby of Black Swan's corporate headquarters, his height and intimidating presence clearing a path for him as he worked his way toward the large security desk near the elevator bank of the skyscraper business complex. He was still ten feet away from the nearest guard, and they were already eyeing him warily.

He knew this wasn't the brightest idea any of them had ever come up with. Walking right into the place and offering himself up like this was probably on the short list of most insane things ever. But when Davina had finally given them the location of the nest—four levels below Black Swan Enterprises off Figueroa—it wasn't like they could simply sit on the info and keep waiting.

The waiting had been killing them. Him most of all.

Gage and the other members of the Pack were only now landing at LAX because they'd been grounded on the tarmac in Dallas/Fort Worth for over an hour thanks to bad weather. Worse, the help that Alyssa's boss, Nathan, sent was still fifteen minutes out. Between the delay in Dallas and the hellish LA traffic, it would probably take at least an hour for any of them to get to Black Swan's headquarters. An hour was too long to wait, especially when they didn't have a clue what the hell was going on in the nest.

Jake had been close to losing his mind while Zane

had been on the verge of throwing up for the past few hours. Neither of them would say it out loud, but the idea that the people they cared about might already be dead was more than they could handle. Zane tried to convince himself he'd know if Alyssa was hurt—or worse. That the bond they had between them would tell him something like that. But the truth was, he didn't know that for sure. After the way he and Alyssa had left things at the club, he wasn't even sure they still had a bond.

That was why he, Rachel, Diego, and Jake had come up with this crazy plan. He'd walk right in and hope security would take him downstairs, where he could find Alyssa and the others, all while keeping things from getting out of hand before backup arrived. As plans went, it was so far beyond dangerous it wasn't even in the same zip code, but it was better than waiting around and hoping for the best.

As he came to a stop in front of the security desk, he wondered if any of the people visiting Black Swan Enterprises ever noticed how many heavily armed security guards were employed there. Certainly way more than one would normally expect to see at an international finance-and-investing conglomerate.

"I'm here to talk to Dario Casteel and Stefan Curtis," Zane said casually.

"Nobody sees either of those gentlemen without an appointment," the man said, not bothering to look up from his computer. "And you don't have one."

Zane put his hands on the counter with a growl and leaned closer. "Oh, I'm sure they're going to want to see me. Tell them I'm waiting at the front desk."

That got the man's attention. He looked up quickly, face pale. Zane bared his fangs, letting his eyes flash gold.

The guard shoved back his chair and got to his feet so fast the thing almost toppled over. He reached for the gun at his hip with one hand, grabbing the two-way radio off his belt with the other. His movements drew the attention of the other guards in the lobby, and they converged on Zane, weapons drawn.

Behind him, Zane heard gasps followed by a flurry of movement as the other people in the lobby gave them some space. That was probably a smart move. They couldn't see his extended fangs or glowing eyes, but they sure as hell could tell something serious was about to go down.

Zane pinned the guard behind the desk with a look. "You might want to get Dario on that radio. Now."

The man stared at him, sweat beading on his brow and migrating all the way up to his receding hairline. Clipping his radio on his belt, he took a mobile phone out of his suit jacket and dialed with a trembling hand.

"Mr. Casteel, it's Edwin at the front desk," he said nervously, his voice low. "Sir, there's a werewolf in the lobby asking to see you and Mr. Curtis."

The security guard on Zane's left thumbed his radio, urgently requesting all available security personnel to come to the lobby. Two other guards hurriedly cleared the lobby, rushing people outside. Apparently, no one trusted Zane not to attack Dario and his human sidekick. He couldn't help but smile at that.

While killing both assholes in the middle of the lobby of Black Swan Enterprises sounded like fun, he was more thrilled about the security guards focusing all their attention in his direction. That would give Jake a better chance to slip in a back door and hopefully give him a chance to find out where Alyssa and the twins were being held without anyone seeing him. If they were really lucky, it might even give the other werewolf time to grab Alyssa and the girls and get them the hell out of there.

Zane smelled the stench of dirt and death even before the doors of the middle elevator opened and Dario stepped out, Stefan at his heels. Dario had a fresh silk shirt that was minus the bullet holes, but other than that, the vampire still looked as pale and cold as he had last night.

As the vampire walked toward Zane, he stepped into a band of bright sunlight streaming through one of the windows. Unfortunately, Dario didn't burst into flames, and Zane had to grudgingly admit Davina had been right. Sunlight wouldn't burn these things to a crisp.

"How're those ribs, chap?" Zane asked, giving Dario a smile. "I know for a fact I heard a few of them crack when I kicked the shit out of you during our little scrum."

"I'm in one piece, as you can see. Which is more than anyone will be able to say about you soon." Mouth curving, the vampire lifted a hand and wiped a thumb across his lips. "By the way, I have to compliment you on your taste in mates. I had a little sip before coming up here and she was exquisite."

Zane moved before he even realized what he was doing. Snarling, he closed the distance between him and Dario in two strides, white-hot rage burning through his veins. Reaching out, he wrapped his right hand around the vampire's neck and squeezed until he heard vertebrae crack. His back bunched up, the wolf inside struggling so hard to get free he thought he might drop to the floor on all fours.

Every security guard in the lobby moved in close, their weapons trained on Zane. He ignored them, lifting Dario off his feet and tightening his grip around the vampire's throat. The only thought in his head was killing this fucking monster.

But Dario simply reached up and put one hand around Zane's wrist, prying Zane's fingers away from his neck with his other hand until he dropped to the floor with an amused expression on his face.

"You can't choke a vampire to death," he said calmly, waving the trigger-happy guards back, then making a show of popping his neck. "We don't need to breathe that often. Side effect of not be able to produce our own blood cells, which is an advantage when you live in a city that has as much smog as LA."

Bloody hell. He hadn't thought of that.

"You might not breathe much, but something tells me it would hurt like hell if I kept crushing until your head popped off," Zane said. "I know from personal experience that vampires don't function well with nothing but a stump above their shoulders. Like those two vampires in the club last night. Hope they weren't friends of yours."

Dario bared his teeth, his lifeless eyes going completely black as he took a step forward, but Stefan chose that moment to interrupt, as if he was bored with all the monster testosterone he and Dario were dumping into the air.

"I'm not sure who the fuck you are or what you're doing in this town, but you're trespassing on private property," Stefan said. "I could have you shot right now, and no one would care. I have a hundred witnesses that will back me up when I say you were threatening us. And before you make some stupid comment about being hard to kill, I'm sure there's enough firepower here to do the job."

Zane growled. "Maybe, but by then I would have taken out a dozen people in here, starting with you."

It might have been an exaggeration, especially if they went for a head shot, but Stefan didn't need to know that.

Apparently, he wasn't aware of it being an exaggeration because he went white as a ghost.

Dario, on the other hand, chuckled. "I have to wonder if the death toll would be as high if they shot you with those wolfsbane bullets my coven spent so much money developing."

Zane resisted the urge to laugh. Those wolfsbane bullets sucked for sure, but the Pack's doctor had come up with an antidote for it months ago, then created a vaccine to protect Zane and every other werewolf in Dallas.

But again, the bad guys didn't need to know that.

"I guess you're just going to have to shoot me and find out," Zane said, baring his fangs and growling again, making the guards closest to him back up. He smirked. "I didn't think so. Now, where is Alyssa? And if you did more than 'take a sip,' as you put it, I will kill you."

Dario thoughtfully regarded Zane for a moment before giving him a nod. "If you'll follow us, we'll take you to see her. I assure you that your mate is perfectly fine."

Stefan looked surprised at that but didn't say anything.

Every instinct Zane had warned him that this was a suicide mission. But he hadn't expected anything less. Going anywhere with Dario was foolish, and while he didn't believe for a minute that the vampire would take him to Alyssa, if there was even a chance, he'd take it.

Zane motioned toward the elevators. "After you."

"Of course," Dario said. "As long as you agree to handcuffs. I can't have anyone so dangerous roaming free in the building."

Mouth twitching, Zane let his fangs retract and put his hands behind his back, ignoring the twinge of pain in his left arm at the movement. "I'd expect nothing less."

He was a werewolf. It wasn't like he was concerned about something as flimsy as handcuffs.

Zane tried to pick up Alyssa's or the twins' scents the moment they stepped off the elevator onto the fourth sublevel, but the vampire stench was so overwhelming down there he couldn't smell a damn thing—not even himself.

As they led him down the long, dimly lit stone corridors of the coven nest, he wondered who the hell did the decorating for these vampires. Whoever it was obviously didn't believe in light bulbs. They also seemed to have a fetish for antique tapestries. Every frigging wall he'd passed so far was covered floor to ceiling with the heavy textiles, most of them so faded he couldn't even make out any of the details. The only thing missing were torches on the walls. Then again, open flames would probably be dangerous with all the material around.

Dario was just ahead of him, Stefan was slightly to the left, and an army of nervous security guards followed behind them. Zane didn't make it obvious, but he moved slower than he usually did, trying to avoid putting any stress on his left arm. Normally, handcuffs wouldn't bother him—not that he wore them very often—but these weren't normal cuffs. Since werewolves were significantly stronger than normal people, Dario had ended up having his men slap what felt like two-inch-thick manacles on him. The damn things were tight as hell and weighed a ton, biting into his wrists and dragging his arms down like an anchor. His injured arm was throbbing like a son of a bitch.

Zane was still trying to hide his discomfort when they walked through a set of huge double doors leading into a theater, complete with more of those damn wall hangings. There were maybe seventy-five vampires there, male and female, ranging in age from young to very, very old, all dressed up like they were going to the opera. Many glanced his way, curiosity in their lifeless, black eyes. At least a dozen men stood guard around the theater perimeter, all of them carrying weapons. Mingling in the crowd were young, attractive men and women in service garb, expressionless and glassy eyed as they carried trays of food and drink.

But everything faded into the background when Zane spotted Alyssa perched uncomfortably on a chair on the dais at the front of the theater. Relief coursed through him when he saw that she wasn't injured. Dario hadn't lied about that at least. Zoe and Chloe were up there, too, as well as three other women he recognized as the missing people Alyssa had been looking for. Even his former boss, Randy Curtis, was there.

He barely paid attention to anyone else as Alyssa caught sight of him and jumped to her feet. The guard closest to her grabbed her arm, refusing to let her go anywhere.

Zane's heart pumped faster, his fangs and claws

extending, his hands clenching and unclenching with the desire to tear apart the man holding her. Then he caught sight of the two small puncture wounds on the inside of her left wrist. The muscles of his back began to twist again at the urge to throw himself onto all fours and race across the room to reach her side.

He strode forward, uncaring that Dario was in front of him, but the guards that had been behind him quickly moved to block his path, shoving the barrels of their guns in his face. He knew trying to charge forward was stupid, but with Alyssa in danger, he simply couldn't think straight.

Zane kicked out with his right leg, sending two of the guards flying. The crowd of vampires hurriedly backed away, no longer curious but fearful as they realized there was a hated werewolf in their midst. Throughout the theater, he heard weapons being locked and loaded, red laser dots appearing all over his chest as the security guards around the room sighted in on him.

He heard Alyssa's breath hitch in terror. Zane looked up to see her staring at him, panic-stricken, two guards holding her back now. He growled long and low, prepared to do whatever he had to do to get to her.

But just when it looked like he was about to get shot, Dario strode up behind the cluster of antsy guards blocking his way, waving them aside. "Let the mongrel go to his mate. I did promise him I'd let him see her after all. We have time before the ritual begins."

The human guards didn't seem to like it, especially the two he'd kicked to the floor, but they obediently stepped aside and let Zane continue on his way to the stage. The men holding Alyssa reluctantly let her go and she jumped down from the dais and ran to meet him. Behind her, Zoe and Chloe made a move to join them, but the two men who'd been holding Alyssa grabbed them. Before Zane could wonder too much about what the hell Alyssa and the other women were doing up there and what this ritual Dario had mentioned was about, she was in front of him, fear and anxiety pouring off her in waves.

"How did they capture you?" she asked softly.

She scanned him up and down like she was checking for injuries before she looked around him to take in the heavy cuffs biting into his wrists. But then her attention quickly moved on, one hand gliding up his injured left arm to caress the scar through the material of his jacket, like she somehow knew it was bothering him. He almost sighed in relief as the pain he'd been experiencing faded immediately. How the hell was she able to do that?

"It's not like I made it difficult for them," he said quietly, resisting the urge to lean forward and bury his face in the curve of her neck so he could breathe her all in. "I walked in the front door of the lobby upstairs and gave myself up. I really don't think they trust me, though. Hence the cuffs."

For a moment, he thought Alyssa was going to berate him for doing something so damn stupid, but then she sighed, continuing to massage the scar tissue that largely composed his left bicep.

"That was foolish," she murmured, leaning close to him as if trying to keep the words from being overheard by all the vampires around them. He didn't know how keen their hearing was, so he wasn't sure if it mattered or not. "They're going to use the other women and me in a ritual to turn Stefan into a vampire."

Fear shot through him. He'd kill every last one of the bloody creatures. "Like hell they are."

Tears glistened in her eyes. "Why didn't you stay away, Zane? I wouldn't have cared what happened to me as long as I knew you were safe."

His heart pounded at her words even if his head couldn't make sense of them. "When you walked out of the club, I thought it was because you didn't want to be *The One* for me. That you couldn't deal with the fact that I'm a monster."

"You aren't a monster." Alyssa gently cupped his jaw with her free hand, her eyes pleading. "Zane, we're standing in a room full of creatures that kidnap innocent humans and feed on their blood while men are pointing weapons at us, ready to let the other women and me die so Stefan can become a vampire. They're the monsters, not you. Don't you see? What you are doesn't make you a monster. It's what you do. And all you've ever done is protect the people you care about." Tears streaming down her cheeks, she wrapped her arms around him, pressing her face against his chest. "When I look at you, I see the man I love, not a monster."

Zane buried his face in her beautiful hair, damn close to tears himself. How the hell had fate found him someone so incredibly perfect? She was more than he deserved. He opened his mouth to tell her he loved her, too—more than he'd ever thought possible—but Dario interrupted him.

"While this is all very romantic," he said dryly, "we have a ritual to perform. I promised you a chance to see your mate. You've done so. Time for her to take her place among the anointed."

As much as he didn't want to pull away from Alyssa, Zane forced himself to take a step back. Then he turned to face Dario, moving in front of Alyssa as he did so. "Did you really think I was going to let you use Alyssa or any of these women for your bloody damn ritual?"

Dario smirked. "Not really. Fortunately, that doesn't matter, since the only reason I brought you down here was to see if the coven's investment in those wolfsbane bullets was worth it."

Zane charged forward, making sure he kept his body between Alyssa and the vampire when Dario's hand came out from behind his back with a Sig Sauer .40 caliber.

Zane would have darted to the side so he could avoid the bullets, but he couldn't do that and protect Alyssa at the same time. So, he ended up taking an entire magazine of large-caliber rounds point-blank in the gut and chest. He only thanked God they were expanding hollow points or some of them would have punched right through him and hit her anyway.

The poison stung, but thanks to the vaccine he'd been inoculated with, it felt nothing like the burning acid he'd experienced when the hunters shot him all those months ago. He went down hard because getting hit with twelve rounds of anything still hurt like a son of a bitch.

Alyssa screamed and dropped to her knees beside him, but he couldn't pay her as much attention as he would have liked. He was concentrating too hard on not passing out. He barely had enough awareness left to see Dario drag Alyssa away from him, across the room, and up onto the dais to join the other women they intended to sacrifice.

Alyssa fought Dario like crazy, punching, scratching,

and kicking the vampire the whole way, but it was no use. Dario was too strong.

Zane strained against the cuffs, but between his useless arm and the multiple bullet holes in his chest and stomach, he couldn't generate enough force to snap the metal shackles holding him bound no matter how hard he tried.

Up on the dais, Alyssa screamed again.

Zane looked up in panic to see five more vampires step onto the dais, the whites of their eyes as black as their irises.

He fought against the cuffs again, ignoring the pain spreading through his chest and stomach, straining his arms until the bones creaked. But other than digging the shackles deeper into his wrists, his struggles did nothing. And he only got weaker as he continued to bleed.

Zane glanced at the dais again to see Stefan shoving his uncle off the stage and into a cluster of vampires waiting for him with open arms. The former chief of police briefly cried in pain as the creatures proceeded to tear him apart. Zane would have considered that to be justice of the most poetic kind if he wasn't so damn terrified for Alyssa.

Zoe and Chloe screamed in terror as each of the old vampires holding them dragged them closer. The other three women simply stood there, paralyzed with fear.

Alyssa was still trying to get loose, kicking and clawing at Dario like her life depended on it. Dario backhanded her with a snarl of rage.

Zane lost it then, all rational thought disappearing as the woman he loved and who loved him in return hit the floor so hard she bounced. He strained so violently against the cuffs his bones cracked again. Only this time, they didn't stop cracking until the manacles slid off his wrists.

He grunted in shock when his shoulders hunched forward sharply at the same time his back began to pop and shift, forcing him to stay on the floor when all he wanted to do was run to Alyssa. It was only when his whole body was twisting into a completely different shape that he realized what was happening. He didn't pause to wonder why it was happening now, considering he'd never come close to a full shift in the entire time he'd been a werewolf. When the transformation was complete, and he was, indeed, a wolf, he made a beeline on his four legs for Alyssa—and the vampire who dared to hurt her.

There was a hiss of pain from the far side of the dais, and he darted a quick look that way to see the vampire who'd bitten Zoe rolling around on the floor, clutching at his smoking face. Everyone was so focused on that they didn't even see Zane coming until he let loose a snarl that echoed through the theater like a rumble of thunder.

Screams and shouts resounded off the walls as guards moved to intercept Zane. In a blur, he was already running full speed across the room, the claws on his four enormous paws digging into the stone flooring as he launched himself at Dario.

Zane didn't realize how fast he was moving until he slammed into the vampire and knocked him backward a good ten feet. There was a pop as a bone in Zane's fur-covered shoulder cracked, but he barely felt it. That was when he realized nothing hurt. Not the multiple gunshot wounds he'd just sustained. Not even the long-suffering wound in his left arm. In fact, he felt better than ever.

Dario rolled to his feet quickly, his clawed hands slashing out and tearing through Zane's side. It stung, but he quickly discovered his thick fur had limited the damage. He lunged forward again, his teeth chomping down on the vampire's outstretched arm right down to the bone. The taste was as bad as the smell.

He and Dario danced back and forth so fast Zane knew they were nothing more than blurs of movement as they tore into each other repeatedly. It quickly became apparent that Dario wasn't interested in a one-on-one fight when he shouted at the guards to open fire, but when the shooting started, it wasn't aimed in Zane's direction. Instead, the vampires' guard force aimed toward the entrance and the eight members of the Dallas SWAT team who came rushing in—Gage and Brooks among them, in their fully shifted wolf forms. Zane's heart pounded even harder when he saw Christine and four other federal agents on their heels.

The theater filled with screams, shouts, and gunfire, but it was the growls and snarls of Zane and his pack mates that sent the vampires running for the exits, crushing their enthralled servants in the process.

Realizing he wasn't going to get any help, Dario lunged for Alyssa, maybe thinking he could take her hostage. Zane cut the vampire off before he could reach her. She scrambled to her knees, her wide eyes taking in Zane in his wolf form as well as the chaotic scene around her.

Zane pushed the vampire back toward the rear of the dais with a snarl, the two of them trading more slashes and bites, both of their blood spattering everywhere. Dario screeched in rage and leaped at him, his clawed hands rearing back to tear him apart.

Zane jumped at the same time, his jaws aiming for the vampire's neck. Dario's claws embedded themselves deep in the ribs on his left side, but Zane's teeth found their mark as well, clamping down tightly on the vampire's neck and sinking in until he felt bone crunch.

Dario tore and slashed at Zane with his claws like a creature possessed. But it did no good as Zane began to shake the vampire back and forth as hard as he could. Dario shrieked, a sound that seemed to paralyze every vampire left in the amphitheater. Zane shook Dario harder, grinding his jaws side to side.

He was actually a little surprised at how easily the vampire's head came off, but that didn't make ending the asshole any less satisfying—though he would have given a hundred bucks for a bottle of Listerine right then, so he could wash the revolting taste of Dario's blood out of his mouth. Well, maybe a bowl of Listerine might work better in his current form.

Zane stopped worrying about bad breath when he realized Alyssa was no longer on the dais with him. Terrified, he looked around and caught a glimpse of her disappearing out one of the theater's side doors at full speed.

He didn't stop to think. He just went after her.

Chapter 13

Alyssa wasn't sure how long she knelt there on the dais and stared at Zane as he fought Dario in his wolf form. When Zane had told her some members of his pack could fully shift into a wolf, she hadn't been able to really envision what he meant. But she'd never imagined in a million years it would be like this. That he would be this…beautiful.

Beautiful.

That was the only word she had to describe the mesmerizing mix of power, grace, danger…and fur. He had fur! How the hell could he ever have called himself a monster?

A large part of her soul had died when Zane had been shot. He'd been hit multiple times in the chest and stomach at a range of less than five feet. Even as Dario had dragged her back to the stage and the start of the ritual, she'd known there was no way anyone could survive those wounds. Not even a werewolf.

But then she'd looked up and seen a snarling gray wolf the size of a small horse charging across the room, trailing torn pieces of Zane's clothes behind him, and she'd known without a doubt in her mind that he'd shifted completely to save her.

Movement out of the corner of her eye dragged her attention away from the fight between Zane and Dario. Stefan was slipping out one of the side exits, using Stacie as a human shield against all the bullets flying around. The girl wasn't even resisting. In fact, she actively put her body between Stefan and any danger even though her eyes were so blank she looked like a zombie.

Alyssa threw a quick glance at Zane. He had Dario by the neck and was shaking him like a rag doll. She was pretty sure that fight was almost done, much to her relief.

She searched for Zoe and Chloe. Jake was herding the twins, Lindsey, and Georgie toward an exit with the help of a huge wolf with dark fur. All around the room, men and women in police tactical gear fought vampires and their human guards. She spotted her FBI teammates as well. Even Christine was there. The place was a complete madhouse. No wonder no one had noticed Stefan leave with the girl.

That made up her mind for her.

Getting to her feet, Alyssa ran toward the door Stefan had disappeared through, slowing down only long enough to scoop up a handgun and extra magazine from one of the dead guards—there were lots to choose from.

She was a little unsteady on her feet. Between the bloodletting, the vampire crap in her veins, and the backhand to the face, she was dizzy as hell. But she made it out the door, avoiding the running battle going on in the corridors and ignoring the acrid smoke coming from the burning tapestries along the walls. How the hell they'd caught fire, she didn't know. The place was going up fast, and it looked like the vampires didn't believe in sprinkler systems.

She passed Rachel and Diego exchanging gunfire with several men and a vampire down one of the side passages. There were already several dead bodies on the floor around the two werewolves, and Alyssa desperately wanted to stop and help Zane's friends, but she knew if she did, Stefan would get away and she'd never get Stacie back alive. She refused to let that happen.

Alyssa let her instincts guide her through the chaos and the spreading fire, until she reached a metal door near the elevators. Her gut told her Stefan had gone that way. She shoved the door open and found stairs. Two sets of footsteps pounded up them, echoing in the close confines of the stairwell.

She took the stairs two at a time, not even slowing to consider whether she was going after the right two people. It was Stefan, she was sure of it. And he had Stacie with him. Alyssa knew that for a fact, just as she knew if he made it out of the corporate headquarters building before she caught up with him, they'd never catch him.

Halfway up the steps, the fire alarm started to ring, the sound so loud it was almost enough to deafen her. Smoke followed, thick enough to make her eyes water. But she ignored both, catching up to Stefan and his hostage just short of the door that opened onto the main lobby—and all the Black Swan employees he could have gotten lost in as they made a dash to get out of the burning building. While Stacie wasn't resisting him as he pulled her up the stairs, she wasn't helping anymore either. Maybe the girl wasn't as far gone as Randy Curtis had claimed.

"FBI! Freeze!" Alyssa shouted loud enough to be heard over the fire alarm.

Stefan spun around and pulled Stacie in front of him, his gun to the side of her head. "Drop it and let me walk out of here or I'll shoot her! I swear it!"

As if to prove he meant business, he pressed the barrel against the girl's temple so hard it almost pushed her head all the way over to her shoulder. It had to hurt like hell, but Stacie didn't make a peep. Yet as glassy as the girl's eyes were, they were still pleading with Alyssa to save her.

Alyssa considered trying to talk Stefan down but knew it would be pointless. The man knew he was never getting out of this, not after everything he'd done. If she let him get out that door behind him, he'd shoot Stacie just to slow Alyssa down.

Taking a deep breath, she lifted her weapon a little higher, planning to aim for a grazing shot to the top of his shoulder. It would be a tough shot, especially since she was still a little dizzy, but she could make it. She had to.

Suddenly, Alyssa heard a scrabbling sound on the stairs behind her followed by a loud growl. Alyssa knew it shouldn't be possible, but she recognized that growl.

Stefan's eyes widened and he jerked his weapon away from Stacie's head, straightening to his full height and pointing it over Alyssa's head, aiming at the wolf behind her.

She didn't waste the opportunity, lining up the shot and squeezing the trigger two times in rapid succession before Stefan could squeeze his. One round hit Stefan in the left shoulder. The other got him in the neck.

Alyssa didn't bother to watch Stefan fall, instead darting forward to catch Stacie before the girl tumbled all the way to the bottom of the stairs. Stacie collapsed into her arms, pressing her face into Alyssa's shoulder and sobbing softly.

"Thank you," she whispered before passing out against her.

Alyssa lifted her head as Zane moved up the stairs in his wolf form and stopped at her side. His beautiful gray fur was covered in blood and she didn't doubt that some of it was his. But he'd survived a full magazine of bullets to the chest and stomach. She doubted a few scratches would put him down.

He lowered his broad face, resting his forehead against hers. He just stood there, breathing her in. Alyssa wrapped the arm that wasn't busy with Stacie around his shoulders, digging her fingers into his fur and hugging him tightly.

"Don't ever think you're a monster again," she whispered. "And don't ever forget that I love you."

Zane sat in the back of the FBI tactical response vehicle, gritting his teeth as his pack mate and SWAT team medic, Trey Duncan, dug an endless number of bullet fragments out of his chest and stomach. He had no idea how Trey was able to find all the pieces, but he was damn happy his fellow alpha werewolf could do it because having all that metal inside him hurt like a son of a bitch. Even though he was grateful to have Trey's help, he couldn't help tensing every time his friend took another piece of lead out. The last time Trey had worked on him hadn't ended well.

Alyssa had watched for a few minutes before finally turning away, refusing to witness Trey alternating between cutting into him with a scalpel and poking around with long forceps. She'd turned green after the first several pieces, deciding to keep watch out the window instead of trying to help.

She craned her neck to look at the circus of activity still going on outside Black Swan Enterprises. "If your injured arm completely healed itself when you went through a full shift, why didn't the bullet holes heal up, too?"

Zane looked over at the back of his left arm, still kind of stunned to see an entire triceps there. A tiny trace of the scar was still there as well, but where there'd previously been a whole lot of nothing, there was now new muscle tissue. According to Trey, it seemed like he'd regrown the muscles while in wolf form and they'd stayed there after he'd changed back to his human form.

"His inner wolf is smart enough to know those fragments would irritate the hell out of him if they stayed in there," Trey murmured as he continued to work. "When he shifted back into human form, it left the wounds open for a while to give us time to get them out. If we didn't, they'd heal over regardless, but they'd hurt and reduce mobility."

Alyssa seemed to take that answer in stride. Truthfully, she was taking almost all of this a lot better than he'd thought she would. She hadn't even batted an eye when he'd turned back into his human form starkers as the day he was born. She'd simply found him some clothes, then helped him continue to get injured people out of the burning building.

Not that there'd been all that many people. Other than Zoe, Chloe, and the three kidnapped girls, the only people who'd made it out of the nest had been a dozen nearly catatonic enthralled servants. Everyone else had died in the shooting or the fire that still continued to burn under Black Swan Enterprises despite the efforts of the fire department. Apparently, fire and vampires didn't mix well.

"Okay, you're good to go," Trey said, putting away his medic tools and handing Zane a T-shirt. Knowing that a good portion of the Pack would be going through a full shift today, the team had shown up with lots of extra clothes. Just in case.

Zane almost groaned as he pulled on the T-shirt. Damn, he'd forgotten what it felt like to get dressed without experiencing pain in his arm. He glanced at Trey, still busy with cleaning up. Trey had been the one who'd had to cut the muscle out of his arm to save his life after Zane had gotten shot a few months ago. Even though he didn't want to admit it, Zane had blamed Trey for his bum arm, and his pack mate knew it. Since that day, neither of them had spoken to each other very much.

"Thanks for fixing me up," Zane said.

Trey didn't look at him as he finished putting his equipment away. "No problem."

Zane knew he and Trey needed to talk, so he could apologize for being such a wanker these past few months, but now wasn't the time. When they got back to Dallas, he'd definitely make a point of it, though. Since giving his pack mate a fist bump was the best he could do right now, he offered his hand. Trey looked at him, his hazel eyes filled with surprise, but then something that didn't need words passed between the two of them and his teammate returned the fist bump.

Giving Trey a nod, Zane led Alyssa out of the response vehicle. Her friend Christine was waiting for them, and she looked up from her mobile phone to give them a smile.

"I was wondering where you were," Alyssa said.

Christine shrugged. "I had a few fires to put out—no pun intended. I just wanted to make sure you guys were okay before I got out of here."

Alyssa's lips curved. "We're fine. Better than fine, actually."

Christine glanced at Zane, regarding him thoughtfully. He got the feeling she wanted to say something about him being a werewolf, but instead she reached out and hugged Alyssa.

"Okay, I have to go." She gave Alyssa a pointed look. "Call me, okay? We have a lot we need to talk about."

Alyssa nodded. "I will."

That was going to be an interesting conversation, Zane thought as Christine gave them both a wave, then hurried off.

As he and Alyssa made their way through the crowd of police, FBI agents, and fire department personnel, it occurred to him that the area looked like some kind of casualty exercise. Except this wasn't an exercise, of course. And there had been a lot of casualties.

Zane tugged Alyssa's hand, pulling her off to the side, so they'd be out of the way of any workers—or roaming reporters with their cameras. He hadn't even realized he was holding her hand as they walked until now. It felt damn nice. He'd never done that with any woman he'd ever been with. He decided he'd been missing out.

They passed by Jake, Zoe, and Chloe, the three werewolves sitting and talking quietly in the back of an ambulance, Zoe messing with the white bandage wrapped around one of her forearms. The alpha and his two betas looked happier than anybody had a right to, considering what they'd just been through. It was obvious they were comfortable together, almost like a brother and his two younger sisters. Zane wondered how it was all going to work out for them. It seemed... complicated.

"So, what do we do now?" Alyssa asked when they stopped a little while later. She wedged her butt up onto a flower bed retaining wall and wiggled around until she got comfortable. "Now that everything is wrapped up, I mean."

Zane glanced over to where his tall, dark-haired boss, Gage, was talking to Alyssa's bespectacled boss, Nathan. Those two were getting way too chummy in his opinion.

"I somehow doubt this situation is going to be wrapped up anytime soon," he said. "That rumor your boss leaked to the press about an electricity fire starting down in the basement during a Black Swan meeting isn't going to hold water for very long. Sooner or later, news agencies are going to wonder why the FBI was down there and why most of the people rescued are men and women who'd been missing."

"That's Nathan's problem to solve." Alyssa gave him a smile. "I was more interested in us. Where do *we* go from here?"

Zane moved closer until he was standing between her legs. He reached out and tucked a stray strand of hair behind her ear. "Since I'm in love with you, I was kind of hoping we could go to Dallas. My flat is kind of small, but we could get a bigger one if you want. Or a house even."

"Move with you to Dallas, just like that?" She blinked. "I know you want to be there for your pack, but what about my job? Are you suggesting that I quit?"

He shook his head. "I'm not suggesting anything like that. You said it yourself—you spend almost all your time on the road looking for things that go bump in the night. Wouldn't it be better to have a place to come back to that you can call home?"

Alyssa regarded him thoughtfully, her heart thumping fast. He hoped like hell he hadn't pushed too hard, too fast. But the idea of letting her get away wasn't something he was ready to do. Not after everything they'd been through.

"Say we do this," she murmured, resting her hands on his shoulders. "How are you going to handle my job? As you pointed out, I'm on the road—a lot. Is that something you can deal with?"

He wanted to howl at the thought. But didn't. "Will I be thrilled that you're out there on your own, going after creatures you know almost nothing about? No, not at all. But it's who you are. I get that. So if dealing with it is what I have to do to have you in my life, then I'm in. As long as you promise me one thing."

She looked at him curiously. "What's that?"

He slipped his hand into her hair, then bent forward until his forehead was resting against hers. He'd done that with her when he was in wolf form and it had been amazing. It felt even better now. "Just promise that if you're out there on the road and run into something you think you can't handle, you'll call me and let me help."

She gazed at him warmly for a few seconds and then tipped her face to kiss him. "I promise."

Alyssa kissed him again, so long and so thoroughly he thought maybe they might need to find a room—or an empty FBI tactical response vehicle. But then Alyssa slid off the brick wall, tugging Zane along the sidewalk with her.

"Where are we going?" he asked.

She smiled at him over her shoulder. "To go talk to my boss and tell him I'm moving to Dallas—immediately."

Chapter 14

ALYSSA SLID ONTO THE BENCH OF THE PICNIC TABLE WHERE Trey, a huge, muscular werewolf named Brooks, and his mate, a high school teacher named Selena, were sitting and glanced around the SWAT compound, amazed at how many people were there. Zane had told her it would be a small cookout for the Pack, their significant others, and some of their closest friends. She now had reason to doubt his mathematical skills, since there must have been at least seventy-five people milling around the fenced-in area despite the chilly weather today.

Rachel was handling the line of grills on the far side of the volleyball pit with the help of Zoe and Chloe. The beta werewolves looked much better than they had when she'd seen them in LA. That probably had a lot to do with the smiles they'd both been wearing ever since moving to Dallas last week with Jake. After leaving Los Angeles, he'd taken them back to their home in Utah—or at least what was left of it—to deal with the aftermath of their parents' murder and their subsequent kidnapping. The worst part out of all of it was that the police in their hometown had no leads about who'd killed their mother and father, other than some grainy footage from a convenience store security camera showing a bearded man in a hoodie transferring an unconscious Zoe and Chloe from a white van to a dark SUV. After that, there was nothing.

Jake had considered taking the girls back to Santa Fe with him but had ultimately decided he wanted them to be around other werewolves—especially betas—so they could learn to be comfortable with what they were and be safe. Gage was trying to talk him into transferring to the DPD so he could join SWAT and the Pack, but at the same time, Nathan was attempting to woo him to STAT. Alyssa thought he'd be an excellent addition to the STAT team, so she hoped he'd take her boss up on the offer.

Zoe and Chloe weren't the only ones keeping Rachel company by the grills, Alyssa noticed. So were the team's collection of mascots and pets—dogs Tuffie, Leo, and Biscuit (the newest addition to the family), as well as Kat the cat. Alyssa was surprised at how patient the animals were, not to mention well behaved. They didn't even fight over the chunks of meat Rachel tossed their way every once in a while. Unlike the pit-bull mix, Labrador, and dachshund, the black cat refused to eat anything that touched the ground. Any morsels Rachel gave her had to be perfectly cooked and placed on the plate in front of her, or the picky feline wouldn't even look at it. Alyssa smiled every time she saw it.

Listening in amusement as Selena tried to talk Trey into asking the medical examiner he had a thing for out to dinner, Alyssa picked up her bottle of water and took a sip, her gaze going to her boss, Nathan. He was sitting at one of the far tables with Gage, Zane, and the SWAT team's two squad leaders. Nathan had been in Dallas for three days now and had spent nearly all that time at the compound in meetings with the commander of the team and the acting chief of police, Hal Mason. She'd overheard snippets of their conversation and had a fairly good idea where those three days of meetings were heading—more joint operations between the STAT team and the werewolf pack. The one in LA had gone well, so why not? She certainly wouldn't mind.

As if sensing Alyssa's gaze on him, Zane flashed her a grin, then got up from the table and headed in her direction, slowing to pick up two cheeseburgers from Rachel on the way. Alyssa had to admit she loved watching him move. It was difficult to believe, but he was even more graceful than he had been when she'd first met him.

Even though the weather was cooler than it had been in LA, Zane wasn't wearing a jacket and she took a moment to appreciate his sculpted biceps. When he sat down beside her at the picnic table, she leaned her head against his left arm. Other than the barely discernible scar along the back of it now, it was almost like the gunshot wound had never happened.

"I saw you eyeing the grills and thought you might be hungry," he said, setting the plate of cheeseburgers on the table.

Alyssa reached for the bottle of ketchup and squeezed out a puddle on the plate big enough for both of them. "I could definitely go for a burger, but I was actually thinking how sweet it is that Tuffie and the other animals help Rachel cook."

He chuckled. "More like waiting for her to drop a whole tray of burgers."

She laughed and dipped her burger in ketchup. "We're still taking Tuffie home with us tonight, right?"

All the members of the SWAT team shared custody of the beloved pit-bull mix, so she went home with a different person every night. They even had a duty roster to make sure everyone got their turn with the adorable pup. Alyssa's family always had dogs when she was growing up—still did—and not having a dog to come home to every night was one of the things she'd missed when she'd joined the FBI.

"Definitely." Zane grinned and leaned over to kiss her. "I love hearing you say the word *home*."

She smiled. "Not nearly as much as I love saying it."

It was the truth. She'd been in Dallas for two weeks now. After leaving LA, she and Zane had gotten on a plane to Washington, DC, packed up her stuff, turned in the keys to her apartment, then flown to Dallas that very same day.

Since then, she'd been living with Zane in his small two-bedroom apartment, and while it was approximately the size of a shoebox—one made for flip-flops—she loved every minute of it because she was with him. And while it was seriously tiny, he'd decorated it surprisingly well. She'd kind of expected the typical bachelor pad, but his place could be on one of those home-and-garden shows. Outside of spending time with the Pack so she could get to know everyone, the two of them hadn't left the apartment much. Heck, they'd barely gotten out of bed.

Across from them, Trey took his attention off his plate of ribs long enough to look at her and Zane. "I overheard Nathan telling Gage the STAT team cleaned up everything in LA. That true?"

Nodding, Zane took a big bite of burger, chewed once, then swallowed. "They went with the human-trafficking angle to explain all the enthralled people, pinning it on Stefan and the muscle heads who worked for him."

"Are those people the vampires screwed up ever going to be okay?" Diego asked as he sat down across from Alyssa.

"Stacie, the girl Stefan tried to escape with, seems to be coming out of it," Alyssa said. "But the ones who had been there a really long time haven't responded to any of the drugs the doctors at the psychiatric facility where they're staying have given them. It's only been two weeks, though, so with time, maybe they'll come out of it."

She hoped. Though she hadn't seen any of the people since they'd rescued them, hearing Nathan describe how they acted was enough to make her want to kill Stefan all over again.

They were still talking about that when some more of Zane's pack mates joined them. Alyssa was amazed how warm and welcoming they all were. She felt like part of their great big family already. Of all of them, Alyssa found herself getting closest to Rachel. That wasn't surprising, since they'd hit it off from the day they'd met. While Rachel hadn't confided in her yet, it was obvious she was dealing with some stuff. Even now, pulling grill duty, Alyssa caught her nervously looking over her shoulder at the training structures on the far end of the SWAT compound several times, her eyes fixed on the darkened windows, like she thought someone was watching her. But so far, Alyssa couldn't get her to open up about whatever she was going through.

"I'm still having trouble wrapping my head around the fact that there are other supernatural creatures out there," Remy said.

Tall, good-looking, and built like the rest of the guys in the Pack, the Louisiana werewolf with the Cajun accent had joined them at the table a few minutes ago, along with his forensic scientist mate, Triana, and her mother, Gemma, a petite, outgoing woman, visiting from New Orleans.

Everyone in the Pack had echoed that same sentiment over the past two weeks. Alyssa found it funny that she had more experience with what was out there in the world than they did, considering she was human and they were werewolves. She'd need to get them caught up.

"What about the hunters?" Remy asked. "Now that the vampire coven is destroyed, do you think they'll still be around?"

"I don't think so," Zane said. "At least not like we've been seeing over the past year, especially since no one is paying them now."

"Plus, when we dug through the computers we confiscated from Stefan's office at the parking garage, we got the name of every hunter he ever hired, so now we have files on them," Alyssa added. "Almost all of them have a criminal past, so when they end up getting arrested again—which they almost certainly will—it will flag our system. Sooner or later, they'll all end up in prison."

Alyssa thought that news would be met with a round of cheers and high fives, but instead, the mood around the table—the compound even—turned somber.

"What's wrong?" she asked. "No more hunters in the world is a good thing, right?"

"Yeah, of course." Diego absently rubbed his thumb back and forth on the label of his beer bottle. "It's just something that Davina mentioned to me back at the club, about there being a balance to the whole werewolf–hunter thing. She pretty much confirmed that more people go through the change and become werewolves—and find their soul mates—when there's a major threat out there. Now that the LA coven is gone and the hunters aren't a factor anymore, that means the likelihood of anyone else in the Pack finding *The One* for them is gone, too. I mean, the whole theory behind why it's been happening over and over again when it never had before was that the Pack was in danger and needed to be stronger. But if the danger is gone now…"

"The magic that pulls soul mates together is gone, too," Trey finished quietly.

Alyssa frowned. Since moving to Dallas, she and Zane had had more than a few conversations about what the legend of *The One* meant to werewolves, but the stuff Diego and Trey were talking about was all new to her. Suddenly, she felt as gloomy as the rest of them. The thought of Zane's single pack mates—*her* pack mates—never finding what she and Zane and every other couple had was almost enough to make her cry.

"Oh, I wouldn't be too worried about that," Gemma said softly, her gaze locked on Rachel over by the grills. "Something tells me there's more than enough trouble out there in the supernatural world for every werewolf in your pack to find *The One*—and then some."

While the idea of more trouble like they'd run into out in LA wasn't a cheery thought, the idea of Rachel, Trey, Diego, and every other unattached werewolf in the Pack finding their soul mates brought a smile to Alyssa's lips. Around the compound, every other werewolf within hearing distance—which was all of them—was smiling, too.

Zane stood up. "Who's up for another round of burgers and dogs?"

Alyssa shook her head with a laugh, still wondering where he put all that food.

They continued to hang out, laughing, talking, and telling stories long after midnight. It was almost 2:00 a.m. when Zane finally leaned in and put his mouth close to her ear. "You ready to get out of here, or do you need to grab some burgers for the road first?"

She chuckled. "I think I'm good. And yeah, I'm ready to go home."

Waving at the few people left at the cookout, including Rachel, they rounded up Tuffie, then headed for the parking lot. When they reached Zane's pride and joy, a sleek, black BMW he was thrilled to admit he'd gotten for a great price at an impound auction, she reached into her back pocket and pulled out her cell phone, then poked a few buttons and handed it to Zane.

"What's this?" he asked curiously.

"It's a phone obviously." She grinned. "London is six hours ahead of us, so it's eight o'clock there. Exactly when I said you'd be calling."

His eyes widened, but even though they could both hear the phone ringing, he didn't put it to his ear.

"I dialed your mother," Alyssa nudged. "She's expecting your call."

He stared at her, something close to panic on his face. *Crap*. She hoped he wouldn't hang up. From where she was sitting beside them, Tuffie looked just as concerned.

She reached out and wrapped her hand around his, gently guiding the phone to his ear. "I'm helping you reconnect with your family, starting with your mom." When he still looked hesitant, she added, "Remember the way you described it to me as the law of inertia? Well, consider me the outside force that's operating on the thing at rest and making it get its rear in gear. You moved on with me. It's time you did the same with your family."

Zane's eyes misted with what she was sure were tears, but before she could be sure, he leaned down to kiss her. Then he pulled away, jerking the phone closer to his ear.

"Mum, yeah. It's me...Zane. Yeah, it has been a long time. It's good to hear your voice, too."

Alyssa started to step away and give him some privacy, but he caught her hand, mouthing the word *stay* and pulling her close as he chuckled at something his mother said.

"Yeah, Mum. Alyssa's actually the one who convinced me to call you." Zane's eyes held hers. "And yeah, she is special."

Alyssa smiled, her heart melting as she leaned in closer to him.

Acknowledgments

I hope you had as much fun reading Zane and Alyssa's story as I had writing it! Zane and Alyssa's book changed a lot over time. When hubby and I came up with the idea, Alyssa was originally going to be a personal trainer who helped Zane with his injured arm, but she wanted a more active role. Which is why she became a kick-butt FBI agent. Then vampires showed up! Totally didn't see that coming! And a special shout-out to our real-life friend, Alyssa, for inspiring the heroine!

This whole series wouldn't be possible without some very incredible people. In addition to another big thank-you to my hubby for all his help with the action scenes and military and tactical jargon, thanks to my fantastic agent, Courtney Miller-Callihan; my editor and go-to-person at Sourcebooks, Cat Clyne (who loves this series as much as I do and is always a phone call, text, or email away whenever I need something); and all the other amazing people at Sourcebooks, including my fantastic publicist and the crazy-talented art department. The covers they make for me are seriously droolworthy!

Because I could never leave out my readers, a huge thank-you to everyone who reads my books and Snoopy Danced right along with me with every new release. That includes the fantastic people on my amazing Review Team, as well my assistant, Janet. You rock!

I also want to give a big thank-you to the men,

women, and working dogs who protect and serve in police departments everywhere, as well as their families.

And a very special shout-out to my favorite restaurant, P.F. Chang's, where hubby and I bat story lines back and forth and come up with all of our best ideas, as well as a thank-you to our fantastic waiter-turned-manager, Andrew, who makes sure our order is ready the moment we walk in the door!

Hope you enjoy *Wolf Rebel*, the next book in the SWAT: Special Wolf Alpha Team series coming soon from Sourcebooks, and look forward to reading the rest of the series as much as I look forward to sharing it with you Also, don't forget to look for my new series from Sourcebooks, STAT: Special Threat Assessment Team, a spin-off from SWAT!

If you love a man in uniform as much as I do, make sure you check out X-Ops, my other action-packed paranormal/romantic-suspense series from Sourcebooks.

Happy Reading!

WOLF REBEL

Prologue

Chattanooga, TN, October, 2017

"SUSPICIOUS ACTIVITY REPORTED NEAR THE SOUTH END OF Forest Lake Memorial."

Officer Rachel Bennett knew the police dispatcher was going to ask her to check it out before the guy called out the number of her patrol car. Why? Because she was just lucky that way. Cursing under her breath, she flipped on the lights, spun her vehicle around, crossed over the median, and headed north on Highway 27.

Rachel forced herself to ignore the chatter on the radio, gritting her teeth as the shift sergeant called out directions to her fellow Chattanooga PD officers, who were setting up a perimeter just north of Lookout Mountain. There'd been a high-speed chase, a crash into a ditch, and lots of gunfire. It was literally the triple crown of fun for a cop on a slow Tuesday night in Tennessee. The chase had drawn half the law-enforcement officers in the area, both city and county. And when the vehicle's two armed occupants had escaped into the woods near the highway, that had drawn every other cop in this corner of the state. Hell, there were probably off-duty officers rolling out of bed right that minute and yanking on their uniforms on the off chance they could get involved in the excitement.

And where was she heading while the rest of the police force ran through the woods looking for two armed felons? To a damn cemetery, most likely to chase off a prostitute and a customer looking to get freaky in a graveyard. Rachel had caught the suspicious activity call because it was her beat, but being forced to deal with sex-crazed perverts the night before Halloween while the other members of her department went after real criminals was frustrating as hell.

As Rachel crossed over the Tennessee River, the more built-up parts of Chattanooga were replaced with stretches of dense woods, interspersed with quiet residential areas. A mile later, the woods disappeared almost entirely.

There was a thriving red-light district just before the bridge, but while that area had plenty of sidewalks for the guys and girls to display their wares, there weren't many good locations to conduct their business. The nearby parking lots were generally well-lit, which scared the johns to death. And the dark alleys behind the buildings were a refuge for the homeless and druggies, neither of which was good for a prostitute's business. Nervous customers took longer to finish in that environment—if they could finish at all.

So, the working men and women of Chattanooga

now had their clients drive them over the bridge to the suburbs, and for reasons that made sense to no one but them, the Forest Lake Cemetery had become their preferred location to get busy. Apparently, the privacy and soft grass made the time it took to get out there worthwhile. Rachel had no idea how the graveyard ambiance affected their bottom line though. She'd definitely never want to do it in a place like that.

Rachel turned into the cemetery, wishing for the hundredth time the place would install a gate that locked. The city had talked to the facility's management about it, but they were resistant to the idea. They claimed it was because they didn't want to keep people from being able to come in and out to visit their loved ones whenever they wanted. More likely it was because they didn't want to spend money protecting a place when there wasn't anything to steal.

She stopped the car a few yards inside the entrance, the beams of her headlights reflecting off the fog drifting silently across the graveyard. She flipped on her search light and swiveled it this way and that, but beyond confirming there was no one parked anywhere near the main building to her left, she didn't see much of anything. Thanks to the fog, she couldn't see more than twenty feet in any direction. Just the silhouettes of headstones large and small, along with a few family-sized crypts.

Nope, not creepy at all. Especially this close to Halloween.

She'd been in this damn graveyard a dozen times in the past month, so she was familiar with the maze-like network of narrow, curvy roads that weaved through the tree-shrouded cemetery. The place had been fashioned that way on purpose to give mourners a sense of privacy while they were there, but it also meant if there was someone in the cemetery looking for some action, it could take a while to find them.

She grabbed her car's radio and thumbed the button. "This is Unit 220. Any additional information from the reporting party about Forest Lake?"

"Negative, 220," the dispatcher replied. "The RP said they heard a female screaming when they drove past the cemetery. No further contact from the RP since, though there was an earlier report of someone seeing a man in a clown costume walking near that same area."

Rachel groaned. She frigging hated clowns with a gut-twisting passion. Then again, was there anyone on the planet who actually liked them?

"10–4," she said into the radio.

She considered asking for backup, but decided against it. Since the call had come into dispatch ten minutes ago, there was little chance whoever had screamed was still there.

Rachel drove around the cemetery, but with the ever-present fog and random patches of trees, she couldn't see a damn thing. Worse, between the hum of the vehicle's heater and the noise from the radio, it was impossible to hear anything either, even with the window down. Knowing she'd never find anything if she kept trying to do this search from her car, she turned around and headed back to the main building, figuring that would be the best place to park while she continued the search on foot.

Letting the dispatcher know she was getting out of the vehicle to look around, she shoved open the door.

She shivered, trying to keep her teeth from chattering the moment the freezing fall wind hit her. Crap. It shouldn't be this cold in Chattanooga already. The weather forecast had mentioned a possibility of snow tonight, and from the way her breath frosted in the air, she could believe it.

She turned down the volume on the mobile radio attached to her equipment belt, putting some distance between herself and the distracting sound of the patrol car's hot engine ticking, straining her ears to pick up anything suspicious. She kept one hand on the weapon holstered on her hip as she moved away from the car and further into the graveyard, letting her eyes and ears slowly adjust to the darkness and the night sounds around her as she swung her flashlight back and forth.

The moon was out tonight, but with the fog, it was like she was walking around in a bubble, cut off from everything around her. She couldn't see or hear anything. There could be someone standing only a few yards away and she'd never know it. Crap, there could be a psycho in a clown costume behind the next tombstone for all she knew.

Rachel shivered as tingles ran up her back. She cursed silently. She refused to let her unreasonable fear of clowns freak her out.

She walked slowly along the paths that separated the various sections of the graveyard from each other, stopping occasionally to shine her flashlight into the woods that lined the east side of the cemetery. After ten minutes, she gave up any hope of finding a vehicle. After twenty, she was convinced the entire call had been a hoax. There was nobody out here.

She hadn't gone more than a half dozen steps back toward her patrol car when a cracking sound from off to the right made her turn.

Any country girl who'd spent time in the woods knew that sound. Someone had stepped on a big stick, breaking it.

She immediately headed that direction, aiming her flashlight in the direction of the noise, her other hand still resting on her weapon. She couldn't see anyone, but her instincts were telling her someone was out there beyond the edge of the glowing beam in the brambles near the base of one of the trees.

"Whoever is out there, this is Officer Bennett from the Chattanooga Police Department!" she shouted. "Stand up and move toward the sound of my voice or I'll release my K9 and you will get bit."

She didn't expect whoever it was to do as she asked. That line about having a dog with her almost never worked, so she was shocked when she heard a desperate scream out in the darkness and then a series of crashing sounds as a young girl ran toward her, slamming through tree branches and undergrowth like her life depended on it.

Rachel immediately had her Sig Sauer out of its holster, ready to take down whoever was chasing the girl. The teen collapsed to her knees the moment she cleared the wood line, crying, shaking, and gasping for breath in the circle of Rachel's flashlight.

Slipping the flashlight in her belt, Rachel dropped to a knee beside the terrified girl, wrapping one arm around her shoulder and pulling her close while keeping her .45-caliber pointed at the dark woods.

The girl wore nothing but a thin T-shirt, leggings, and ragged socks. No wonder she was shaking. She didn't even have any shoes on. The socks and leggings were shredded from running through the woods, and she was bleeding from myriad cuts and scrapes. But it was the deep, bloody lacerations crisscrossing the kid's back and one arm Rachel was more concerned about. The girl had a hand clasped over the wound on her arm, but blood was still leaking out from between her fingers.

Rachel let the girl go long enough to reach up and thumb the button on the mic attached to the webbing on her vest. "Dispatch, this is 220. I need immediate backup and EMS at my location. One female victim with severe lacerations across her back and arm as well as possible hypothermia. Unknown assailant."

The dispatcher asked a few questions about Rachel's exact location in the graveyard and how far she was from her patrol car, but the best she could do at the moment was provide a general direction and distance from the entrance. She also couldn't answer the most pressing question—whether the scene was secure.

"Who did this to you?" Rachel whispered to the girl, glancing quickly at the wounds along the girl's back before looking off into the trees again. "Do you know where he is?"

The girl only cried harder, latching her arms around Rachel's waist and holding on for dear life. The poor thing might be too traumatized to even speak.

"It was a clown," she whispered brokenly, her face buried in Rachel's shoulder.

Rachel thought for a minute she'd heard wrong. Then she started praying she'd heard wrong. But when the girl lifted her head and looked up at her with terror in her eyes, she knew she hadn't heard wrong at all.

Crap.

"A clown?"

The girl nodded, seeming to draw strength from Rachel's presence. "He wasn't wearing a mask though. He had on face paint. Like you see in a circus. I was in the backyard near the fire pit talking to my friend on the phone when he grabbed me and dragged me into the woods. I tried to fight him, but he has a knife. I thought he was going to kill me." She swallowed hard. "I still can't believe I got away."

"Where is he now?"

The teen shook her head. "I don't know. I hit him in the head with a rock, but I didn't knock him out. I heard him come after me."

Cursing silently, Rachel called the dispatcher again with an update on the attacker, saying there was a man somewhere in the cemetery wearing clown makeup and carrying a knife. The dispatcher immediately put the information out on the radio. A moment later, officers began calling in their locations and ETAs—estimated time of arrival—to Forest Lake Memorial. Unfortunately, they were all on the far side of the city, which meant Rachel was on her own for at least ten minutes.

That might not seem like much, but those ten minutes were a lifetime when there was some weirdo out there with a knife.

She didn't hear anything right then that made her think the clown was nearby, but that didn't provide much comfort. The truth was that she hadn't heard a peep out of the girl either and she'd been hiding in the woods twenty feet away. She sure as hell didn't like the idea of the clown being that close to her and the kid.

Rachel couldn't sit in the middle of the graveyard waiting for help to arrive, letting the girl bleed to death. She needed to get the girl back to the car and put some bandages over those wounds.

"What's your name?" she asked gently, sliding her free arm around the girl again while still keeping one eye on the fog-shrouded night.

The girl stared at Rachel for all of a second before a slight smile creased her lips. After everything that had happened, it was amazing she could still smile. "Hannah," she said even as her teeth chattered from the cold. "Hannah Harris."

"Nice to meet you, Hannah. My name is Rachel. What do you think about getting out of this place? I have a nice warm car waiting back at the entrance. How does that sound?"

Hannah's smile widened for a moment, but then disappeared. "That sounds good, but I'm not sure if I can walk that far."

It was Rachel's turn to smile. "No problem. I can help you."

She would have preferred to slip an arm around Hannah's shoulder and help her walk back to the car, leaving her right hand free for her handgun, but it quickly became obvious that wasn't going to work. Hannah's legs were complete rubber. There was no way she'd be able to walk back to the cruiser, even with help. Rachel had no idea how the girl had made it this far.

Hating to do it, but having no choice, Rachel holstered

her weapon, then scooped Hannah up in her arms. The girl cried out softly in pain as Rachel's uniform jacket scraped against the open wounds on her back.

"I'm sorry," Rachel whispered as she turned and headed back toward her patrol car. "I know this hurts, but there's no other way to do this."

"I don't care." Hannah's hand came up to clutch Rachel's jacket in a death grip. "Just don't let him hurt me again. Please."

"Shh." Rachel's heart seized in her chest at the pain in the girl's words. Damn that effing clown, whoever he was. "I won't let anyone hurt you. I promise."

Hannah buried her face in Rachel's tactical vest, somehow making herself even smaller than she already was. A few more sobs that sounded almost like relief slipped out and all Rachel wanted to do right then was squeeze her tight and make her feel safe again. But giving her a hug wouldn't do that. Getting her back to the car and some medical help wouldn't, either. Finding that damn clown and getting him off the streets was the only thing that would do that.

Rachel moved quickly, glad Hannah was so petite. Rachel was strong—you had to be with this job—but if the girl had been any heavier, there was no way she could have carried her. She considered retracing her steps back to the car, but then realized it would be a long trip with Hannah in her arms. Plus, keeping to the roads and gravel pathways would force her to go past several areas heavily shrouded in trees. With that damn clown still out there somewhere, it was a risk she wasn't willing to take, especially since her hands weren't free.

Hoping she was making the right decision, she turned

off the path she was on, heading straight across the fog-shrouded cemetery in the direction of the main building and the front entrance. It was risky going cross-country like this, but if her sense of direction was right, they'd be back at her patrol car in half the time it would take if they took the long way around.

Within seconds, the path they'd been on had disappeared into the mist and the blurry outline of various shaped headstones and grave markers began to appear out of the darkness ahead of them. Rachel strained to hear the sounds of approaching sirens, but so far the only noises were her footsteps in the cold, crunchy grass, Hannah's occasional moans of pain, and the chatter of the radio as her fellow officers called in their updated ETAs.

Hannah was nearly unconscious in her arms by the time Rachel saw the hazy outline of the main cemetery building. She picked up her pace, almost running across the parking lot. In the distance, sirens echoed faintly and she prayed the paramedics would be part of the first group to arrive.

Rachel was so eager to get Hannah into the warmth and safety of the car, she didn't hear the crunch of gravel under foot until it was almost too late. She snapped her head around in time to see a huge man in clown makeup sprinting out of the fog, a big knife in his hand.

For the first time since becoming a cop, Rachel froze. Between the white grease paint covering his face, the blood red markings around his eyes, and the menacing black grin permanently etched around his mouth, he was like a nightmare come to life. Even his teeth, which he'd somehow tricked out to make it look like they'd been filed down to sharp points like some kind of monster, screamed evil. A bright orange fright wig completed the look, turning the big man into the most disturbing thing she'd ever seen, despite the big, bright red nose he sported.

The clown was less than a foot away when Rachel finally snapped out of her daze. She instinctively curled around Hannah in an effort to protect her, praying the Kevlar fibers in her tactical vest would protect *her*.

Rachel flew forward like she'd been hit by a Mack truck. Her knees slammed into the gravel and Hannah sailed out of her arms with a high-pitched scream. A lightning bolt of fiery agony beneath her right shoulder blade let her know the demented clown's knife had punched right through the vest. Shock kept her from feeling the full extent of the damage, she was sure, but she had a feeling the blade had gone deep enough to puncture a lung. The pain from the wound made her whole body go rigid and for one terrified moment, she thought she might not make it home that night.

She screamed as the clown ripped the knife out. Crap, it hurt even more coming out than it had going in. Fighting off dizziness, she rolled to the side to avoid the next attack she was sure was coming her way. Another piercing scream echoed in the cemetery and she worried the man was going after Hannah, but when she looked up it was to find the psycho coming at her again.

She managed to get her Sig out, but the stabbing pain in her back kept her from moving as fast as she usually did and the damn weapon slipped out of her hand when the clown landed on top of her, crushing what seemed like every trace of air out of her already damaged lungs.

Rachel punched, scratched, kicked, and shoved, but the man on top of her easily weighed over two hundred and fifty pounds, and most of it seemed to be muscle. He was insanely strong—or maybe just insane. Eyes practically glowing red, he went for her throat, and those teeth she'd thought only looked sharp were actually as pointy and dangerous as they looked. The pain as they tore through the course fabric of her uniform jacket and into her shoulder was nearly as bad as the knife he'd plunged into her back had been.

She tried to reach her Taser, but the a-hole had her left arm pinned. There was no way she could get at her telescoping baton with him on top of her, either. So, she did the only thing she could. She reached down to the other side of her belt and grabbed her radio. She brought it up and smashed it against the side of her attacker's head, hard. The plastic shattered into pieces, but it got the madman's attention—and his teeth out of her shoulder.

She dropped the remnants of the radio and punched out blindly, feeling her fist connect with a jaw that felt like steel. Something popped in her clenched hand with a spasm of pain, but she ignored it, punching him over and over. One of the blows caught him in the eye and he reared back with a shout of anger.

Rachel was sure she had him on the ropes then. Until the knife slashed down again with a thud so solid she thought at first he'd missed her completely and struck the gravel-covered ground. But then searing pain exploded in the left side of her chest and she knew he hadn't missed. Her scream of agony must have shocked the hell out of the clown because he jerked back, tilting his head sideways like a confused animal.

She grit her teeth against the pain and threw another punch at him. Her aim was crap and she completely missed his face, but she hit him in the throat, which was actually much better. The clown tumbled backward, clutching at his neck with both hands, coughing and gagging like he was dying. She followed that up with a kick to the face, knocking off his stupid, red clown nose and breaking his real one with the heel of her heavy patrol shoe. Blood running down his face, he collapsed to the ground, coughing harder. Hopefully, she'd crushed his larynx and he'd choke to death.

Just in case he didn't, she spun around on the ground, trying to figure out where her Sig had gone. She couldn't find it in the dark, but the move sent a spike of pain lancing through her chest. Crap. The knife was still in her. How the hell hadn't she noticed it?

Rachel glanced down and almost passed out when she saw how deeply the knife was buried in her chest, and she momentarily wondered how it was possible for her to still be alive. Taking a breath, she wrapped her hand around the handle. She remembered a first-aid class saying something about leaving the knife where it was, that it could cause more damage on the way out. They were probably right, but there was no way in hell she was leaving it where it was. Not with that idiot clown already dragging himself to his feet. And definitely not when he could take it out and stab her again.

Tightening her grip, she clenched her jaw and tugged on the knife. It took more force than she would have thought necessary, but the first stomach-twisting sensation of the blade sliding out distracted her from that fact. Then the soul-searing pain arrived, threatening to overwhelm her. For a moment, she was tempted to give into the blackness threatening to consume her, but then Hannah screamed.

Rachel lifted her head to see the clown turning his attention to Hannah. If Rachel lost consciousness, Hannah was dead. And Rachel had promised not to let the bastard hurt her again.

The sirens in the distance were gradually coming closer, but they were still too far away to matter.

Tossing the knife away, Rachel scrambled to her feet to go after the insane man in the clown makeup. It might have been smarter to keep the weapon, but in truth, she feared that in her condition, he'd take the blade away from her and use it on Hannah.

For a big man, he was ridiculously fast. He lunged for Hannah, wrapping his huge hand around her ankle and dragging her toward him with a grunt. Hannah kicked at him with her free foot, trying to get away by pulling herself across the gravel as she screamed at the top of her lungs.

The clown continued to crawl forward, moving like some deranged monster, so focused on Hannah it was like Rachel didn't even exist. Maybe he assumed she was too weak to come after him—or already dead. Either way, he didn't notice her come up behind him and point her Taser at his back.

Rachel waited until she was two feet away to squeeze the trigger—so close she couldn't possibly miss. The barbed probes deployed with a pop, stabbing him through the shirt he wore. The Taser clicked like crazy in her grip as it dumped thousands of volts into the man. He groaned, but didn't seem nearly as fazed by it as she'd expected.

Not wanting to lose even that small advantage, Rachel reached behind her back and pulled out her cuffs, then jumped on his back. If she could get his arms restrained, she and Hannah might just make it until backup—and EMS—arrived.

The clown immediately lost interest in Hannah, releasing his hold on the girl and turning on Rachel with a vicious growl. She still had the trigger on the Taser depressed and it was still clicking like it should. By now, he should have been screaming in pain and writhing around on the ground, but it wasn't having any real effect on him. Wrapping one hand around her throat, he grabbed her left shoulder with the other, nearly crushing her bones as he shoved his thumb into the stab wound in her chest.

Rachel tried to scream as the pain hit her, but the hand around her neck made that impossible and all that came out was a strangled sound. She swung a punch at him, hoping to get him to release her. She didn't realize until her fist connected with the side of his face that she was still holding her cuffs in her hand.

His head rocked back hard, but it seemed like he'd barely noticed the blow from the heavy steel cuffs, despite the line of blood that ran down his paint and blood smeared cheek. If anything, it seemed to piss him off even more and he tightened his grip around her throat.

Rachel's vision started to dim and she knew she was going to die. This freak was going to kill her, then he was going to kill Hannah.

Like hell.

She punched him again and again and again. She

didn't aim, didn't even think, but simply fought for her life…and for Hannah's.

Rachel wasn't sure how many times she hit him, but at some point she realized he wasn't moving and that his hand was no longer wrapped around her neck. Her arms were so weak she could barely lift them any longer. She had no idea where the Taser was. And those damn sirens still seemed so far away.

She used what little strength she had left to roll the clown over onto his front, then yanked an arm behind his back and got one of the cuffs around his wrist. Even semiconscious he was strong enough to resist her efforts and she couldn't get his arm around to cuff that wrist. It didn't help that his arm was coated in so much of his blood she couldn't get a grip on it.

That was when she realized it wasn't his blood, but hers. She was bleeding to death.

Refusing to think about what that meant, Rachel tried to pull the man's left arm around, but the stab wounds in her chest and back were making it difficult to get a breath. Her vision was getting fuzzy, too. Suddenly, it was like she was viewing everything through a curtain. One that was getting thicker by the second.

She was close to giving up when a slender pair of hands reached out and covered her own. Rachel lifted her head to see Hannah kneeling beside her. Even in the darkness, the young girl's face looked pale. She'd lost almost as much blood as Rachel.

Hannah didn't say anything as she helped get the clown's left arm back behind his back, then worked with Rachel to get the cuff on his wrist. Once that was done, it was like every ounce of energy left in Rachel's body evaporated and she slumped to the ground on one hip, the hands she had planted on the gravel the only thing keeping her from falling over face first.

Suddenly, she was surrounded by warmth as Hannah moved close and settled at her side. The girl wrapped an arm around her, resting her cheek on Rachel's shoulder. "Thank you for saving me. And for not leaving me. Or letting him hurt me."

"I made a promise," Rachel said softly. "I never go back on a promise."

Hannah didn't say anything for a moment. "He's not really a clown, is he?"

Rachel shook her head, alarmed at how dizzy even that simple movement made her. "I'm pretty sure he's not. But if he is, then he's the worst clown in the world."

Hannah lifted her head from Rachel's shoulder to gaze into the fog at the flashing lights of the police cars that were coming closer. After a moment, she put her head on Rachel's shoulder again.

"I don't like clowns," Hannah said.

"No one likes clowns," Rachel agreed.

Her vision was getting dimmer by the second and breathing was almost too painful to bother with. She wasn't going to make it until help arrived.

"Rachel!"

She jumped at the panic in Hannah's voice. That's when Rachel realized she'd fallen over and was lying on the ground near the clown, staring straight into his open eyes. She freaked, horrified he'd fully regained consciousness at the same time she was losing hers. The thought of what he could do to Hannah even though he was in cuffs terrified her.

"Rachel, you have to stay awake!" Hannah shook Rachel's shoulder. "They're almost here. I can see the blue lights."

Rachel tried to do as Hannah asked, but her eyelids were suddenly so heavy. Nothing hurt anymore, so that was good. On the downside, it was getting harder to breathe. It struck her that she was dying. The fact that backup had arrived and that Hannah would be okay made her feel better about that.

But as she lay there on the cold ground, staring into the clown's glowing red eyes, Rachel realized she was still scared. Of leaving Hannah behind after making her a promise. And of being so close to this creepy-ass clown. More than anything, though, she was scared of dying. There was still so much she'd never had a chance to do with her life. Like learn to play a musical instrument, travel to exotic places, or even fall in love. Panic began to overwhelm her as she realized she was never going to get a chance to do any of it.

As that fear threatened to choke out what little breath she had left in her lungs, the clown grinned at her, his bloodied lips pulled wide as if he could sense her terror and it was the most amusing thing he'd ever seen.

That nightmarish smile of his—and the all-consuming fear she felt—was the last thing she remembered before everything went black.

Chapter 1

Dallas, Texas, Present Day

"DON'T TAKE THIS THE WRONG WAY, BUT YOU LOOK LIKE crap."

From where she sat on the bench lacing her boots in the SWAT team's locker room on the second floor of the admin building, Rachel glanced up to see fellow officer Khaki Blake regarding her with concern. Tall with long, dark hair and brown eyes, Khaki was the only other female werewolf on the Dallas PD SWAT Team. But more than that, she was Rachel's best friend. And when friends started a conversation with *don't take this the wrong way*, it was because they knew you would.

"We just ran ten miles cross-country for physical training this morning," Rachel pointed out, returning her attention to her boots. "How do you expect me to look?"

"I didn't say you looked tired. I said you look like crap."

"What's the difference?" Rachel asked, not sure she wanted to know.

"Tired means you stayed up late binging something on Netflix," her friend said. "You look like you haven't slept in a week."

Rachel finished lacing her boots, then sat up with a sigh. In addition to the showers and locker room, there were also a handful of cots as well as a kitchenette. If you had to work a double shift, it was nice to be able to come up here to catch some rest.

"I haven't been sleeping much lately," she said quietly.

Khaki frowned. "You're still having nightmares, aren't you?"

Rachel nodded. She hated admitting it, but it wasn't like Khaki didn't already know about the hellish dreams. Her friend had quickly picked up on the fact that something was bothering Rachel after she and some of their pack mates had come back fresh from a fight with a nest of vampires in Los Angeles a few weeks ago.

It might be stupid, especially since she and her pack mates were werewolves, but discovering vampires existed had shocked the hell out of all of them, including Rachel. So, when Khaki assumed she was a little off because of what happened in California, Rachel hadn't corrected her. It'd seemed easier to let her friend think she was suffering PTSD from the fight with the bloodsuckers than to admit she'd been dealing with nightmares—and other things—ever since werewolf hunters had attacked the SWAT compound two months ago. That night she'd screwed up and let one of the hunters get away, even when she'd had the man right in her sights.

A little while after, she'd started picking up bizarre scents that none of the other werewolves in her pack seemed to notice. Scents that both attracted and scared the hell out of her. Even worse were the shadows she caught out of the corner of her eye, shadows that were frequently horrifying but other times almost comforting.

As bad as her waking hours were, it was the nightmares

that were causing her the most distress. She'd been having traumatic dreams ever since going through her change that night in the cemetery in Chattanooga, but they'd been nothing compared to the terrors she was experiencing lately. The endless horrors of being chased, hunted, and savagely attacked she revisited on a nightly basis would jerk her out of sleep, heart pounding and sobbing in fear. They were the kind of things that made a person never want to go back to sleep for as long as they lived.

"You know," Khaki said as she stood up and strapped on the last of her gear. "There are people you can talk to about stuff like this. I know Cooper talked to a psychologist a few times and really thinks highly of her. I'm sure he could get you in to see her."

Rachel hadn't realized their pack mate had even seen a psychologist. Before she could answer, footsteps at the base of the stairs interrupted her. She breathed a sigh of relief as she picked up Senior Corporal Xander Riggs's scent. It wasn't that she didn't appreciate Khaki's help, but she seriously didn't want a shrink poking around in her head. She already knew she had a few screws loose. If a therapist confirmed it, the department would put her on administrative leave. She couldn't let that happen.

Xander's voice floated up from below. "You two almost done up there? The guys and I would like to clean up in this century. Unless you're cool with the idea of working alongside a bunch of sweaty male werewolves all day."

Rachel looked over at Khaki, who returned her smile.

"I could think of a lot worse ways to spend the day," her friend admitted. "Especially if we can convince them to take their shirts off."

Rachel laughed as Xander grumbled down below, making out like he was jealous. It was all an act, of course. No one could ever come between Khaki and Xander. He might be Khaki's squad leader on the SWAT team, but he was also *The One* for Khaki—her soul mate—just as she was for him. In any other SWAT team in the country, cops would never be allowed to have a relationship with a fellow officer. But in their world, it was something that was accepted. Finding a soul mate was extremely important to a werewolf. Not to mention rare.

Too bad there wasn't a chance of Rachel finding her soul mate among the Pack. While there wasn't a single guy on the team who wasn't sexy AF, unfortunately they were all like brothers to her. The idea of getting busy with any of them was enough to make her want to yak. Just her luck. Here she was surrounded by the most amazing men she'd ever seen in her life and none of them did a thing for her.

"Oh, and Rachel," Xander called from below. "Gage wants to see you in his office."

Rachel had to fight to keep her inner wolf from coming out in pure self-defense as an inexplicable terror overtook her.

Sergeant Gage Dixon was the commander of the Dallas SWAT team, as well as alpha of their pack of alphas. When Rachel had shown up at the compound out of the blue eager to join the Pack, he'd gone out of his way to welcome her and make her feel like this was the place she was supposed to be. But while he was a great guy and the best boss she'd ever worked for, there was a reason Gage was the head of the Pack. The man was completely in charge and nothing ever got past him.

What if he knew there was something wrong with her and was going to tell her he was putting her on leave—or worse?

The panic must have shown on her face because Khaki sat down beside her and gently touched her arm.

"Relax," Khaki said. "There's no way Gage could know about the nightmares. He probably just wants to talk about work stuff, maybe even something to do with that STAT unit you worked with out in LA."

Rachel's inner wolf retreated as she considered that. The Special Threat Assessment Team was the joint CIA and FBI task force that had helped Rachel and the guys take down the vampires. Apparently, the feds had been aware of the existence of werewolves and other supernatural creatures for some time. While it was a little scary to have the Pack on the government's radar, at least the organization seemed to be interested in developing a working relationship with them. They'd even asked Gage if they could use members of the Pack to help them deal with some of their more dangerous cases. But the thing that had really convinced Rachel and the others to trust the STAT people was when they'd discovered that fellow werewolf and SWAT cop Zane Kendrick had found his soul mate in a member of the task force.

She gave Khaki a small smile. "You're probably right. I'm just tense from lack of sleep."

Standing up, she headed for the steps.

"Don't think I didn't notice the slick way you avoided giving me an answer about getting some help with those nightmares," Khaki said, her voice making Rachel pause and look over her shoulder. "You have to stop going it alone, Rachel. If you're not going to see a psychologist, then at least find some good-looking guy and engage in a little pillow-talk therapy."

Rachel laughed and started down the stairs. "I'll keep that in mind."

Khaki's advice might be sound, but the truth of the matter was that Rachel hadn't slept with a guy since being attacked in Chattanooga and going through her change. At first, her life had been too insane trying to learn how to control her inner wolf. Between moving to Dallas and spending time in LA, she hadn't had time to even think of dating. These days, she couldn't imagine simply picking up some random guy for a booty call. She wasn't sure she knew how to do that anymore. Even if the idea did sound inviting.

COMING NOVEMBER 2019!

About the Author

Paige Tyler is a *New York Times* and *USA Today* best-selling author of action-packed romantic suspense, romantic thrillers, and paranormal romance. She and her very own military hero (also known as her husband) live on the beautiful Florida coast with their adorable fur baby (also known as their dog). Paige graduated with a degree in education but decided to pursue her passion and write books about hunky alpha males and the kick-butt heroines who fall in love with them.

Visit Paige at her website at paigetylertheauthor.com.

She's also on Facebook, Twitter, Tumblr, Instagram, tsu, Wattpad, Google+, and Pinterest.

Also by Paige Tyler

SWAT: Special Wolf Alpha Team

X-Ops